LOST IN EVERLYNIA

JEWELS HUSSEIN

To those who read not to get lost, but to be found.

CHAPTER 1
EVERLYNIA

EVERY FAIRY TALE begins with a tragedy. Mine came in the form of a raven.

We've all heard about the two most compelling human origin theories: the creation theory suggests that Adam and Eve—and life as we know it—were created by a divine being, and the evolution theory proposes that humans descended from ape-like species and have since evolved. One night, however, I discovered that what I had been taught in school was only a brief overview of the actual theory.

Naturally, I was skeptical at first, but what my mother told me and what I saw for myself made perfect sense. The entire world was a fantasy and not the kind where wishes were granted by a singing genie. As a seventeen-year-old junior in high school, it wasn't exactly what I needed, and certainly not what I'd asked for.

My name is Alexandra Cage. Ironically, I'd been a captive in the mortal realm for as long as I could remember.

My mother was a mystery, to say the least. She raised me

on her own, and never spoke about my father or any other family ties. In truth, she seldom speaks to me about anything, and when she did, I found us even more driven apart by her strange requests to move halfway across the country for no reason other than her mysterious job.

We've lived in nearly all fifty states, and every time it felt more like running away from my mother's past. I didn't understand what that past was until it finally found me: the note that started it all, sitting atop my copy of *The Story of America* in my locker.

A chill ran down my spine as I sensed a pair of eyes pinned on my back. I turned, but there was no one in sight. *Is this a prank?* I thought of the slim possibility of that ever happening. No, no one in my school would take the time to prank me. I picked the card up and read it.

Found you, princess!

What did that even mean? I looked around once more and caught a glimpse of something dark at the end of the hall; I couldn't make it out. Whatever it was, it moved too quickly for the human eye, though I was certain it was staring at me. Goosebumps covered my entire body. I returned my gaze to the card, my hands trembling and palms sweating. My eyes widened to the madness unfolding before me. Letters appeared on the card at random to form new sentences.

Is Her Highness alright? I can smell your fear ... tempting.

I must've gasped loudly, because the passing couple stopped and stared, whispering something rude before they turned away. My heart sank to my stomach, and everything was gone in no time. There were no words written—just a blank notecard.

The school bell rang, both making me jump out of my skin and announcing that I was late for my debate class. I slammed the locker behind me, leaving the blank card inside. I decided that whatever I had seen had merely been a figment of my imagination.

Mr. Lozano divided us into two groups: those who adhered to the creation theory, and those who adhered to the evolution theory. I decided to stick to the bigger group to avoid further questioning. A classic strategy used by many introverts to survive high school.

I hoped Mr. Lozano would forget about my existence much like the students did, but the universe had another plan for me.

"Ms. Cage, please explain why you believe in the creation theory." He smiled, moving closer to hear me more clearly. He peered through his clear glasses that covered half his face and made his eyes appear twice their normal size.

"Well, I-I would like to believe in something greater," I stammered, stepping back slowly. I felt my cheeks burn. A few students snorted. The pressure of having everyone's focus on me did not help at all. "Um … I think there's a powerful being capable of creating life from nothing. The evolution theory, although it may be true, doesn't provide much space for the imagination." I gripped my hands tightly to prevent them from shaking, feeling my heart pounding in my ears.

From the look on Mr. Lozano's face, I knew my argument wasn't nearly enough, but he accepted it anyway.

Perhaps he didn't want to hear my stupid argument after all. I know I didn't.

"Dreamer you are, Ms. Cage." He smirked once more before turning to face the other side of the classroom. "Any rebuttals?" he asked.

Those last few seconds seemed like a lifetime of embarrassment. I could hardly hear anything. My mind was replaying my childish response over and over again. *A dreamer.* That's a nice way of calling me delusional. The rest of the class was inaudible. Students argued back and forth like real scholars, but I was still lost in my thoughts.

The bell rang to dismiss me from that Hell class my mother made me take. With my lunchbox in hand, I zigzagged my way to the oak tree where I ate lunch alone, occasionally accompanied by some friendly squirrels sharing my snacks.

I munched down on my sandwich as I read my favorite novel for the hundredth time that year.

Just as I reached my favorite chapter, high-pitched screams shattered my reading bliss. Peering through my tangled curls, I saw the cheerleaders scurrying back inside the school, leaving their pom-poms scattered on the football field.

Startled, I dropped my sandwich, peanut butter and jelly staining my pants. A shadow appeared at the corner of my eye and vanished. Someone was watching me again. Before I could think of anything else, my flip phone buzzed, announcing a new message. I opened it immediately, expecting my mother to inform me of how busy she'd be at work, and how I would have to take the bus. Instead, it was a message from an unknown contact.

How long will you refuse to acknowledge my existence, Your Highness?

I had to read the message several times to believe it. I wasn't imagining things this time. The text message was real. The date and time, it was all real.

Who is this? I texted back.

A few moments later, another buzz made my heart skip a beat.

A loyal subject.

I sighed and texted back, **I believe you have the wrong number. I'm not who you think I am.**

You are Alexandra, daughter of King Alrick, the rightful heir to the Faye Throne, Your Highness.

Who? I pondered in confusion. I began typing my response when my mother suddenly called me. Her name flashed twice on the screen before I picked up. My mother would never call me during school hours. What was so pressing that had caused my mother, Helia, to break the no-calling rule?

"Hello?" I answered.

"Oh, thank God! Lexi, are you okay?" she asked in a shaky voice.

"I'm alright, mother."

"Has anything … strange happened today? Anything at all?" she asked.

How could she know? "Um … yes, I suppose today was a bit odd. I feel like I'm being watched." I nodded as if she could see me from over the phone.

"Lexi, whatever you do, don't trust anyone! And don't talk to anyone. I'll pick you up after school, so don't leave on your own, and don't take the bus. Do you understand?"

she said with persistence. I felt her worry from over the phone.

I still couldn't believe what was going on, all those messages, the shadow, the feelings. "I understand. I'll see you then," I said and hung up the phone. Looking back at the messages from the unknown contact, they were all deleted. Only the messages I'd sent remained, which proved that all the surreal events that had happened were not hallucinations.

Time felt like it barely passed and when the last bell rang, I picked up my notebook and colored pencils and tossed them in my backpack. I hadn't paid attention in any of my classes today. I was too busy thinking about the strange events that took place earlier on. For once, school didn't matter.

I called my mother, but she didn't answer. I texted that I would wait for her near the bus stop instead. The school buses left one by one as I waited for her. The longer I waited, the more anxious I became. *Has something happened to her?*

Another thirty minutes passed, and I was the only one waiting in the pickup area. Everyone, including faculty and staff, had left. My terror grew as the parking lot became darker. *How much longer do I have to wait?* Pulling my phone out, I began to dial 911 but stopped immediately. What would I tell them? *Hello, I'm a seventeen-year-old high school junior, and I need a ride home because my mommy's playing hide-and-seek with her phone. She told me to trust no one, and I'm scared.*

Groaning, I stuffed my phone back into my bag, but a familiar, haunting chill lingered in the air like a mysterious mist. It was as if an unseen presence stood steps away, fixated on me. Swiftly retrieving my phone, I was determined to call the cops this time.

"I wouldn't do that if I were you, Your Highness," someone said from beneath the bus shelter across the street from me. A second ago there was no one there. His face was entirely hidden by the shadow. He leaned against the glass back panel, both feet firmly planted on the ground and his arms were crossed over his chest. Something dark fell from his back to his feet.

"Who's there? Show yourself!" I demanded, "Are you stalking me?"

He straightened his back, slid his hands into his leather pockets, and took a couple of steps forward, spreading his shoulders. It was evident he had wings attached to his back; long black wings with sharp feathers spread wide to intimidate me. Golden eyes came into the light. "Stalking? Hardly," He said, a menacing grin stretched across his face, revealing his long, pointy fangs.

"Who are you?" I asked. "What do you want from me?"

"My, my," his tongue brushed against his teeth as he tilted his head, "I'm whoever you wish me to be," he said, Stepping closer. I could see his sharp features in the light. His eyes were sharp and cunning, like a fox's, framed by thick eyebrows. His hair, the darkest shade of black, was slicked back. A single strand fell on his face as he clicked his tongue. "What a waste."

"What?" I asked, my voice tinged with panic. "What did you just say?"

"It's a waste to kill someone like you, Your Highness," he

said softly, leaning down to meet my gaze. His scent was wild and somewhat spicy. Nothing like a human. "One look at you—at your freckles, your hair," he whispered, fingers weaving through a strand of my hair as if testing whether the ginger would come off, "and those hazel eyes." He *tsked*. "It really is you, Carrots."

With every step I took backward, he followed. My back slammed against the wall as he pinned his hands on both sides, caging me in. There was no way out, and no use in hiding my fear.

"Why do you want to kill me? I haven't done anything to you. Let go of me!" I shouted.

He leaned closer and whispered in my ears. "Not because of what you've done, but because of who you are." He pulled his head back, so our eyes met again. He opened his mouth slowly, his fangs growing longer and sharper as he readied to attack me. My heart sped. I closed my eyes tightly as I tried to push him away. He was impossible to fight.

Suddenly, a bright light blinded me, and a loud honk startled the both of us. When I opened my eyes, I saw my mother in her black minivan, death-staring at the raven-like creature. A look that terrified me. She said something, but I couldn't understand; something only he did.

Grinning, he stepped away without looking at me. His wings flapped back and forth until black dust began to form around him. In just a breath's span, he vanished, leaving no trace behind.

"Hurry, get in the car!" my mother shouted. I was still afraid of her and that scary look she had on her face. A knot tightened in my chest as I sat in the front seat. My mother drove off before I could even properly shut the door. Her hands were shaking, and I could see her sweating under her skin. "Did he hurt you?" she asked as soon as we stopped at the red light.

"No, but he said he wanted to," I stammered. "He said someone told him to kill me," I continued nervously. "What took you so long? Did you know that this would happen?"

"Of course not! I knew they were after you, but to *kill* you?" Her brows drew together in a frown.

"Mother, what is going on? Who's after me, and why?" I asked. Three hours before, I'd been a nobody, and now those *creatures* were after me. I didn't know what was going on, but I was sure my mother did.

"Lexi, I'm not sure if you're ready." The light turned green, and she drove ahead. "I-I have a lot of explaining to do. I didn't think I'd have to tell you so soon." She sighed.

I desperately wanted to know everything, but the fear in her eyes hinted that I should hold off on pressing for answers until we got home at least. We drove for another fifteen minutes in silence. I thought about what had happened to me and tried to make sense of it, but I couldn't. Finally, we were home.

As we entered our one-bedroom apartment, I observed my mother's movements to see if it was appropriate to question her about everything. She paced around the kitchen for a minute before grabbing my shoulders and pulling me into a chair. "Alexandra, you have to listen to me carefully."

Alexandra. Not Lexi, but Alexandra. Which only conveyed the depth of seriousness. I responded with a solemn nod.

"Okay, okay. First, I need you to know what I've been doing since you were born," she said, her big green eyes staring right into mine. "My sole duty is to keep you safe and out of their reach, no matter what."

"What do you mean? Keep me safe from who? Mother, what is going on?"

She rolled her eyes. "Oh, Alexandra, stop asking questions. I'm going to explain everything to you. Seriously, if my duty was your concern, I don't know how you'll react to what's coming." She shook her head. "I didn't tell you about my job because I needed an excuse to move around freely without you suspecting anything. In truth, I've been running trying to protect you from faeries."

I tried to keep a straight face. A giggle slipped. I couldn't help it. *Faeries?* My mother smacked her forehead so hard that it made me jump, and she turned away. She scratched her head for a good minute and quickly turned around to face me as though she had discovered something new. "Okay, let me make this easy for the both of us. I'll tell you a story, and all you have to do is listen. Don't make any faces and don't ask any questions until I'm done. Got it?" she asked. I nodded. "Good. Let me start from the *very* beginning."

She grabbed another chair and sat across from me. She cleared her throat and took a deep breath. "Once in the land of Everlynia, there were two regions to keep the fairies and faeries apart: Solmark and Icymark. The fairies, kind, and lovely beings, lived in Solmark, where they were ruled by Summer and Spring in the Faye Throne. The faeries, evil and horrid beings, lived in the Icymark, where they were ruled by Autumn and Winter by their Fae Throne. They kept peace by following strict rules, agreed upon by all seasons' rulers. Everything fell apart when one fairy fell in love with a fae; such union was strictly forbidden. To keep rules in place, the two creatures were exiled from Everlynia. They sought shelter somewhere else and began their own life by taking a new form and erasing all memories of Everlynia from their descendants. Those two creatures were known as Adam and Eve.

"The exile rule remained in effect, but throughout history, only three people were ever exiled. Those were Adam, Eve, and the queen of the Faye Throne. The queen was accused of conspiring with the enemy of Solmark. As a punishment, the king exiled his queen. However, no one, not even the queen herself, knew she was carrying the king's child; the rightful heir to the throne. The queen gave birth to a beautiful daughter and took all the risks to keep her alive and protected," my mother said.

She gave me one long stare, hoping I understood the story. She pressed her lips together and raised her eyebrows as high as they could go.

"The end?" I asked.

Her eyes softened, and she shook her head slowly, "No." She placed her hand on my cheek and brushed my tangled curls away from my face, "It's only your beginning."

She took another deep breath, "Alexandra, I am the exiled queen. And you…you are the rightful heir to the Faye Throne."

All my life, my mother had refrained from sitting down with me and sharing any details about herself or her past. She'd never given me advice or pretended to be a loving mother, and now this?

Her hand came up to touch my cheek, but I smacked it away from my face. "How do you expect me to believe or trust you? If any of what you're saying is true, then why didn't you tell me before? How does hiding something like this in any way protect me?"

She covered her face with both of her hands and sighed. Her straight, brown hair fell to her shoulders as she gracefully leaned back in her chair like a queen. "I admit, I made a mistake. I should've told you sooner. But you must believe me when I say I did everything for you. I lost everything the moment I got here, to this world. I don't belong here, and neither do you. My only purpose in life is to keep you safe and away from danger. I don't know how, but someone in Everlynia is aware of your existence and is threatened by it."

She ran her fingers through her hair, holding back her tears. "I thought I was doing the right thing, but I was wrong. We can't stay here, Lexi. We must leave. Now," she said as she quickly rose from her seat and opened the cabinet above the stove.

My head was spinning. "Great, we're running away again?" I asked, crossing my arms. "Where to this time? Back to Texas?"

A couple of wooden spatulas and a ladle fell from the cabinet to the kitchen floor as my mom searched for something in there.

"No," she said, still looking around, standing on her tiptoes. "No more hiding. We're going back to Everlynia." She snatched a small red velvet bag from the back of the cabinet and swung the bag between her fingers as she turned around. "Where we belong."

"Um…what?" I tilted my head in confusion.

Helia sniffled. Still holding onto the red bag, she walked slowly toward me and dropped to her knees. "Alexandra," she said in a low voice, "I know it's a lot to take in, but you have to trust that everything I told you is true. I can't keep you safe on my own, not after what happened today."

She took a brief pause before reaching out to grab my hand firmly. "Darling, I can't imagine what horrors you must've seen today. But if we stay here, you will be approached again and again by faeries like the one you saw today. I'm not enough. I need someone powerful to protect you." She gazed straight into my eyes. "I need the king, your *father*. Will you trust me? Trust that I see no other option but to let your father know that you're in danger?"

I shook my head. "No, what if… What if he already knows? What if he was the one who ordered that raven thing to kill me?" I narrowed my eyes. "Why would he be merciful toward me, if he wasn't toward his wife, the queen?"

Just as I said those words, my mother started sobbing uncontrollably. I'd seen her show more emotions in one night than she had in my entire life. She gently let go of my hands and wiped her tears away from her soft face. "No, Lexi, your father was ready to go to war for me, but I couldn't let him. Solmark was already weakened by my accusation. And when I learned I was pregnant with you, it was already too late. I assure you, he's more merciful than you'd think," she said with a controlled smile and teary eyes.

A searing pain pierced my heart as my mother unveiled her suffering. I despised myself for ignoring her feelings and focusing solely on mine. I had no right to blame her. None at all. My mother had given up so much for my father, and so much more for me. I knew I couldn't offer a lot in return, but I'd do anything to ease her pain. "I trust you, Mother."

A small smile lit her face. "Thank you, Lexi."

"Well then, how do we…go to Everlynia?" I hesitated. "Do we have to make a sacrifice or something?" I blinked, waiting for a response.

She placed her hand over her mouth as she tried to contain herself. I could see her laughter in her eyes. She wasn't very good at hiding that. Then she gathered herself and said, "No. To enter the land of Everlynia, we need to consume pixie brew. Luckily, I have some," she said as she held the small bag high, almost poking my eye with it. "Before I was exiled, I collected a small amount, just in case I needed to return for any reason. But…it's only enough for one grown woman."

Seriously? No going down rabbit holes or entering closets? Or even human sacrifices? "So…what does that mean?"

"It means we'll most likely be transported further away from the Faye Throne. You see, the less pixie brew you have, the further you'll be from your desired destination," she said. "All we have to do is mix this brew with water and… bottoms up! Simple, right?"

I nodded. *Okay, not so bad. I can do this.*

I jolted upright when I heard a loud bang against our window. Another followed a few seconds later. My mother and I dashed to the living room. She pulled back the curtain just enough to see who it was. I peeked over her shoulder and saw a cloud of ravens circling around outside our apartment. Harsh croaks filled the sky. A couple of ravens flew right into the window, cracking the glass with their sharp beaks.

"We have to leave now, Lexi," my mother said, running back to the kitchen. Opening the dishwasher door, she pulled two clean glasses from the silver racks, filling them halfway with tap water, and evenly sprinkled the black substance from the vial. "Come, Lexi," she said with a quick glance.

This is it; we're doing it right now. I hurried to her side as she stirred the mixture with a wooden spoon, working as fast as she could. "It might not taste good," she said, "endure it. You'll feel dizzy and you'll start to see things until we're in Everlynia. It's all normal. Now, bottoms up!"

To my surprise, the mixture did not have a bad odor; in fact, it did not smell of anything at all. I gulped the entire drink in one go, just as my mother did. I didn't feel anything at first, but the taste of expired vinegar began to fill my stomach and throat. The sourness burned my insides, and I began to sweat from the heat. The kitchen appeared to be much larger at one point and very small at another. My legs were barely supporting me; one step and I'd fall flat on my face. I felt someone wrapping their arms around me; it must've been my mother. In the blink of an eye, I was in complete emptiness.

My eyelids felt like they were made of metal. It was almost impossible to blink. Colors began to emerge from beneath my feet, many of which I had never seen before. Angelic voices began to sing in a language I didn't under-stand. In an instant, I went from slowly breathing to not breathing at all. The sensation of my brain being squeezed made me doze off on the spot.

For what seemed like hours, I was floating in nothing-ness. When my breathing returned to normal, I slowly opened my eyes to a beautiful fairy staring down at me as I lay in her lap, motionless. Her skin glowed in the dark. In one breath, I smelled various kinds of flowers and spices. I glanced at the fairy as she spoke to me, but I couldn't hear a single word she said. The fairy shook her head, smiled down at me, and gently tapped my forehead once, sending me back to sleep.

CHAPTER 2
THE VILEFOREST

I WOKE to the sound of jingle bells over my head. When I opened my eyes, I found myself in the company of small fairies—pixies, I supposed. Around twenty of them, each with bright wings stared at me strangely. One of them moved closer to touch my face and waited for my reaction. I had no idea what they expected of me, but my body refused to move. My attention was drawn to my surroundings; I was in a forest, encircled by giant trees that blocked my view. The drowsiness clung to me like a stubborn leech.

A fairy, much larger than me, shooed the critters away from my face and helped me up. It was her, the same fairy I'd seen the night before. She had the same captivating aura. This time, I tried to concentrate on her face; she had large eyes, tinted lips, and pointing ears. Her silky, brown hair fell to my face as she kissed me on the brow. She smelled like a garden of roses. "Good morning, Lexi," she said.

"Mother?" I asked with a fond look on my face.

She nodded. "How are you feeling?"

"Tired," I said as I leaned back against the tree. Everything remained spinning around me. I tried to keep my head still, and my eyes on my mother. "I'm feeling a little lightheaded."

She rose silently and disappeared behind the massive trees. I couldn't see where she was going; I was completely out of focus. She returned moments later, cradling a flower filled with shimmering liquid. "Drink this," she said, handing it to me, "it'll help." The teal liquid inside glistened, barely enough for a single sip.

Oh, great. Another round of fairy drinks. Fingers crossed it doesn't taste like the pixie brew, or else I'll gag.

I took a deep breath and gulped down the liquid. Surprisingly, it was nothing like the pixie brew. Heavenly sweet, and delicious. A symphony of flavors that awoke my senses in pure bliss. The drowsiness and headaches vanished in an instant, and my insides yearned for more.

My mother surveyed me and gently touched my forehand to check for a fever. "Are you feeling any better, Lexi?"

"What was that? It's delicious! Can I have more?"

She breathed a sigh of relief. "I'm afraid not," she said. "A small amount of tealoxica can heal you, but too much of it will make you blind. Be careful, Lexi; the sweetest and prettiest things in this land are the most toxic. Remember that, dear."

I gave an affirmative nod. "So, how far are we from the Faye Throne?"

"Far. We're somewhere in the Vileforest. A wicked territory inhabited by some of the nefarious dark fae, like the one you've encountered in Mississippi. Most of them are traitors and untrustworthy. They are not of the Solmark or the Icymark, but outcasts. Often, they trespass on our territory, facing serious consequences if they're caught. They know this land better than anyone," she said, shaking her head.

It made sense; this must've been the ideal home for that dreadful raven thing. I realized it wasn't the time to think about him; I needed to concentrate on what was next. "So, what now?"

My mother sobered. "I have already sent word to my trusted advisor; he should arrive in a few hours. First, I'll request an audience with the king to explain everything that has happened since my exile. If everything goes as planned, I will summon you to the Faye Throne."

"What do you mean, *if?*" I asked, confused. "I'm not going with you?"

She pressed her lips. "Alexandra, I can't put your life in danger. I'm sure I would have to pay a price for keeping you hidden these past years; everyone would expect that. But if I can speak to your father first, perhaps I'll make him understand. Caz will take care of you until then. I only need a day or two."

Not sure if my brain decided to take a vacation, or whatever was in that drink sedated my rage, but I had no words. My mother would entrust me to this 'Caz,' a stranger in a place I'd never visited before. "Great, and what am I to do with this *Caz*?" I sneered.

She crossed her arms and shifted her weight to one side in a *very* Helia way. "I'm serious, Lexi. Caz can keep you safe until the king agrees to see his heir. He has never failed me. I trust he'll take good care of you."

"Fine," I mumbled as I stepped on the fallen leaves

beneath my feet. "I'll do as you wish, Mother," I said, plastering a faux smile on my face.

A violent, chilly wind blew away my hair, burning my eyes. Suddenly, the smell of sweat and gas filled the air. I almost gagged at the horrible scent. For a split second, there was a familiar smell, but it vanished before I could recall what it was.

My mother delicately covered her nose with the back of her hand. "It's time to go before those horrid fae attack us."

Twigs snapped all around us as we ran through the Vileforest. The dark faeries pursued us like determined predators. The sound of their footsteps grew louder and louder, and I caught a glimpse of a small green goblin through the tree branches.

Our feet were deep in the muddy fields, sludge splattering up to our knees. My feet started to cramp, and the cold air filled my lungs. Exhaustion clawed at me as I pushed through the pain, just as the dark fae finally lost interest and faded into the shadows of the dense forest. My mother and I collapsed to the ground, grateful for the chance to rest. My heart pounded so loudly it drowned out all other sounds, and it took a while for it to slow.

My mother sat beside me, panting. "Well…that was fun, wasn't it?"

I looked around again to see the *fun* she was talking about. What about being covered in dirt, barely breathing, and fleeing from hungry creatures I'd only seen in graphic novels was fun?

She groaned as she got up. Her white dress was soaked in mud, giving her a wild appearance. "Oh great," she mumbled as she looked down. "How am I supposed to meet the king looking like this?"

Marvelous. We'd almost died running away from those weird fae, and all she cared about was how she'd look in front of the king who'd exiled her. Talk about fairy-tale drama.

My stomach growled, reminding me that I hadn't eaten anything since lunch the day before. "Mother, is there anything we can eat here?"

She hummed as she cleaned her dress as best as she could. "Well…the goblins aren't far from here," she said, placing her hands on her hips.

"Are you serious? They were chasing after *us*." I pointed back to the muddy field. "They nearly killed us. Besides, I don't want to eat a *goblin*." I narrowed my eyes.

"Why not? They taste like chicken." She shrugged.

My teeth were still exposed in disgust. There was no way I'd ever eat that creature. My mother knew that, and she couldn't help but sigh. "Fine, we'll find something else. In the meantime, we need to keep going or we'll end up on some fae's plate."

We must've walked for hours. I couldn't tell what time it was, but the bright sun was directly above my head. The further we went into the Vileforest, the darker and colder it became. The aroma of damp moss and life flooded the air. Flowers painted the ground in colorful hues, and the trees stood like skyscrapers, stormed by pixies and other small-winged fairies.

I noticed a half-foot-tall mushroom-shaped fairy peering

at me and hiding away behind a giant oak tree whenever I turned my head to look at it. It had large blue eyes that covered half its face and a tiny round nose. A dirty beige rag wrapped around its body like a strapless dress. By far, it was the most innocent-looking creature. My neck ached from looking around. The sight of that enchanted forest made me forget about how hungry I was and how much pain my feet were in.

My mother walked through, without glancing at any of the fairies in the forest; perhaps because she'd seen them before. After all, that had been her home, and she was once their queen.

A few minutes later, she stopped and glanced up. A smile tugged at the corner of her lips as she pointed to a tree ahead of her. "Want to try a pixie pear? The best you'll ever taste."

She wasn't exaggerating. I took one bite and the sweet, juicy, soft fruit melted in my mouth like cotton candy. A sigh of pleasure escaped me as my mouth curved into a smile that I couldn't stop. After twenty pears, I was finally full. I stuffed a handful of pears into the pocket of my hoodie to enjoy later.

My mother laughed as she graciously ate a couple of pears. "You know, your father planted a garden full of pixie pears just for me." She blushed. "This was before our coronation. I first met him at the annual gathering of the seasons' rulers. He was charming and offered to lead the way. All eyes were on us that night. We danced for hours until the music stopped, at which point, the Prince of Autumn stepped in and offered me a pear from his land. It was my first time trying pixie pear, and it was delicious. My face couldn't hide how much I enjoyed it, and your father was a jealous man. Three weeks later, he invited me to his court and presented me with the pixie pear garden. It was then when I realized I was in love with him."

I could see that she was overjoyed, and it made me happy. Amidst everything, the silver lining was how close we'd become—the deepening of our connection. I decided I liked this version of her.

A loud canter startled me, and I turned around to find a dark rider approaching from the middle of the forest. A cloud of smoke appeared as the rider pursued us. I couldn't stop my body from trembling. My chest tightened. I took a step back to hide behind my mother.

She threw her hands up in the air as she stepped forward fearlessly. "Finally!" she said. "He's here, Lexi. Caz has arrived."

The rider came to a halt a few feet ahead of us. The source of the smoke trail was clear then. The black horse itself was lit up in flames. Its tail hair was strands of lava, and its eyes were glowing red. The horse snorted fiery ashes, standing proudly before us as the rider gently climbed down from the saddle.

Caz kneeled before my mother, his long lashes casting a shadow on his cheekbones. Strands of wheat-blonde hair fell as he bowed his head lower. "Your Majesty, former queen of the Faye Throne," he said in his euphonious voice. "I'm at your service." When he finally opened his eyes, gleaming like twin sapphires.

"Rise, Caz," my mother said. Stepping aside, she rested

her hand on my shoulder, pushing me toward him. "This is my daughter, Alexandra."

I stood before him with my hair tangled, my clothes dirty, and sweating profusely from the heat. Still, Caz greeted me with a gentle bow, unconcerned about my appearance. "I'm honored to meet you, Princess Alexandra of Solmark."

"The honor is mine" I mumbled shyly. He straightened his back, giving me a glance from head to toe, running his hand through his wavy hair, before turning his attention to my mother, disregarding me entirely.

"Caz, I need you to tell me everything I've missed since my exile."

He hesitated. "Your Majesty, I'm afraid you won't like what you're about to hear," he said, lowering his gaze. "Many things have changed, and none of them are in your favor."

My fairy mother's smile faded quickly. She crossed her arms and stood firm. "Go on."

"Your Majesty, King Alrick has taken a bride after your exile." He said, "Lady Rose proposed a union that would strengthen the Solmark region. With Your Majesty gone, he needed the next ruler of Spring by his side, for he is the only ruler of Summer."

Tension gripped her muscles as she narrowed her eyes at Caz. "Rose? My little cousin Rose?"

"Yes, Your Majesty." He affirmed with a nod.

Her nostrils flared as she turned her head to me. "Lexi, wait by the oak tree. I need a moment with Caz," she commanded in a tone that wasn't inviting. I retraced my footsteps silently.

Under the oak tree, I watched my mother and Caz deep in their conversation. She kept shaking her head at every comment he made and spoke with her hands. I imagined she was very displeased with how things had turned out.

The sound of breaking twigs made me realize I wasn't alone.

I turned my head to find the little mushroom-looking fairy standing behind me. He held a Teal flower in his hand and offered it to me. "Shroom," he said, his voice a squeak. His large eyes were fixed on me as I carefully grasped the flower. He offered a smile and placed his hands behind his back as he shook his body from side to side. I tucked the flower behind my ear and took out a pear to give him in exchange.

"Shroom?" He tilted his giant head and blinked rapidly, unsure what I wanted him to do.

"This is for you," I said in a friendly tone. With his tiny hands, he hugged the pear like it was a watermelon. "Shroom!" He ran away with it, jumping on the broken branches and vanishing into the forest.

"We need to leave, Your Highness." Caz's voice startled me. He held out his hand and pulled me up to my feet.

Looking past him, I couldn't see my mother anywhere. The dark, fiery horse was gone too. "Where is my mother?" I panicked, stepping away from him.

He held my gaze for a second. "She's on her way to the Faye Throne, Your Highness. To meet your father, the king," he said. "I suggest we get moving too. The darkness is creeping in."

Somehow, I half-expected she'd do something like this, especially in the wake of the latest bad news. "So, where are we going…sir?" I felt stupid not knowing what to call him. He looked young, but I've learned from books that age and fairies don't mix. For all I know, he could've been millennia old.

"I know a place nearby. We can rest there until dawn." He turned back. "Call me Caz," he said, making it sound like an order. I came to realize that while he may have had an obligation to protect me, it didn't necessarily imply that he liked it, or me.

I gave a curt nod, following him.

The forest grew quiet as it got darker. We had been walking for hours, with Caz unsure of which path to take. I remembered how my fairy mother had explained that the Vileforest was an abandoned territory that wasn't part of the Solmark region. Still, I didn't think someone like Caz could be lost in it. My legs screamed from the pain, and I wasn't sure how much longer we'd be walking.

Breathing became more difficult, and my body refused to cooperate. I collapsed onto a pile of dried leaves that crunched beneath me. Through my hazy vision, I saw Caz kneeling beside me, his brows drawn together before gently picking me up in his arms. He shook his head, murmuring something. That was the last thing I remembered before drifting away.

I jolted awake with a ringing in my ears, a loud buzzing that faded away as I opened my eyes wider. Cold sweat covered my forehead and neck. My body felt sore. I glanced around, panicking at the sight of the small dwelling. For a moment, I forgot where I was. Tree branches were tightly stacked to form walls, and vines hung from the roof. The floor was covered in grass tiles, and a giant rock in the corner passed as a chair. I found myself wrapped in a chunky knit blanket, warm and cozy. My mind raced as I tried to figure out how I'd gotten here. Then, he broke the silence.

"Did you get a good night's sleep?" Caz asked, leaning against the open doorway, his head was only a few inches from hitting the roof. The sun shone behind him, casting his long shadow on me.

I shook my head, stretching my limbs like a cat.

"No? How unfortunate," he said, sounding slightly discontent. "Was the ride uncomfortable for you, princess?" He had an unreadable expression on his face.

I glanced at him in confusion. The eerie way he looked at me brought back my memories from the night before. *Caz had carried me here.* He noticed the embarrassment starting to creep over my face and effortlessly smiled.

"I could do without it," I answered.

His expression did not change. I leaped out of bed and sprinted past him out of the dwelling. "In fact, I command you to never hold me in your arms again," I said, crossing my arms over my chest.

Caz stood speechless, raising his brow, and staring back momentarily. Finally, he stepped away from the doorway and approached me, so close I could feel his heartbeat. I stood my ground as he bent down to my face. His high cheekbones and elfin ears caught my attention. "Would that please you, princess?"

"Yes, it would," I said in a direct tone.

He placed his hands in his pockets and straightened

himself. "Let's make one thing clear, princess: should I deem it necessary, I *will* carry you. After all, my duty isn't to please you, but to protect you in any way *I* see fit." He gave me an odd look.

What's up with this guy? I didn't know much about him, but anyone could see how truly blinded by arrogance and duty he was. "And how would the queen respond if she found out about your improper conduct?"

"The queen would most likely be grateful that I kept you alive, rather than how I did it," Caz retorted. "Now, we should get going before the orcs find their breakfast."

Arrogant fool, I wanted to say, but decided he wasn't worth it.

We scurried through small wetlands, ponds, and fields of thorns that varied from a centimeter to a few inches long. By the time we were out of there, my jeans were ripped. To make everything worse. My hair was filled with small twigs, spikes, and leaves that fell from the trees as we walked by. My stomach growled with hunger. I took out the last couple of pixie pears and ate them in one bite. It wasn't enough, but I was satisfied for the moment. The air became increasingly foul as we continued from one location to the other. Distant howling made my insides twist in fear, but Caz didn't even turn an eye to any of that. Eventually, the sounds faded away. "Keep close," Caz said without looking back at me.

Moments later, we entered a dark hedge maze with hundreds of paths divided by tall hedges, stormed with caterpillars and ants. A cloud of colorful fog hovered over the maze, brightening the way. Strangely, my body felt numb as the world around me began to sway from side to side.

Angelic voices sang and my head pounded. My vision went fuzzy in an instant. I tried to concentrate on Caz, but there were four of him, each taking a different route. I didn't know which one to follow. I tried to call out to him, but my voice echoed back in my mind. Only one of them turned to me and said I should keep my eyes on him. His soft voice oddly hypnotized me.

I followed him closely until we reached an enormous stump with a door in the center of the maze. Caz cackled in a high-pitched tone and suddenly dissolved into dozens of crows that flew in a tornado-like fashion around me. I lowered my face into my hands as fast as I could. Their beaks and claws cut into my flesh as they forced me into a wooden cage that appeared out of nowhere. My throat clenched from screaming as I waved my arms around to scare the crows away. The cage door dropped closed, releasing me from the crows' clutches.

When the territorial caws stopped, I opened my eyes to find my hands covered in scratches, leaving my skin swollen and discolored. The more I looked at it, the more it stung. I was sick with the fear of being alone in a maze and away from Caz.

Trapped in a small wooden cage across from the stump, anxiety crept over me as I heard the stump door creaking.

Three old boggarts stormed out of the stump, holding pikes with sharpened bones twice their height. Two were mirrored reflections of each other, and the third appeared much older. Hideous short hags with a few strands of silver hair falling to their pointed chins. Their skin was saggy and zombie-green. They had big, hooked noses like witches and huge lumps on their backs. My heart began to beat quickly as they reached the cage.

They stood side by side, peering into the cage with their wide, stained eyes. The twins climbed up on the bars and hissed at me.

"At last," the older one said with a lopsided grin. "Something fell right into our trap."

CHAPTER 3
BOGGARTS AND FATETELLER

THE AIR CRACKLED WITH HISSES, rendering me motionless as the short hags pointed their pikes at me. Filed bones dug into both my calves like knives, tearing the seam from the knees down. I gasped, holding my tears inside as I tried to calm myself.

"It bleeds," the oldest said. "It's good meat."

"It may be, but it doesn't have any fur," the second said. "I wanted a new rug."

"But…what is it?" the third asked.

"I don't know," said the oldest as she narrowed her eyes to get a better look at my ears. "It looks weird."

"And what is it wearing?" the twins said in unison.

Their giant noses crinkled as they sniffed me through the bars. "It even smells weird. What is it?"

"Is it a faun?"

"No! Not a faun, you idiot," the second said. "Fauns have those hairy legs. This one doesn't. This one looks like an elf, but much smaller."

"Oh, but I wanted a new rug."

The oldest hag slammed her hands on the wooden bars and snarled. "It doesn't matter, you boneheads. If it bleeds, then it's good meat. Though it's not enough. I should eat it before the juice runs out."

"Why you? Last week, you ate the satyr alone. I haven't eaten anything in two weeks," the second said.

"I haven't eaten in three weeks!" the third yelled.

"If it wasn't for my crows, we wouldn't have caught this thing in the first place!"

Cold sweat prickled over my skin as I watched them fight among themselves. I looked for a way out, but there was none. I was trapped in the middle of nowhere and soon to be eaten by one of these boggarts. Caz wasn't there to save me, and my mother had left me in that strange world without even saying goodbye. I was on my own. I didn't know what to do, but I knew I couldn't just stand here and let them decide whose plate I'd be on that night. "Shut up and stop fighting, you old hags!"

Immediately, the boggarts stopped pulling each other's hair and turned their gazes to me. Their wide, devil-red eyes bore into mine. They leaned forward, almost getting their heads caught between the bars of the cage. "Did you boneheads hear that? This one speaks."

"Yes, I can speak." I inched forward, scaring them back. "So, you can either continue fighting like the idiots you are, until one of you dies, or you can keep your trap shut and listen to me."

The oldest boggart frowned and drew her lips back in a snarl. "And what do you have to say, meat?"

I raised an eyebrow. "I propose a solution to your problem. A game. First, we must make a contract. Each participant is only allowed one guess. If none of you guess right, you'll have to let me go, unharmed. Will you abide by these rules?" The only thing I knew for certain about fairies from reading books was that once a contract was made, it couldn't be broken.

The old hag hummed and gripped the bars tightly, almost breaking them into pieces. The twins lifted their shoulders in a shrug, scratched their heads in unison, and glanced at each other silently. They hugged their weapons closer to their chest and slowly nodded. The older one hesitated. Eventually, she came to terms with it. "Alright." She sighed loudly. "We'll abide by your rules, meat. Now go on with it. What's the game?"

"It's a riddle." I clapped my hands to start the game. "A harmless spy that has no feelings and no size. It's weightless and painless—brainless and speechless. Always by your side, never complains, and never lies. What is it?"

One of the twins guffawed. "Easy, it's a goblin."

"You idiot!" the other said. "She said it was harmless."

The boggart twisted her face. "Oh…yeah. But she also said it was brainless."

"Yes, like you, I suppose," the second one said. "My guess is the air. It's weightless and painless. Am I right?"

I shook my head. "Nope. Both wrong," I said as I shifted my gaze to the older hag. "Now it's your turn."

She growled, showing her yellow broken teeth as she let out a harsh breath. "Harmless spy, you say?" She walked around in circles. "Ay…ain't an easy one. I'd say…the sun." She puffed out her chest and raised her pike. "Right, meat?"

I took a deep breath and let out a sigh of relief. "Wrong." I grinned. "The right answer is your shadow."

The old hags froze in disbelief. Their faces went blank as they stared at each other. It took them a long moment to understand. "How did you know we didn't have the right answer, meat?"

"I didn't. I just hoped your intelligence matched your beauty," I said solemnly.

The one who wanted a new rug blushed. "Thank you," she said, beaming.

"None of you guessed right. Now, you'll have to abide by the rules and let me go unharmed." I felt my stomach churning inside as the oldest boggart held up her pike and lifted the cage door open. They hissed as I got out of the cage slowly, scrutinizing their every move.

The oldest boggart gave a mirthless laugh as she watched me back away. "Be cautious, meat. We aren't the only hungry creatures in this maze," she said. "Some are said to be even nastier than the treacherous queen."

My blood began to boil when I heard their sickening cackles. The terror inside me quickly turned into anger. Those ugly old hags were talking about my mother. Intrusive thoughts overtook me. I wanted to rip their throats out.

Instead, I ran alone through the cold, dark maze. Tears streamed down my face as I dashed from one hedge to the next with bleeding and trembling legs. I wanted to get away from there; not just from the maze, but from Everlynia. I yearned to return home and be with my mother once again. I missed my imaginary friends and our one-room apartment. I missed the squirrels and my books. Stabbing pain flooded my head as I reflected on what was my normal life.

Trapped in the ghastly maze, turning left and right until I bumped into someone who'd emerged from a hedge wall.

His arms wrapped around me tightly, trapping me in yet another cage.

Choking back tears, I couldn't scream for help. I scratched his arms with my nails to escape, but the more I resisted, the tighter he held me. "Let go of me!"

"Stop," Caz said in a quiet voice. He lowered his head to meet my gaze. "It's alright, princess. It's me." His pupils flared as he carefully examined me from head to toe.

I gasped and tried to push him away from me, but he refused to loosen his grip. After many failed attempts, I gave up. "Let me go." I sighed. "Please."

Caz paused for a long moment before finally releasing his grip on me. He kept his gaze fixed on me as I wiped my eyes, the salt stinging my cut skin.

After a few minutes, my tears stopped pouring. I sniffled softly and turned back to face Caz. In my torn jeans, I shivered with cold, barely standing on my own.

Caz's eyes softened. "I'll hold you now," he whispered, and I nodded slowly. He slid one hand behind my back and the other under my thighs. I grunted as he gently picked me up. Wrapping my hands around his neck, I rested my head on his shoulder.

I peered out to observe the maze for the last time. Fireflies gleamed in the shadows like the stars at night, dazzling the maze as they flickered on and off. I was too scared to notice the beauty of the place. Caz picked up the pace, and we swiftly found our way out of the maze.

Near a glistening pond surrounded by luminous grass, Caz carefully set me down on a moss-covered stone. I stretched out my wounded legs and grumbled at the sight of blood running down my calves.

Caz clenched his jaw and gazed intently. "I asked you to keep close," he said. "The maze isn't a place for solo exploration, princess. Let me know the next time you're determined to go for a walk on your own. It helps to do my duty properly."

My face flushed with rage. I despised the way he interpreted what had happened. "I know what a maze is!"

"Then why didn't you follow me?"

"I did! There were four of you, and I followed the one who instructed me to. How could I possibly have known it wasn't you?"

"The boggart sisters," he whispered, looking down at my legs once again. "Did they do this to you?"

I let out a harsh breath. "Yes."

He shoved his hair away from his eyes and walked toward the pond. After washing his hands, he aggressively snatched a couple of lily pads that were floating on the glistening water. Placing my feet in his lap, he wrapped the lily pads around my wound and held it in place. I felt his palms burn against my calves as he pressed down before letting go after a few seconds. The pads stuck to my skin like bandages. Caz got up on his feet and leaned closer to me. I pulled back as his fingers slid behind my ears and pulled something out. A teal flower twirled in his fingers. I had completely forgotten about it.

"Tealoxica," he said as he handed it to me. "Drink the liquid inside. It'll help."

I did, and my body went numb as I drank the sweet liquid.

The scratches on my hands vanished in an instant. I was finally free from the unbearable stinging pain. I suddenly remembered how badly I'd scratched Caz when he'd clutched me. When I looked at him, I noticed that he'd been staring at me like a predator, his eyes locked on me like a cat on a mouse. He quickly ducked his head to avoid interacting with me, something I'd always done throughout my life. I knew I needed to apologize to Caz, but I never imagined it would be so difficult.

"I-I'm sorry, Caz," I stammered. "I'm sorry I hurt you."

"Don't apologize," he said. "Never apologize for fighting back, princess."

What a surprise, another lesson. "Forget I said anything." I crossed my arms and turned my head in annoyance.

"You've got a lot to learn," he said, "if you intend to stay alive in this land."

Sarcastically, I raised my eyebrow as high as they could go. "Oh, yeah? Enlighten me."

Caz sat on the edge of the pond, crossing his arms and legs. "For starters, control your temper," he said easily. "Your tone and attitude are your biggest adversaries. I don't know anything about the world you came from, but in Everlynia, there's a cost to everything. Especially your manners, princess."

I bit my lip hard. I expected the tealoxica to calm my anger like last time, but it didn't. "Are you suggesting I'm impolite?"

His brows knitted. "Everyone in Solmark would think so," he said with certainty. "You need to understand that first impressions matter. You came here to claim your place in the Faye Throne, in Everlynia. You must act as the ruler you are, not the girl you were."

"Wait a moment," I said, holding my hands up. "I'm not here to claim anything. The only reason I'm here is to be safe from your kind." I paused for a second to remember my mother's exact words. "The king's protection. That's what I'm here for. I'll leave this land as soon as my mother and I have his protection."

Caz pressed his lips together in anger. His veins visibly popped out of his neck. "What?" he said. "Your mother is not here for protection, princess. She's here for you. No one can protect her but you. If you're the rightful heir, then you'll have to claim your place and your safety shall be granted. There's no other way."

A rush of adrenaline blinded me. *Is he telling the truth? Was mother lying to me the entire time?*

"What do you mean?" I stammered with rage. "*I* have to protect her?"

His muscles stiffened. "Being the first daughter of Spring and Summer, when the time comes, you'll hold much more power than the king of Solmark."

"And what am I to do now, beg the king to put me on the throne?"

"It's not that simple, princess.

"Then what?"

"I guess you'll have to find out," he said, laying on the soft moss with his hands behind his head.

That night, it took me hours to fall asleep. My mind flooded with thoughts and questions I didn't have the answers to. Caz's words made me more worried about my mother. *What exactly is she doing right now? Is she safe in the Faye Throne? Is she thinking of me as her daughter or as an heir she wishes to crown? Is there another reason she brought me here, another secret she's hiding from me?*

A breeze swept away my worries, and I fell into darkness.

I was staring at my reflection in the pond. The girl before me was nothing like me. She wore a crown on her head and a frown on her face, ginger curls framed her face. She had elf-like ears and high cheekbones. Reaching out, she pulled me into the pond. The ice-cold water filled my lungs as I struggled to free my wrist from her grip. In a heartbeat, I found myself standing in the middle of an empty throne room, surrounded by giant golden windows that reached the roof. Gold dust sprinkled across the floor. The walls were decorated with colorful crystals that reflected every ounce of sunlight. The ceiling was covered in paintings of fire-breathing dragons inside a dark cave. In every corner of the room stood twelve-foot-tall sculptures of different winged dragons—some coiled into a ball, others poised to strike. I could have sworn I saw one of them turn its head to look at me, but its unnatural stillness convinced me it was just my mind playing tricks.

"She's here," someone whispered behind me. "I told you she's in Everlynia."

"Shush! We're not supposed to be here, remember?" came another voice.

I swung around, but I couldn't find anyone. "W-who's there?" I stammered. "Show yourself."

A soft giggle echoed throughout the room. "Did you hear that? She commands, like a queen."

"We'll be doomed if she's the queen. She still looks funny. Nothing has changed. I thought those ears would suit her."

My hands were immediately drawn to my ears. Like my mother and Caz, I had long, pointy ears.

"I think she looks lovely."

"You think that of everyone, Rue."

My eyes scanned every inch of the room, but I couldn't find the owners of the voices. Behind one of the dragon sculptures, I caught a glimpse of a moving shadow. "I can hear you both." I trembled as I walked slowly toward the corner. "I heard everything you said. Now, show yourselves!"

I quickly peered around the sculpture and found a couple of stock-still squirrels. From afar, the figures looked completely ordinary, nothing weird. Recklessly, I leaned forward to get a closer look at them. One of the little critters wore a red waistcoat and carried a toothpick-sized sword. The other wore a short puffy dress with a pinafore on top. Their bushy tails curved like a cane against their backs, long and bristly.

"What a pretty little thing," I whispered as I touched the lady's pinafore.

"Oh, thank you!" she said courteously. *She answered me. The motionless figure spontaneously came to life and responded.*

My body shook with fear as I dropped to the ground, screaming. The little dressed squirrel shared my reaction, and we took turns shrieking at each other. The other one covered his ears and cringed in response. "Enough!" he yelled, finally stopping us.

I gasped, struggling to get up from the dusty-gold floor. "What are you?"

With one hand, the angry squirrel raised his sword in my direction and pushed the lady squirrel behind him with the other. "Are you blind, Ginger? I'm a knight." His nose crinkled. "You've seen and bothered us many times before."

"I have?"

"We're the same squirrels from your school in that other world, fool."

"Oh, but…you can talk," I muttered stupidly.

He sighed and lowered his sword. "We can do a lot more, Ginger Head."

"Don't be rude, Max," the lady said. "She's the princess, remember?"

The angry squirrel shook his head in disapproval. "You believe it? Take a good look, Rue," he said as he gave me a once-over. "She's far too young and naïve. Scared of talking squirrels; how on Everlynia will she ever defeat Vironnos—"

Rue stepped on Max's foot to shush him before he said too much. I didn't understand a word Max had said, but I knew I wasn't supposed to. Not yet apparently. Rue jumped and gripped my hair as she ascended to my shoulder. "Don't mind him, princess. He's just a rude boy," she whispered and giggled afterward.

I took a deep breath to collect myself and calm down. That world kept getting weirder and weirder by the second. I tried to communicate with the Rue, but my words were halted by a loud chime that filled the room in its entirety. The squirrels made a high-pitched squeaking noise as they scurried to hide behind the dragon's head. Footsteps echoed louder, and an unsettling sensation rippled through my body at the sight of a powerful Fayestorming inside the throne room, followed by dozens of guards. The crystals trembled from her raging aura. As she approached the throne, her long, emerald medieval gown brushed against the gold beneath her. She sat on the throne and gripped the arms, almost breaking it. She was a queen.

"Why is she here?" she asked quietly.

My insides tightened into a ball. *Is she talking about me?* I wondered. The guards stood speechless with their heads lowered in respect—or fear. No one was looking at me. I was completely invisible to them.

"Why is she here?" the queen yelled. Her voice was loud enough for the crystals to fall from the ceiling to the floor and shatter like glass.

The color drained from the guards' faces as they shuddered in place. A brave one stepped forward, kneeling before her. "She requested a private audience with the king, Your Majesty."

The queen drummed her fingers on the golden arms of the throne. She gnashed her teeth and narrowed her jade eyes at the guard. Her poisonous glare took their breaths away, and mine. "Ah, the wench requests an audience," she said, "with my husband." She rose from her throne and walked gracefully toward the guard, who was still kneeling before her. "Rise." He quickly stood up, bowing his head still. "What does she want with my husband?"

The guard hardly swallowed. "She didn't say, Your Majesty."

"What do you think she wants from my husband?" She leaned forward, scaring him back a few steps. "Speak!"

Too frightened to lift his head, he looked up at her

through his eyelashes. "Perhaps…she wants his forgiveness." His voice was filled with terror. "Y-Your Majesty."

"Tell me," she said, "if you were the king, who would you choose?" Her hand slid under his chin and lifted his head forcibly. "If you were Alrick, who would you be with? Her? Me?" She offered a wicked grin. "Speak the truth." The words escaped her mouth like a spell that completely controlled him. Her sharp nails slowly buried into his neck, scratching deep into his flesh. "Speak the truth, only."

His eyes darkened and his fear transformed into desire. "Me? The king…" He grinned. "I'd choose the fairest queen of all." His jaw tightened. "Yes, the beautiful Helia."

Fear flooded my body as I heard him say my mother's name. If I remember correctly, the vicious queen standing in front of me must have been Rose, my mother's cousin. Queen Rose was breathless with fury. Her eyes flamed as she let go of the guard's face, releasing him from the spell.

The guard let out a loud gasp as if he was finally able to breathe. He cowered on the floor and pleaded for mercy. "Please, Your Majesty! Please forgive me, I wasn't in my right mind. No, I didn't mean—"

With a snap of her finger, she turned the guard into gold dust, falling like a glittering ashen snow to the ground. Her breaths quickened as she gave a deadly glare to the rest of the guards, who stood in complete silence, shivering uncontrollably. With a wave of her hand, she dismissed them all. "Utter lunatics." She sighed.

The guards hurriedly left the throne room, relieved to be in one piece. I turned to face Queen Rose, only to find her gazing at me with her malevolent forest eyes. Her wicked stare was enough to slay a grown man. I felt sweat dripping from the back of my neck as she regarded me with disdain. *Can she see me?* Panic surged through me while she stepped in my direction. She stopped only a couple of feet in front of me. That close, I could feel her growing heat like an open stove.

"Helia… Just when I thought I'd gotten rid of her."

I turned around to find my mother riding Caz's dark horse, marching toward the Solmark Court, swarmed with guards ready to arrest her as if she were a criminal.

"And so, the wench arrives," Rose said. "I won't play nice this time, cousin." I flinched with terror at her venomous energy and the realization that nothing could save my mother from her wrath.

In a split second, everyone vanished into thin air.

The room shifted, and my crowned reflection appeared. "You've seen enough," she said as she stepped out from the cloud of smoke, dressed in a sheer gown. "For now, that is." Her gaze fell to my shaking hands, and she gave a bitter laugh. "You're worried for her? That is good."

"Of course, I am," I said. "My mother is in danger—"

"Oh, yes. She is," she said. "In danger, and alone."

I knew my mother wasn't safe, but to have someone confirm it made my heart twist. Everything Caz had told me came flooding into my mind. I remembered his words, no one can protect her but me. "There must be a way to help her. I must help her."

She smirked and rolled her eyes at me. "You want my help? Ask for it properly."

"Who are you?" I frowned.

She sighed, annoyed. "My dear, I'm a Fateteller. There are many choices you must make, and you must be careful.

Choose wisely or you'll end up in Nothingness. I can guide you away from the danger you and your mother will face."

I took a few steps back before asking her another question. "You're interested in helping *me*? Why?"

"My dear, you are the daughter of Spring and Summer. A promise of power. It would be a waste if you ended up slaughtered by a wicked queen…or something else." She brightened.

A sharp bolt of horror struck me as she leaned forward, examining me. "Will I die here?" I shivered.

"Did you not hear a word I said? You'll only be harmed by your wrong choices." She shook her head. "I can't tell you what to do." She paused briefly. "I can only tell you what *not* to do. However, my help is quite expensive, living one." She plastered a grin on her face.

Of course, she would want something from me. No one would do good for no reason in this land. *You need all the help you can get, Lexi.* "What will it be?"

She rubbed her palms together vigorously. "We'll discuss that later, living one. I only ask for payment after I've delivered my help. Do we have a deal?"

I need her help, I reminded myself. "Fine. Now tell me, how can I help my mother?"

Her eyes gleamed, and she raised a finger at me. "Your first night at the Solmark Court will define your future. Queen Rose will offer a proposal that will end you and our mother if you accept it. Be wary, for the offer is tempting and the wicked queen is waiting," she said. "The nights will be long, but I'll always be by your side, living one." Her voice faded away as she disappeared into the smoke.

I woke up confused, but remembering every detail of my dream as if it were real. My eyes bulged out of my head as I glanced around wildly. I found myself alone near the shining pond, infested with pixies, and with no sign of Caz anywhere. Did he leave me?

I walked slowly toward the pond, staring at my reflection in the water, hoping it wouldn't reach out to drown me. An elf-like girl stared back—leaf-shaped ears, sharp cheekbones, and defined jawline. My wild curls begged for a comb, but at least no crown, frown, or a strange gown.

For no particular reason, all the pixies started flying around fiercely. Multiple twigs broke behind the bushes, and I swiftly snatched the largest pebble I could find and crouched behind the moss-covered stone, ready to throw it with all my might.

The footsteps reached closer to the pond. Only a few feet away, someone—or something—stood their ground, looking for prey.

I gripped the pebble tightly, jerked upright, aimed, and threw the stone as hard and as quickly as I could. I immediately regretted what I did.

Caz quickly tilted his head, easily dodging the pebble flying at him like a bullet. A look of surprise swept across his face, and he regarded me with distaste. "We'll need to work on that later, princess," he said casually. Raising his hand to my face, he held the mushroom creature I encountered before. "Hungry?"

The little creature smiled at me, unaware of Caz's intention to make a meal out of him. "Shroom!" he said, excited to see me again.

"No!" I said, making Caz flinch in response. "No one is going to eat him."

"Why not?"

"Because he's my friend," I said as I picked the little creature up like a baby. Caz raised an eyebrow, glancing back and forth between me and the happy mushroom. "No one is going to eat him," I repeated slowly to make myself perfectly clear.

"Does your friend have a name?" Caz asked, voice full of doubt.

"Um…" I glanced down at the critter, its huge eyes blinked up at me expectantly. "Spore?" I offered, the name spilling out before I could second-guess it. Spore let out a delighted trill.

Caz nodded once and turned back to the pond. "I see you're all healed," he said quietly.

He was right; I'd been too distracted to notice, but the wounds on my calves had healed entirely, leaving no traces behind. "Y-yes, I think so."

The ground shook beneath me. I looked up to Caz and found him glaring at the other side of the pond. His muscles stiffened, ready to battle an army single-handedly.

From a distance, I saw dozens of red riders approaching us. Caz let out a deep sigh and tsked in aggravation, while Spore buried his face in my hoodie and whimpered quietly. Riding on gold-painted horses, the guards marched directly toward Caz.

As they broke into a canter, a tall figure appeared, riding on a black panther. Dressed in a long red coat, he looked like trouble, reeking of bad news. He had straight, charcoal hair lavishly tied with a rubber band into a ponytail. His sky-blue eyes cast a skeptical look on Caz, then glanced briefly toward me. The corner of his mouth turned up into a grin as he gave me a curt nod and turned back to torment Caz. "So, this is what you've been hiding from us, bastard brother," he said in a chilling voice, sending the pixies scurrying to their homes. "The queen won't be pleased."

CHAPTER 4
COURT AND TRIAL

THE WIND HOWLED, sweeping the dried leaves aside and bearing an unpleasant surprise. The riders surrounded me from all sides. Unable to run anywhere, I turned to hide behind Caz. The rider continued to stare at me with a wicked grin, sending a shiver down my spine. Caz sensed my discomfort and edged closer to me.

The panther rider chuckled. "You know, I was hoping for a warm greeting from the old hags, but all I found in their stump was their ashes. Do you have any knowledge of that?"

Caz shrugged. "Only that their time was cut short. Why, were you fond of them?"

"I can't say I wasn't."

"Are you going to say why you're here, or do I have to guess, Liam?" Caz asked in a tired tone.

Liam laughed as he gently patted the giant panther, who stared at Caz in disbelief.

"I DESPISE CRIMINALS WHO CLOAK THEM-

SELVES IN INNOCENCE," the black panther said. His voice was both alluring and calm.

Caz appeared completely unfazed, as if animals speaking were a normal thing. Maybe it was a normal thing in Everlynia, but not for me, I was still stunned by the talking squirrels I'd met in my dream, which had felt very real. "Criminal? And what crimes have I committed, Liam?"

"Oh, plenty, I'm sure. This time, you're convicted of conspiring against the crown," Liam said.

"Conspiring against the crown?" Caz repeated quietly. "Me? What made you come to this conclusion?"

"Don't pretend otherwise. You conspired with the exiled queen to seek a private audience with the king, yes? To further the exiled queen's agenda, you've been keeping a *possible* heir to the Faye Throne away from the eyes of the rulers. All of those are crimes you've committed against our queen," Liam said with conviction. "You made a promise to the throne. You should have been more mindful of the company you keep."

Caz cocked his head. "Since when do you care for Queen Rose, brother?"

Liam shook his head. "Oh no, you cannot accuse me of indifference. I've always been loyal toward my rulers, the saviors of our beloved Solmark," he said. "However, I do it *my* way. That's more than you could claim."

"I, too, am devoted to the throne and I honor my promises. I remained faithful to the one true queen, Helia," Caz said, a whisper of a growing rage in his voice. The veins in his neck stood out as he pressed his lips in displeasure. "Just as you should've done."

Resembling a troublesome brat, Liam forced a smirk on his face. "I did serve Queen Helia for as long as she reigned. As long as she *deserved* to reign. Even rulers aren't immune to making mistakes, and hers was unforgivable." He tilted his head so his eyes could meet mine. "Isn't that right, princess?"

My lips tightened into a thin line. He wanted to see me cower under the weight of his gaze, but I wouldn't give him the satisfaction.

Caz shot me a glance before turning back to face Liam. "That's enough," he said. "If you're here to take me back to the Faye Throne, do it quietly."

"I will, brother." Liam's eyes darted to mine. "However, your companion here will join us."

Caz swung his arm around to push me behind him. "Make no mistake, Liam. You've been given the order to bring *me* back for my crimes. Leave her out of this—"

In one breath, Liam drew his sword, crafted from stone, and aimed the sharp tip under Caz's chin. One wrong move, and he'd be done for. "I've been ordered to bring you back, *dead or alive*. Your choice," he said. "As for the princess, she *will* come with us. Even if it means I have to kill you first." He pushed his sword closer to Caz's throat, slightly pricking his skin.

I'd only spent a couple of days with Caz, but that was more than enough time to know how persistent he was. If I had to wait for them to settle their differences on their own, I'd have to wait a year—or a lifetime, perhaps. I took in a long breath and loomed closer to Liam who appeared astonished by my attempt at intimidation. "Cut it out." I glowered at him. "You can take me to the Faye Throne. I won't fight you. I'll come with you willingly. There's no need for violence." I shoved his sword away from Caz and kept my cold gaze on his brother, hoping he wouldn't notice how scared I truly was.

Liam slipped his sword back into his leather scabbard and gave a curt nod again. "Wise decision, princess," he murmured. "You'll ride with Caz. We should reach the Solmark Court before the trial begins. Hang tight, princess. It won't be an easy ride." He smirked and rode off with his panther ahead of us, while the army of guards rode behind him in a single line.

One of the gold-painted horses cantered toward us. He appeared much older than the other horses. Ancient as time, his silver braided hair fell from his back to a few inches above the evergreen moss-covered ground. He bowed his head as low as he could and greeted me. "Welcome to Ever-lynia, my lady."

I looked at the horse in awe. I wasn't sure if I'd finally gone mad or if nothing seemed impossible in this world, but I'd grown fond of the talking animals.

"Thank you, uh..." I gave him my best curtsy, but apparently, it was terrible, as Caz and Spore couldn't help but giggle a little.

"Call me Valor, my lady."

I nodded. "Thank you, Valor." A smile refused to faint away from my face. Ever since I came here, I've been running away from goblins, escaping old boggarts, and being looked down upon by people who hate me but don't even know me. This was the first time I'd been treated well by someone whose intentions seemed pure. It made me happy to think there might be some good in this land.

Caz gently lifted me onto Valor's back. "Get acquainted later, we don't have time," he sighed deeply and swiftly sat behind me, glaring at Spore. "Is your friend coming with us?" I lowered my head and found the creature's giant glistening eyes looking up at me, he smiled and ducked his head. I didn't want to leave him behind, not with the goblins and dark fae unleashed in the Vileforest looking for their next meal. "Yes, he will."

We rode for hours through the Vileforest. Went up and down hills, over and under fallen trees. Moving at what seemed to be the speed of lightning, everything around me was flashing before my eyes. I almost fell many times, until Caz grew tired of it and wrapped his arm around my stomach to pin me back to him. The cold wind burned my cheeks in a new and painful way. The sound of trots breaking twigs and branches beneath Valor's hooves filled my ears. My heart pounded with fear, not of falling, I was sure Caz would prevent that, but fear of facing the rulers of Solmark.

I asked Caz several times how far we were from the Solmark Court and every time he replied with the same answer: not far. We've been riding for more than five hours with no breaks, food, or water. *How long can a fairy survive in these conditions?* I wondered.

"SHROOM!" Spore blurted as we entered a massive dark tunnel, so dark I couldn't see Valor below me, his clacking steps and bouncing movement the only indication he was still there. That was short-lived as suddenly, Valor's and the other horses' trots became inaudible. We were still moving fast, even faster than we were before, but there was no sound at all. The air became foul and warm, it smelled of blood and bones. I felt Caz's breath against my neck as he held the reins tighter and pulled me closer to his chest.

"Ca—" I began to speak, but Caz shushed me immediately.

"Keep quiet," he whispered in my ears. His warm breath froze the blood in my veins.

In the darkness, I fought a rising panic. I didn't understand the sudden silence that surrounded me. Hisses and grunts filled the tunnel as we rode on. The riders didn't want to confront whatever was hiding in the shadows.

It wasn't until we were out of the tunnel that the sound of the horses' trots resumed to bombard my ears, much to my displeasure. Caz loosened his grasp, and I could finally breathe again. Nonetheless, I didn't dare to open my eyes. Caz let out a sigh that quickly turned into a groan. "We're here, princess," he said in a false cheerful voice. "The Solmark Court, where friends and family smile proudly as they stab you in the back. You'll enjoy it here. I know I do," he added with a sigh of irritation.

My eyes snapped open at the name of Solmark. We'd finally arrived, and all it took was a wave of nausea and the world's worst headache to get here.

Blinking my eyes rapidly, I gazed around at the paradise before me.

A thousand different flowers of various colors and sizes adorned the beaming courtyard that stretched further than the eye could see. Clear glass fountains were scattered about, releasing liquid gold that splattered on the pristine green grass. Pixies, nymphs, trolls, and other fairies I had no name for danced around the fountains, covering their bodies in a shimmery golden glitter. They sang and played heavenly-looking instruments that produced the most beautiful sounds I ever heard.

Valor kept a steady pace, allowing me to enjoy this beautiful side of Everlynia. "Beauty is always found, my lady. Even in the most hideous places," Valor said courteously.

"Ironic, isn't it?" Caz added.

Too distracted by the heavenly view, I agreed without fully comprehending what they had meant. The fairies' gaze locked onto me. Many faces with unreadable expressions. Spore pulled down on a curly strand of my hair, and I snapped back to reality.

"SHROOM," his voice seemed sorrowful.

"What is it? What's the matter?" I asked him as he wrapped his tiny arm around my fingers. He gripped them tightly, nearly breaking one, and continued to whimper. He was clearly anxious but about what? I didn't have the slightest idea how to comfort a friend. How could I, when I had no friends before?

Caz exhaled slowly. "Your friend is scared," he said, "Fairies like him rarely survive a night at the Solmark Court. The weak-looking are devoured within a week at most. And if not for food, he'll be hunted for fun."

What a horrible way to live. I wondered how long *I'd* survive at the court. I'd be every curious faerie's target. I gradually came to believe Caz, that the only person who could save me was myself. That is if the king of Solmark believes I am his daughter, as my mother claims. "Don't worry," I released my fingers from his grip and carefully patted him on the head. "You're not alone. I'll keep you safe. I won't let anyone hurt you, I promise."

The word promise echoed in my head.

Valor gave a terrifying snort. "My lady, try not to make promises to anyone within the Solmark Court. Promises are a cage of iron, unbreakable. They will weaken you until there's nothing left. Nothing, but the darkness within you."

My eyes darkened with worry. As a child, I read many books about promises and favors in Fairyland and what they meant. *A cage of iron.* I've never heard that one before. My body went cold at the thought of it.

A fresh gust of cool wind whipped against my skin as the massive plant-covered gates opened, revealing the magnificent Solmark Court. My worries and thoughts seemed to blow away with the passing wind. Tall, firm stone walls were decorated with large colorful windows, perfectly symmetrical and elegant. Eleven statues of terrifying dragons encircled the building. With holes carved into their chests, it was as if the dragons' hearts had been mercilessly gouged out. Some appeared newer, and others were of ancient stone. Their frightening gaze sent a shiver down my spine. The fact that they seemed frozen in time didn't help calm me down. I had the impression that each one of them would come to life and attack me with their razor-sharp claws. I wouldn't stand a chance against a starved dog, let alone hungry dragons.

Outside the court, elven guards in red and green uniforms were stationed throughout the vast courtyard. They greeted us as we rode through the gates and came to a halt just a few feet from the stone bridge. Liam and his guards dismounted in unison. With a sickening grin and a lazy bow directed at me, Liam crossed the bridge first and entered the court, disappearing through the large jeweled door with his panther by his side.

Caz let me down slowly and his mouth twisted in disapproval. "You're a mess," he sighed. "You must behave when you enter the court. Only speak when you're spoken to. Be respectful, kneel before your king and queen, and…" he paused for a moment, "just try not pull a stunt. You know, first impressions—"

"Matter," we spoke in unison. "Yes, I know," my eyes rolled in impatience.

Valor's nostrils flared. "Cold as always, Caz," he sounded bored. "Never mind him, my lady. Be yourself, that is all," Valor said. "You're not a guest at the Solmark Court. You're *home*."

Caz led the way, and I followed him down the corridor, which was infested with fairies of all kinds. Both familiar and unfamiliar. My heart hammered in my throat, and I forgot to breathe for a while. The fairies must've sensed my terror as they turned their predatory gazes at me, making my stomach contract into a ball.

The corridor grew quiet, the only sound being my echoing footsteps. Glancing around, I met the eyes of many frightening fairies, and I tried not to focus on any of them. Some fairies in the audience bowed with respect, while others stood speechless, their mouths dropping as I passed by. Spore wailed silently and hid his face in my hoodie. Good god, I envied him. At least he didn't have to endure their haunting stares.

I cowered behind Caz until we reached the throne room. Two guards, one dressed in red and the other in green uniforms, greeted him with their hateful looks. Completely ignoring me, they opened the double door and gestured us in.

It's real what they say—dreams do come true. The throne room, to my surprise, looked exactly like the one I saw in my dream last night. The same sculptures in the corners, the same paintings on the ceilings, and the same crystals covering every inch of the walls. At the end awaited a pair of elegant thrones, too distant to reveal the features of Solmark's rulers.

Everything was the same, everything except for the separated seats of what I can only assume was for the noble fairies of the court. Twelve chairs were arranged symmetrically on either side of the Faye Throne. On the right sat six elves, all dressed in luxurious aristocratic clothes with green velvet cloaks that rested on their shoulders. The elves on the left wore similar clothes but were adorned in red cloaks that reached the sparkling-clean floor.

A strong, poisonous aura clouded the room as the nobles were seated elegantly in matching golden armchairs that faced each other. Their chins were held high in haughty pride while the rest of the fairies stood on either side of the throne room, clearing the middle for what seemed to be a trial.

I felt nauseous at the amount of unwanted attention I got simply by standing there. Then, my breath seemed to be pulled out of my body as my eyes landed on my mother, surrounded by four armed guards. She was still dressed in the white satin cloth that she hated so much after it had become muddy. My heart fluttered with excitement. I wanted to run to her, but the moment I moved, Caz grabbed my wrist and shook his head slowly. Giving me a fearsome look that drained the blood from my skin, and I knew better than to run to her, though I badly wanted to.

I stood behind Caz, as a voice, loud and true as a judge, echoed throughout the room. I traced the source to a dwarf who shifted swiftly in his seat at the center of the room.

"You stand before me today for your outrageous crimes against the crown," he began with a sigh. "Robbery, burglary, violence, and intruding the Solmark region. Are you innocent of these crimes, Lucien?" he asked. I couldn't see the figure kneeling on the floor, but the guards swarmed around him as if he would attack at any moment.

"I'm not," the faerie spoke as he raised his head towards the judge. His voice sounded familiar to me; I was sure I heard that voice before, but I couldn't remember where. "But…" he added, "I *am* guilty of intruding in the Icymark region as well. Your enemy, you know. I've killed a couple of their guards; I did your kind a favor." The fairies in the room broke into a low laughter, and the guards drew their swords, aiming at his neck.

The dwarf sighed again. "They're not our enemy, and the criminal acts you commit in the Icymark region are none of our concern, Lucien. I will add it to your long list of violations, however, would that please you?"

"Yes, it would. As you all know, I do care greatly for the well-being of my reputation," he joked, and the fairies burst into quiet laughter once more.

The dwarf groaned as he scribbled on an ancient piece of parchment. "You're a resident of the Vileforest, your reputation precedes you." The dwarf shook his head vigorously. "Someone with your crimes would surely be dragged around until they're ripped limb from limb. However, you are the last of your kin. For that, the crown would pardon your crimes. This time, *only.* If you're brought here again, you *will* suffer the consequences. Have I made myself clear, Lucien?" The dwarf gestured to the guards to let him go.

As he stood up and his face became visible to me, I was certain I knew him. The winged fae that tried to kill me in the mortal world. That horrid raven thing. I turned to my mother, hoping she'd notice him, but she was far too distracted—brushing her hair with her fingers and cleaning her dress as best as she could.

Lucien bowed and waved goodbye to the fairies. "Same time, tomorrow," he cheered, completely ignoring the dwarf's warnings. With just a wink at the crowd, they went crazy. His massive wings spread as he dragged his feet to enjoy more adoration and applause.

Before he could exit the room, our eyes met, and a look of surprise crossed his face. The eerie grin on his face brought back the fear I had when I first encountered him. He remembers me, I'm sure he does. *Will he try to kill me again?* At the prospect, my heart sank to my stomach. Raising an eyebrow at me, a corner of his mouth lifted, and he walked out as if he didn't see me at all.

For a split second, I was grateful for his spectacle. The attention of the audience was drawn to him and his foolish charade. Now that he was gone, all eyes drifted back to me, and I realized I was next.

Caz pushed me forward and we started walking down the hall. With every step, a sharp nervous pain stabbed my chest. My mother joined us with a deafening silence. A few fairies whispered among themselves and laughed as we continued walking on eggshells, our eyes focused on the ground, until we reached the foot of the Faye Throne. Dropping to our knees and bowing, Caz and my mother spoke at the same time.

"Long live the rulers of our beloved Solmark."

As I raised my head, a surge of adrenaline burst through my veins. Queen Rose sat on the right throne, a slim figure with overwhelming power and hatred in her eyes. She looked exactly like the woman in my dream, with a ridiculously large crown on her head. On the left throne, sat the King of Solmark. I've always wondered what my father looked like since my mother failed to mention anything about him.

All the traits that I despised my entire life—the ones that made me an outcast wherever I went, those that only made me a target to school bullies—were all thanks to my father.

The Solmark King had the figure of a Roman god. His orange hair fell in beautiful curls to his bust. A crown made of golden thorny vines rested on his tangled eyebrows, and a sun-shaped pendant dangled from his neck. A threatening and intimidating aura surrounded him like a visible layer of radiance. His lazy crystal green eyes were pinned on my mother, who didn't bother to return the stare.

The room went utterly silent until a wicked voice spoke up. "How dare you stain my throne room with your presence, cousin?" Queen Rose sat her palms flat on the armrest and leaned forward. "Haven't you disgraced us enough? The Solmark Court is no place for a two-faced wench like you."

My mother swallowed a witty retort. She's always been

great at those. "I have returned for my daughter's safety," she inclined her head to show nothing but respect.

"Your daughter?" Rose mused. "Her? Why on Everlynia would we care for that lowly elf?"

"Your Majesty, I'm starting to be concerned about your vision. I advise you to drink less tealoxica henceforth," my mother said without hesitation, making the nobles in red chuckle at her comment. "Alexandra isn't a lowly elf; she is of royal blood. The Solmark King's blood."

Gasps went around the room as my mother made the announcement. The noble elves, on both sides, gave me deadly glares that snatched the air from my lungs. Each gave curt nods that were more like a punch to my gut, and I had to lower my gaze to draw my next breath.

"Liar!" Rose shouted as she slammed her fist against the throne. "I should have your head for your false claims. You dare trespass in our Solmark after my husband banished you, and now you're claiming that mortal isn't a daughter of Adam and Eve, but of royal blood? On what grounds should we believe a traitor like you?" She erupted in a fit of rage that shook the floor.

My mother smirked at her accusations. "Fairies cannot lie, dear cousin."

In a quick motion, the dwarf got up from his chair and approached us gracefully. His oversized coat trailed behind him as he whirled in circles around me. "At last, someone speaks the truth in this court. Fairies cannot lie," he said in a calm, loud voice. "Lady Helia, as a former ruler of the Solmark, you are well aware of our unbreakable laws, which is why I must ask you this. How come you have not approached the Solmark King about this matter sooner, knowing the dire consequences you'd face if you did not?"

I'd expected my mother to be nervous, vulnerable, and powerless right now, but she was as tough as steel. Either bold and fearless, or a master deceiver, I could not tell which. "I simply didn't care about my fate. Only the safety of my daughter. An exiled queen's child would not survive long in Everlynia, of that much I was certain," my mother answered quickly.

"I see…you've decided to wait until your daughter, Lady Alexandra, was older. Old enough to inherit the Faye Throne, yes?" The dwarf gazed through his silver Windsor eyeglasses.

"Yes."

Nothing in the world could have prepared me for this. It was true what Caz had told me; my mother *did* want me up on the Faye Throne, to protect myself, but more importantly to protect *her*. I wanted to storm out of the Solmark Court and flee from the lies and the burden my mother wanted me to carry.

"Lady Helia, you stated that your daughter is no longer safe in the mortal realm, and that is why you've returned to Everlynia. What made you come to this conclusion?" The dwarf waited impatiently for my mother to respond, running his fingers through his long bushy beard.

She drew in a long breath. "There was an attempt on her life recently, by a dark fae," she continued calmly. "As you are all aware, heirs are constantly threatened."

Whispers filled the room. My heart continued to beat loudly in my ears as I received all kinds of looks from the fairies. Some expressed sympathy, while others were outraged at the thought of some fae attacking their king's daughter. The audience hissed and growled in aggression until my heartbeats became inaudible to me.

"Silence!" Queen Rose stomped her foot, sending the ground shaking throughout the court. "This is absurd! This ridicule will not be tolerated in my court. Go on, word-smith," she commanded the dwarf, "make your judgment, and let us be done with this mockery of a trial."

The dwarf clasped his hands behind his body and turned to face the raging queen and the wordless king. "Your Majesties, I'm afraid I cannot deliver my judgment on this matter, only my advice," he bowed his head. "Lady Helia has violated yet another rule by disobeying the king's orders and returning to Everlynia after being exiled for her wrongdoing. Furthermore, she had deliberately kept the *only* heir to the Faye Throne away from Everlynia. Those crimes are enough to label her a traitor and demand her execution." Queen Rose's face lit up with a smile.

"No-" I began to protest but was quickly silenced by everyone's stares. Words froze in my throat, and I struggled to keep a hold of my temper. I couldn't see my mother through the shroud of terror coming over me. I hated that she didn't tell me the truth, still, I couldn't stand the thought of losing her. Trust was out of the question, but she was my mother and the only person I truly cared about.

"However," the dwarf continued as he pointed back to me. "Lady Helia did what she believed was the right thing to protect her daughter. She had returned despite the consequences she might face, to warn us of a serious threat to our heir, and an even greater foe to our Solmark. Lady Alexandra is the daughter of Spring and Summer; an attack on her is an attack on the king and Solmark. So, I urge you, my lord, to not let the anger get the best of your judgment. To not punish for the crimes, but to reward for the integrity and bravery that Lady Helia had shown us today."

The King of Solmark finally shifted his gaze away from my mother. You could hear a pin drop in the silence as everyone waited for the king's response. He eventually rested his gaze on me while staring out at the crowd with an expressionless face. My heart pounded against my chest, and I bowed my head, mostly to relieve the tension. As I lifted my head, I felt everyone's gaze on my back. Finally, the king graced us with his euphonic, spine-chilling voice.

"I have many enemies, none of whom I fear," King Alrick said, "and they will not threaten me, my daughter, or any of my subjects. Whoever tries to take away my heir will face my wrath."

His words echoed in the throne room as he raised his voice higher. "Alexandra will be under my protection until I deem her worthy of the Faye Throne."

My mother sighed in relief and looked back at me with a faint smile on her face.

"As for Lady Helia," he paused for a moment, "she will not be harmed. Not in my land."

"You cann*ot* do that!" The queen rose from her seat and stomped by the king's side. "I will not allow you to treat that elf with respect, she's the daughter of a traitor," she said, shooting me a look of disgust. Her eyes were like needles jabbing into me.

"Careful, Rose. She is my daughter as well," his tone with Rose wasn't kind.

"And you say it with pride?" Rose gritted out. "Everyone

will mock us for this, is that what you want? I am the Solmark Queen, and I command you to rethink this matter."

Alrick narrowed his eyes and tilted his head slightly towards Rose. "Do not let jealousy blind you, my lady. You may be the queen of Solmark, but I am its king. I follow no one's command. I've given my word that no harm shall be done, and my word is absolute. You're welcome to stay longer if you wish, my lady. If not, you may leave. The trial is over." He dismissed her with a wave of hand.

Rose pursed her lips angrily, holding back screams and curses. The audience fell on their knees bowing in fear as Rose's steps shook the ground like thunder. She stopped only a few feet before my mother and gestured to the guards standing behind us. "Take her!" She sneered. "Take Helia to the Spring Court dungeon and keep her locked away. She is not to speak to anyone." Fiercely, she turned to face the king. "No harm, husband. I, the jealous queen, cannot stand her presence in the court."

"Lady Rose," the king leaned forward, and his throne creaked in protest.

"Oh, I insist, my lord. Allow me to relieve you of this burden." She gestured again and the guards drew closer to my mother, waiting for the king's approval to take her away.

He let out a sigh. "Very well, do as you wish, my lady. So long as she is unharmed."

"Not even a scratch," she faked a smile.

The guards pulled my mother to her feet and walked behind the queen as she led the way out.

"Stop!" I cried out, pleading for them to release my mother, but they paid me no heed.

Queen Rose blocked my way like a giant wall. There was no way around her, and most certainly no getting through to her. "Did you not hear him? The king's word is absolute," she shot the unbothered king a final look before walking out.

The green nobles gave me the side-eye as they followed their queen like dogs, one by one, they stormed out of the throne room.

A rush of terrible emotions washed over me. "Please, stop this. Do something!" I pleaded, but the king showed no sympathy.

"Take Alexandra to her chamber," the king ordered, and twin female selkies appeared behind me. They had light blue skin and solid black eyes; their dresses were damped from their dripping hair. They bowed their heads as they stood before their king. "Attend to all of her needs and be sure she is comfortable here."

"Yes, Your Majesty," The twins spoke together in a low, warm tone. I turned to the king one last time, hoping he would notice how distraught I'd be without my mother. I received nothing but a nod from him. A simple nod that told me to forget about it.

And with that, the trial ended, leaving me in utter despair and alone once again.

CHAPTER 5
THE QUEEN'S PROMISE

I FOLLOWED the selkies down the narrow halls. I couldn't see a thing through my teary eyes. Thousands of disturbing envisions plagued my head. *What am I to do here alone?* I thought I would see my mother again. I thought I would talk to her and be with the one and *only* person I truly know in this land, but now I'm stuck in a court with countless eyes on me, but with no one who truly sees me. The twin carrying Spore patted my shoulder in an attempt to ease my worries. Her gentle touch interrupted my train of thought and jolted me back to my current situation.

I gazed up at the giant golden double doors standing in front of me as the twins opened them. Inside, a luxurious bed in the middle of the room, covered with expensive-looking silky sheets caught my attention. The walls were decorated with painted and live flowers dangling every-where. The floor was glowing with shimmery patterns that flowed like a river. A sweet scent came from a corner that was filled with fresh bakery items and drinks.

"This is your chamber, my lady," the other twin spoke

up and beckoned for me to follow her inside. Behind a red curtain, a small steaming pool called for me. Thank heavens I could wash myself at last. "I suggest you get washed first—"

I needed no encouragement from the selkie. Quickly, I took off my muddy clothes and went for a swim in the heated pool. The clean warm water hugged my body, relaxing my aching muscles. For several minutes, my mind went blank, and I felt at ease. The vapor carried away every last trace of discomfort I had experienced while staying in the Vileforest. I didn't want the comfort to end. If it were possible, I would spend the rest of my life in the rose-petal-scented pool. A sudden splash made my eyes open wide in alarm, and I found Spore floating in the pool beside me. I closed my eyes again and surrendered myself to absolute bliss.

Time passed quickly. How much time? I'm not sure. I awoke to candle lights and will-o'-the-wisps flying above my head like a dancing chandelier. I lay motionless in my bed, unaware of where I was or how I got there. I groaned as my memories slowly returned to shower me with the dreaded feelings of the past few days.

Whispers jolted me upright and I nearly screamed at the shadows that stood behind the sheer bed curtains. "Please forgive us, my lady," the twins stammered nervously. "We didn't mean to wake you up, but…Queen Rose has asked for your presence in the throne room. We must get you ready."

"What?" I frowned. "Oh, Rose. What does she want from me?" The words barely escaped my throat as I thought of the raging queen and what she would do to me.

"We know not, my lady."

I shuddered at the possibilities. I always try to mentally prepare myself for the worst-case scenarios, but this time it wasn't working. Nothing could prepare me for what was to come. I'd seen the queen angry before, and I would be a fool to look forward to this meeting.

I sat on a wooden stool as the twins styled my thick hair. I kept my eyes on Spore, watching him munching down on mini cupcakes to distract myself from the pain in my scalp as the selkies brushed through my tangled curls.

"You have lovely hair, my lady," said one of the sisters. I wasn't sure if she meant it or was just trying to ease my nerves, but I thanked her anyway. The other walked to the closet and carefully grabbed a long flowy dress.

"This one will suit you, my lady." She held a soft-looking evergreen gown, masterfully rendered with tiny flowers and gold pearls at the bottom, and long lantern sleeves attached to the corset top. "It's not much, but it'll do for tonight," she added.

For the first time in my life, I slipped into a gown. I'd never felt so exposed before; the dress was weightless. Stepping into view, the sisters couldn't help but burst into joyous cheers. They grabbed my wrists and ran towards the dresser mirror, eager to show me the outcome of their work.

I gasped as I met my reflection. The beautiful evergreen dress complimented my braided hair, adorned with lilies, and falling down to my waist. I almost liked my reflection had it not been for the sharp elf features that made me look like a completely different person.

"What do you think, my lady?" They stared in the mirror, patiently waiting for my reaction.

"I-I think I like it," I said, carefully inspecting the dress and its details. The selkies let out a sigh of relief, retracing their steps to Spore, and began cleaning up the mess he had made.

Out of the corner of my eye, I noticed my reflection move and my head jerked toward the mirror. A whisper of my name drew me in like a force of gravity. *Alexandra, Alexandra, Alexandra,* the voice continued. My heartbeat quickened as I stepped towards the dresser. Everything around me began to fade away until I saw nothing but a glowing princess before me. She grinned from ear to ear and held a finger up to her lips.

I swallowed dryly. I've seen her before, but where? My mind couldn't function like I wanted it to.

The air became thick with smoke, and she inched forward. "Don't forget," she said in a deep, commanding voice. "Tonight will seal your fate. A proposal shall end you and your mother if you accept. Do *not* trust the wicked queen."

Her words paralyzed me, body and soul. I remembered a similar speech she'd given me the last time we met, in my dream. She's the Fateteller. I bit my lower lip to wake up but instead felt a sharp pain. This certainly wasn't a dream.

Horrified, I leaned closer to the reflection. "Simple, no one in their right mind would trust Queen Rose anyway. Whatever offer the queen makes, I will not accept it. Is that all?" I struggled to keep my eyes on her unnerving expression.

"*Simple?*" She snickered in response, raising an eyebrow at me. "You make me laugh, living one. You'd be a fool to accept, and a greater fool to reject the wicked queen. The game has only just begun, and you're already at a disadvantage if you think any of this is *simple.*"

"I don't understand," I stared at her in disbelief. "You said I mustn't accept the queen's offer, or my mother and I will end with a terrible fate."

"If you call it that," she nodded. "A terrible fate, or no fate at all. Those are your choices, living one."

I stood rigid with terror. "No fate at all? The queen would kill us, is that what you mean? You're lying. The king had promised our safety in his land. No one would dare to harm us, not even the queen."

The Fateteller frowned. "I'm a fae, I do *not* lie. What use would I have of you if you were dead? We have a deal, remember? I will help you survive Everlynia, and you will pay a price later. You have my loyalty and service until you are crowned queen. Our contract was sealed the day you agreed to use my services, and you can no longer back out."

My heart rose to my throat. "That...that wasn't a dream?" I recoiled.

"It wasn't," she confirmed. "Your dreams are visions, living one. A token of gratitude, and a way to uphold my end of the bargain, I will show you the past, present, and future. Rest assured, I'm on *your* side."

The ice-blue cloud of smoke twirled, and I knew my audience with the Fateteller was coming to an end. "Never forget, the queen cannot be trusted. Consider yourself warned." She snapped her fingers and the mirror shattered into millions of fragments that showered around me.

Before I could blink, I was back in the present, staring at the perfectly intact mirror and my puzzled reflection.

"My lady, we must head to the throne room soon. Queen Rose hates waiting." One of the selkie spoke. The other looked wary as to why I had been staring in the mirror for so long, but said nothing.

I considered bringing Spore with me but decided against it. I doubt Queen Rose would welcome the little critter. To my surprise, the throne room was almost empty. Only a few satyrs served the queen drinks and fruits, while the rest waited patiently to be of service to her when she needed them. Rose sat on the throne, with her chin resting on her palm. She looked utterly bored until her gaze met mine.

I bowed, hoping she wouldn't turn me into golden smoke right then and there. "Finally, you've blessed us with your presence. Come closer," her voice sent chills up my spine. My legs trembled as I took a few steps closer.

Rose sighed. "Do not make me repeat myself, *heir*."

My body grew tense, and I ignored every fiber of my being that told me to stay back. I came to a halt a few feet in front of the throne before the queen raised her hand to stop me. "Stop there, that's close enough."

Her gaze danced over me, scanning me from head to toe and twisting her face in disgust. "Odd looking," she said at last. "Not even the slightest hint of a Solmark heir. What a joke we have become. And to think someone like you could ascend the Faye Throne," she scoffed. "Oh, that vicious mother of yours hid you well. Surprises, surprises, that is her way of playing the power game. She made the king forgive her crimes simply by dangling you before him. She told a false fairytale, and the idiots believed her. Playing the hero who returned with a cheap heir to save Solmark from another humiliating Seasons Gathering. How considerate of her."

Rage shot through me, and my nerves were on fire. "Why do you hate my mother so much? All she wants is to save me from danger. She will do anything to protect her daughter from harm. She doesn't deserve to be locked away for that."

"No?" Rose chuckled. "You think your mother is a saint? Do you think you're truly free from danger here?" She tapped a fingernail on the throne arm, and a satyr rushed by her side, holding a glass of a black drink I'd never seen before. She sipped the drink and gave me a scornful look. "If anything, you've fallen into a far more serious threat. Have you any idea what the Solmark's throne represents?"

"No," I didn't want to hear the next part.

Her eyes darkened as she leaned closer. "Blood," she went on, "blood of the sacrificed, or your own. Tell me, Alexandra, have you ever fought a dragon?"

Completely serious, she grinned coldly, and I noticed a glimmer of satisfaction in her dark eyes. My jaw trembled in fear as my mouth fell open without a scream. The windows were suddenly struck by lightning, and the shadows of the dragon statues fell over the room. Flinching, I glanced back at the windows and saw nothing but a clear quiet night outside. I must've jumped three feet in the air, for everyone in the room was now making strange faces at me.

Queen Rose laughed as she leaned back in her throne, almost choking on her drink. The satyrs giggled and buried their faces in their hands. Something about my reaction made them crack up. "My dear, if you intend to spend your remaining days at court, I advise you to get used to illusions. Overwise, you'll be labeled as a fraud."

"Am I to thank you for this advice?" My voice trembled as I spoke, unable to gather my thoughts.

"No need to," Rose said, taking another sip. "Anyone would tell you the same. Heir, you're not prepared for what is to come. Perhaps you'll never be. The only way to prove yourself worthy of the Faye Throne is to battle Solmark's sworn enemy, and you're no match for a fire-breathing dragon, my dear. In that regard, no one can help you. Not even the king himself."

"Suddenly you care?" I clenched my fists. "I know what you're attempting to do, but it won't work. You won't scare me away."

"Oh, dear. You don't believe me?" Rose gestured with her cup like a drunken sailor. "You're already scared, I can see it in your eyes. I don't blame you. Tonight, you might be free, but not for long. When the moon begins to bleed in the night, the sacrifice must be made. The Sea of Flames battle may only have one victor. You could become an heir to the Faye Throne…or a useless dead elf, there's no in-between. The Faye Throne, no matter how powerful, can only have one queen."

I was on the verge of having a panic attack. I couldn't tell if Rose was being honest or not. Her wicked grin never faded, and I felt clutched in fear. I knew my mother was hiding something from me, but I never could have imagined the sheer gravity of it. How could she put me in such jeopardy? Part of me wanted to see her, to let her explain herself, but the other part was blinded by emotions. My face felt like it was on fire, and I turned to glare at the Solmark Queen. "What if I don't want to become a queen? What if I don't want any of this?"

The queen rose from her throne and walked swiftly around me, still holding her cup firmly in her hand. "You can't," she said calmly, "it isn't up to you anymore. You've been recognized by the king as his daughter, there's no turning back…however," I stiffened as she pressed a finger into my shoulder. "*I* can offer you a way out if that is what you wish," she said with a snake-like smile.

Here it comes, the queen's proposal.

"I propose you leave Everlynia for good. Take your mother and go back to the mortal world. No one needs to know of this. In Solmark, you'll be forgotten as if you've never existed. Return to your normal life and leave the mess behind. Everlynia isn't your home. If you agree, I will have my guards escort you and your mother back to the Vileforest. From there—your mother knows the way," Rose giggled. "I'd say she's an expert."

I was torn between the two choices. Accept the queen's offer and return home with my mother or reject her and stay in Everlynia to face an unpredictable fate. The right choice should have been obvious to me, but it wasn't. I wanted to go back and forget about all of this. I wanted to go back to being no one, to forget about all of this. Still—

Rose snapped her fingers and time gradually slowed down. A second felt like an eternity.

"Do we have a deal?"

I felt dizzy. The world spun around me, and I began to lose control. Drawn deeper into a void, I couldn't think at all. I heard the queen mumble words I didn't quite understand, and the more she said, the less control I had. I felt as though my lungs might burst. *Her proposal shall end you and your mother if you accept. Do not trust the wicked queen*, the fate-teller's whispers consumed me and pulled me out of the void.

Queen Rose seemed surprised when I gasped for air. Startled, she took a step back and narrowed her eyes in confusion. "How—"

"We don't have a deal!" I interrupted, thankful that my voice was convincing. "You're a manipulator. I would *never* trust you, Queen Rose. Do you take me for a fool? If I had accepted your proposal, I would have been taken to the Vileforest with my mother, a land that does not belong to King Alrick, so by killing us you won't be breaking the king's promise. Am I mistaken for assuming this?" I thought of every word the king had said during the trial; he promised us safety within his land but said nothing about the outside of Solmark.

She cocked an eyebrow to my response. "My, my, how unexpected of you to read my mind. Yes, I wanted to spare you and your mother some measurable pain. You are weak and unfit to rule. Miles away, your mother will rot in the Spring Court dungeon, and you will soon face one of Solmark's strongest foes. You understand your path will not be pleasant. Why bother trying, heir?" She threw her head back.

I sucked in a breath. "No matter how unpleasant the path may be, I'll decide when to end it, not you. If there can only be one queen, so be it."

Rose threw her cup to the floor as she bared her teeth. "You dare challenge me? Careful, a dragon might not seem so scary compared to me. I will turn you to ashes of gold before you'd think to cross me again." A couple of satyrs rushed to clean up after their queen. "I have offered you mercy and you refused it. Remember that when your heart will be torn out between the flames of the Summer and the Shadows. As your blood turns cold, your memories will fade. You'll drown in the Nothingness, lost forever and forgotten, that is the alternative."

My veins throbbed in my neck. A surge of power overtook me, and for a brief moment, the vicious queen did not frighten me. "You will not bully me into accepting your offer, Queen Rose. I have made my choice, and I am prepared to face whatever grievances you may cast on me."

"Get out," Rose gritted, her eyes blackened with hatred. "Get out of my sight!" She sneered, and the crystals shook overhead, a few fell inches from my feet.

I started to walk away from the queen when she clapped her hands once to stop me.

"One more thing," she said, her eyes lowered to mine. "I'll send your regards to my dear cousin. However, I doubt she would care for anyone right now. Poor thing, she must've reached the Spring Court dungeon as we speak. What can I say, it's not a pretty place. Not for a lady, anyway," Rose smoothed down her dress as she sat back on the throne. My eyes filled with tears. "Oh, how rude of me to remind you. Don't you worry, heir. At the very least, *you* will get to enjoy your time at the court." Rose's eyes gleamed and she drew a sickening smile on her face. "Off with you now."

I wiped a tear off my cheek as I fled the throne room. The further I ran from the wicked queen, the more tears flowed down my cheeks. Everything the queen said had finally sunk in. Inside, I was smoking with rage. Rage that the queen might've been honest all along. I know I did the right thing, but I felt very empty, as if I'd lost everything just now. The pressure in my brain rose as I remembered my mother. I begged to wake up from this nightmare and return to my normal life, with my normal non-ex-fairy-queen mother. I nearly tripped over a brownie fey that cussed out so many words I'd never heard of. Before I could turn to apologize, a dark shape emerged from a corner with a tiny window and pulled me into the darkness. With a hand over my mouth, I couldn't scream even if my life depended on it.

"Hold your breath," he whispered in my ears and pulled me closer to his chest. I did. In an instant, I felt my feet were off the ground, and my body became light as air.

Sneers and hisses filled the corridor as a group of redcaps marched down the hall with a troll secured over their heads. They dug their claws into him and tore his flesh. Pure evil little things laughed as the little troll cried out his last screams. One of the redcaps mimicked his screams, and the rest burst out laughing.

"Shut up, ya filthy caps!" Shouted a larger one in the back. "Let us deliver the damn message and get out of this filthy court. We ain't here to hunt the bloody trolls. Say another word and I'll rip ya heads off."

The laughter died, the rest carried the dead troll, and passed by us as if we weren't visible to their eyes. Perhaps we *were* invisible, for even *I* didn't feel myself present. The voices faded as they turned into a different hall and vanished from sight.

"Icymark redcaps? Why are they here? The Seasons Gathering is a fortnight away," the dark figure spoke to himself. Either forgetting I was beside him or simply didn't care.

I blew out my cheeks after he released his hand from my mouth. My feet hit the ground as if I'd been falling from cloud nine. I yanked myself free from the his grip and whirled around to meet his eyes.

Caz shot both of his eyebrows up. His mouth opened, but he couldn't get a word out. Instead, he regarded me in silence with his solemn blue eyes, giving me an *are-you-okay* look. That is when I realized that my tears were still warm on my face.

Embarrassed, I turned away from Caz. I wished on every shooting star that he wouldn't ask me anything, but as always, my wishes were not answered. "What's the matter?" I didn't answer. Caz grabbed my wrist and turned me back around. "What's the matter, princess?" he asked again, this time a little louder.

"It's none of your business. Let go of me!" I shouted.

"Yes, it is," he said, pressing harder on my wrist. Enough to make me flinch. "I made a promise to your mother. *I* am responsible for you as long as she remains away. Now, tell me what made you think it was a good idea to wander the halls alone at night. Have you no regard for your safety?"

Caz has jumped to conclusions yet again; it must be a

habit of his. One that I'm sick of. "You're hurting me," I whispered, too tired to raise my voice. Caz loosened his grip but didn't let go entirely. "The queen requested to speak with me, that's why I'm out here. Very kind of her to explain my duties to the crown. Something my mother failed to mention, or perhaps she didn't think it was important enough."

Caz sighed. "She wanted to tell you at the right time," he murmured. "Princess, there's nothing you should worry about. You are—"

"I am lost! That is what I am, Caz!" I shouted, throwing my hands up in the air. "Every second I spend here takes a piece of me away. I barely recognize myself anymore. I feel as if I'm paying for every breath I draw, every step I take. I used to be an outsider and free, but now I'm enslaved to this role, this act that I'm forced to play. And all for what? To become a worthy heir? How's any of this supposed to make me feel safe? So don't tell me I have nothing to worry about when all I *can* do is worry." I didn't mean to explode with rage, but I did. I fought back tears that threatened to spill again. My chest rose and fell with rapid breaths.

I gradually began to gather myself. Oddly enough, I felt somewhat relieved, as if a massive boulder had been lifted off my shoulders.

Caz went completely still for a long moment. Waiting for me to compose myself. Waiting for the fire within me to be put out. Finally, his shoulder sagged, and he raised a hand to scratch the back of his neck. "You ask far too many questions, princess," Caz whispered, managing to put on a smile.

Good God, was he trying to be nice? His gleaming blue eyes locked on me, and every last bit of rage died away. "Yeah? Well…you hardly answer any, Caz."

"What's the point? You won't listen anyway," he said, matching my tone. "Follow me. Oh, and this time," he turned back with a stirring glance, "try to keep close."

"Where are you taking me?" I asked, trailing behind him as he turned from one hall to the other. This Caz was nothing like the one at the maze, he knew exactly where he was going, making quick left and right turns without hesitation, like he owned the place. I thought he was ignoring me for a while, but then he surprised me with yet another faint smile.

"I know someone you'll listen to. *He* knows everything. Everything you need to know and more," Caz said, taking my hand in his and gently pulling me closer to him. We stood speechless in front of a white wooden door that had been conjured out of nowhere. I doubt I'll ever get used to the oddity of this place. If I do, that'll be the day I've lost my sanity. "Even *you* might run out of questions, but he will never run out of answers." He pushed the door open with one hand, and together we stepped inside.

CHAPTER 6

CHAOS AT THE SOLMARK COURT

THE ROOM WAS DARKER than a starless night. A vast space of nothingness welcomed us as we stepped inside. The white door creaked behind us, sending eerie echoes around the room. My heart pounded in my ears, and I shifted from one foot to another, waiting for something to jump out at us and drain the blood from my veins. That is what I imagined anyway. For a long time, nothing happened. Caz squeezed my hand and stood behind me, breathing down on my neck. My heart drummed faster and louder as he whispered in my ears.

"Ready, princess?" A blinding rainbow portal opened beneath me. A refreshing minty breeze gently lifted my hair and dress.

Caz held my other hand, and we jumped.

My eyes widened with excitement as we slid down the colorful portal. Vibrant colors flew past me like a dream. Some were so bright for my eyes, I thought I'd go blind by the end of this ride. Nauseous, I began to hear soft voices in the background, whispering my name and giggling. They sang a song about the Sea of Flames, the sacrifices, and the pain. My emotions were out of control; I wanted to laugh, cry, dance, hide, scream, and fly, all at once. Although I could see Caz behind me, I couldn't *feel* him at all. Quickly, I became sick with the overwhelming pressure surrounding me from every side. Every time I thought the fall was coming to an end, a new portal appeared, and we continued to slide through it.

One after another, until we finally arrived at our destination. I was on the verge of collapsing on my face, my life flashed before my eyes, and I thought this was the end. Instead, I stopped a couple of feet above the marble floor, floating in the air as if gravity no longer existed. Caz, on the other hand, landed on his feet with a feline grace. He snapped his fingers once, and I dropped to the ground. Cursing, I bounced to my feet, thankful I didn't break any of my teeth.

"Seriously? Was there no other way?" I asked with irritation, glaring at Caz.

He shrugged. "We could've taken the stairs, but...I wanted to see that face," he said, and I rolled my eyes at him. Caz looked down at my dress, then back at me with an unreadable expression. He seemed a little *different*, or perhaps it was the fall's side effect that was making me see things. "Come on, the little man knows we're here. Let's not keep him waiting."

I followed Caz into a secret door behind a leaf-covered wall. My mouth fell open at the sight before me. Inside was the largest library I'd ever seen. Hundreds of captivating shelves rose to kiss the sky, filled with books of all sizes and colors. Some of the books moved by themselves, rearranging their order, and flying from one bookcase to the next as they pleased. Flowers and plants adorned every inch of the shelves, adding to the enchantment. Countless floating candles, like fallen stars, illuminated the large room.

"Does my lady like books?" someone asked, standing behind me.

I spun around, half surprised, half frightened. Caz caught my back with one hand to prevent me from falling and making a fool of myself. The dwarf dipped his head in a nod as he gave me a heartwarming smile. Silver beard stroked the floor as he did, and his large eyeglasses teetered at the edge of his nose. Dozens of books floated behind him, waiting to be placed in his hands. The dwarf shot his eyebrows up at me, reminding me there was a question I still needed to answer.

"Oh, yes. I do enjoy reading," I said, swallowing.

"What a surprise," his face lit up. "I must admit, I never imagined a Solmark Princess to share my hobby. I do feel somewhat…special."

Caz crossed his arms over his chest. "Well, you'll feel more special when you learn the purpose of our visit." Caz grabbed one of the flying books and began skimming through the pages. "The princess has a few questions for you. You think you can help, wordsmith?"

My breath caught in my throat as the dwarf reached for my hand. "I'm delighted to be of your service, my lady," he said, nodding. "Allow me to show you the way, princess. Feel free to join us, Caz. I'd rather have you where I can see you."

Caz followed quietly behind us, his head buried in a book he picked up along the way.

We followed the wordsmith to his work area where old maps of the human world and books lay scattered across the marble floor. It wasn't that the wordsmith was messy, but there were far too many books in such a small workspace. If my mother were here, she would discipline him in the same way she does me, after paying a visit to my so-called "side of the bedroom." The wordsmith motioned towards the tree stump. I sat awkwardly across from him as he settled behind his desk. Caz leaned against a shelf, flipping through the pages of his book.

The wordsmith shifted incessantly in his seat, rocking side to side until he finally stopped. "Please forgive me, Lady Alexandra; being this close to you scares me," he said with a soft laugh.

I couldn't help but frown when I heard his comment. I've been called many things before, but *scary*? That one was new, and I had no idea how to respond.

The wordsmith noticed my confusion. He quickly clarified, his voice growing an octave higher. "I only meant that you greatly resemble your father, King Alrick," he shook his head, certain that he made a mistake.

Oh, wonderful. If only being a smaller version of the king would make things easier…

"It's alright," I said, acting as if it meant nothing to me.

The wordsmith let out a sigh of relief as he comfortably leaned back. "What questions do you have for me, Lady Alexandra?"

At last, I could ask the questions that have been eating me alive. "The Sea of Flames," I blurted almost too quickly, "tell me all about it."

"As you wish, my lady. However, I must warn you that it

isn't a pretty tale," the wordsmith said, motioning to a pile of maps on the floor. An old one emerged from beneath, flying above the wordsmith's head and leaving a trail of dust in its wake. "Since the beginning, Everlynia has been home to five powerful guardians, Summer, Spring, Fall, Winter, and the Shadow. Each guardian defended their region with honor and dignity, and they were all united by a greater force. A force that granted powers and wishes to the most virtuous guardians and created life itself. In time, the Shadow guardian began to seek more powers, more than he could ever possess. The stronger he became, the weaker the force grew, and soon it vanished.

The days turned into nights, and the moon bled for a fortnight. Darkness descended, and Everlynia suffered terribly from its wickedness. Without the great force, the seasons drifted apart, and unity crumbled. The Shadow guardian destroyed his region, but it wasn't enough for the monster he'd become. Slowly, he sought to wipe out the other seasons. The Shadow believed that the power he possessed made him absolute, that he could take whatever he desired."

The magical map translated his words into motion pictures. Switching scenes every time the wordsmith paused.

"One by one, the guardians succumbed to the great darkness. Only the Summer guardian was successful in defeating the shape-shifting Shadow, putting an end to his greed, and restoring light to Everlynia. Little did they know, the light would always be accompanied by the Shadow. History seemed to repeat itself over and over again, as the Shadow creatures continued to hunt for power. Draining the life out of Everlynia, and everyone living in it.

"Ever since, the Summer and the Shadow have been the worst of enemies. It became a ritual for the Solmark heir to defeat a Shadow dragon in the Sea of Flames battle in order to ascend the Faye Throne. This practice will finally end the day you'll kill the last living dragon, Vironnos. Unlike the Summer guardian, you, my lady, will end the Shadow once and for all."

The wordsmith gazed at me with his ghostly white eyes, stirring fear within me, until I couldn't take it anymore.

"Why me?" I whispered, feeling a little stupid for asking.

"You're the first daughter of Spring and Summer, Lady Alexandra. You're Solmark's promise. The only one who can save Everlynia from destruction," the wordsmith explained, leaving me choked with horror. One day I was an average high schooler, and now I'm expected to defeat the last dragon.

"No," I muttered, shaking my head. I couldn't do what they were asking of me. I couldn't kill a dragon, even if I wanted to. *How could my mother possibly believe otherwise?* The thought made me shudder.

"Yes, being born in the mortal realm may have left a mark that sets you apart from the rest of us. Your tongue may not be bound to tell the truth, but it doesn't change who you are. It doesn't have to."

"You don't understand, I can't do what you're asking of me."

"My lady is afraid," the wordsmith's voice broke through the jungle in my head, "but, you don't have to be. A Shadow dragon can't defeat you; it has never happened, and it never will. All Summer fairies are immune to fire. As the daughter of King Alrick, you are no exception."

I stole a glance at Caz and saw him nodding slowly. His eyes were still glued to the book he was holding firmly in his hands, but he was attentively listening to our conversation.

A sudden steamy gust of wind made the flying candles flare in aggression. Both Caz and the wordsmith leapt to their feet like they were being summoned. I froze, clinging to the tree stump chair, unaware of whatever it was that they seemed ready for.

"We have to go," Caz said as he pulled me to my feet. We rushed out of the library of fallen books, candles, and torn papers. I tried to remember the way out, but it was impossible. We had made a hundred turns and walked out of dozens of gates. I couldn't remember the path, even if I had a map in hand to guide me.

In the halls, fairies of all kinds crowded the corridor as they waited outside of the Faye Throne room. It didn't take long for their murmurs to reach our ears.

"There was an attack on the Spring Court. That's all I heard," someone said. Shushes filled the air as they saw us coming from a distance.

Caz stopped in the middle of the hallway where the redcaps had savagely killed the little troll. I nearly bumped into him. He whirled around and regarded me somberly. "Perhaps you shouldn't be here, princess. This doesn't concern you. It's best if you return to your chamber—"

"Nonsense," someone interrupted, walking up to us, "I believe the future heir of Solmark should hear this. Learn a few things about our politics and the way of Solmark. And *maybe* avoid making the same mistakes as her mother. We wouldn't want another disappointing queen, now would we, bastard brother?" Liam grinned, showing off his fangs. Good god, I wanted to punch him in the face.

Caz's face became solemn. He, too, felt the same anger boiling up inside. Instead of responding, he drew me alongside him as we walked down the corridor.

The crowd's knife-like gazes followed us until the throne gates closed behind us.

We stood amid chaos. The king and queen sat quietly on their thrones, while the Spring and Summer nobles squabbled.

"Another foolish act! Hasn't Spring done enough ruin to Solmark? How long would we have to endure your shame? With your actions, we're weakened by the day!" The eldest Summer noble rasped, sending a prickling sensation up my spine.

"Careful now, Lord Damien," A spring noble stepped forward, far too close to him. The two were at each other's throats. "Spring has no part in this. Lady Helia is no longer the Spring ruler, nor a subject of ours. She is not our concern."

"Nothing is, so it seems," Lord Damien chuckled. "It's humiliating to have some filthy Icymark redcaps report to us your failure. It's hard to believe you had no hand in this, Lord Aries."

Liam sprinted by Damien's side, ready to lash out whenever he commanded it. "Just say the word, father."

"You dare accuse the Spring of Helia's absence?" Lord Aries shot back, threateningly enough for both sides to draw their swords. Caz threw his hand to his side, and a sword of flames and ashes slowly began to appear as he swiftly gripped the burning hilt. The ground trembled beneath my feet, from the nobles' gazes.

"Stop this madness!" King Alrick commanded; his voice frightened even the still dragon sculptures in the corners. "There will be no bloodshed in my court. We have enough enemies as it is. I did not summon you to fight, but to find a solution," Alrick said in a cold tone. His eyes darted through the crowd of nobles like an eagle's, and then they met mine. With a curt nod, he directed the attention of the nobles toward me.

I recoiled. Not from their resentful stares, but from the queen's wicked smirk. "My king," Lord Aries said in a measured voice, "an attack on the Spring Court is an attack on you. On Solmark. We mustn't stand by and do nothing—"

Lord Damien interrupted the Spring Lord. "And what do you suggest we do, Lord Aries? Start a war for someone who isn't worthy of our sacrifice? We don't know for certain who is responsible for tonight's attack, as Lady Helia had countless enemies before. If the Darklings were to blame, no one in their right mind would go against them. Surely, she must've known something like this would happen when she decided to return to Everlynia. She brought this on herself!" Lord Damien raged.

I stood there in the throne room, my heart racing and a shuddering sigh escaped me. My mother was abducted, and no one seemed to care. The one person I needed the most had been taken away from me, again.

"Where is my mother?" I managed to ask, too frightened to control my shaking hands.

The last person I wanted to hear from was the wicked

queen. "Who knows?" she mused. "Perhaps in the darkest part of the Vileforest or the coldest region of Icymark. If your dear mother is still alive, that is," she said, sounding anything but empathetic.

King Alrick sighed. "Your mother's been abducted by the Darklings, no doubt." He pinched the bridge of his nose. "Do not fret; the Darklings will be dealt with," he announced.

I shook my head. "It's not the Darklings that I'm worried about, it's my mother!" I gritted out. Something I surely never imagined doing in front of a fairy king, surrounded by heartless elves, but I couldn't care less. I wanted nothing more than to be with my mother again, alone in our one-bedroom paradise. No fairies, Darklings, dragons, and no Everlynia. Just the two of us.

"Your mother…" King Alrick seemed unsure of what to say. "She had my protection for as long as she remained in Solmark. Things have changed now. It's best if you forget about her."

The world stopped spinning, leaving me in utter disbelief. I couldn't breathe, his words suffocated me like a snake tightening around my neck. The possibility of not seeing my mother again made my heart sink. My eyes quickly filled with tears, but I wasn't going to cry. I wasn't going to let him tell me what to do either. King or no king. "You're not nearly half the man my mother described you to be," I seethed in my croaky voice, hoping my words were as distressing as his.

Thrashed by the nobles' glares, I left the throne room without an ounce of regret in me.

My mind became a jumble of thoughts as I made my

way back to my chamber. I wasn't sure what to do, but I knew I had to do something. *If the Solmark King and his nobles have no intentions of saving my mother, then I will.* I wished determination was enough to bring her back, but in a world full of unknown dangers, I'm at a complete disadvantage.

Outside my chamber, the twin selkies paced restlessly in the hall. Their faces were chalk white as if they had seen a ghost. They stood frozen when they saw me coming from a distance. "My lady!" they both called out, voices shaken with terror. "W-we only left for a little while. We had no idea any of this would happen," they went on, pointing to my chamber.

My heart pounded. I ran inside, unintentionally knocking over the sweets-filled table as I came to a halt. Exactly as I've envisioned. Spore was nowhere to be found, and the room was a total wreck. I didn't know what to make of it, only that I was beginning to hate this place more and more as time passed. Things and people appear and disappear as they wish, and I have no control over them.

"My lady, look!" one of them shouted, bringing me back to the present.

On what once was a mirror-clean floor, ashes and dust spontaneously gathered in the shapes of letters and began to form words:

Carrots,

. . .

Though the night was dark, I have seen it all.
If you wish to make a deal, meet me inside
the Pixiehouse at dawn.

Worry not, your fungi is safe and sound.

By the time I read the last word, the wind swept away the ashes, and I felt a spark of hope in me. Someone is willing to help me find my mother; the odds may not be against me after all. My heart fluttered with the thought of our reunion. Drowned in my joyous hallucination, I awakened to the twin shrieks.

"My lady!" I jolted upright in response.

"The message! It was right here; did you see it?"

"Y-yes," I fell to my knees, tracing out the words that drifted out of sight far too soon. "I did."

"Whatever does it mean?" The other sister asked with a wry grin, "And who's Carrots?"

Carrots. Suddenly the world went fuzzy and dark. Those repulsive familiar words resounded in my head, squeezing my throat shut. Those words belong to the one person responsible for all of this, the one who forced my mother to tell me the truth and bring me here, the one who tried to kill me, that raven thing. No, Lucien.

Everything fell into place, yet I was desperately puzzled.

Why would he help me now? Why would he want to? I wondered if this was another trap. I wondered if he still intended to get rid of me. Nothing made sense, but I didn't have the time to waste.

I tried to persuade myself that things would be different now. This time, I have Caz by my side. I'm not a nobody; I'm an heir of Solmark. He couldn't hurt me, nor trap me.

I'm on the horns of a dilemma; if I wanted to save my mother, I would require Lucien's help, but if I didn't accept, I might lose her forever.

I hurried to the closet door and flung it open, looking for anything remotely comfortable. I only found a lace-up ruffle hem pinafore with a dirty white smock. When it came to clothing, my options were very limited, but at least it didn't scream "Look, I'm of noble birth!" I finally slipped into the mossy green pinafore that hung just below my ankles. *They've got talking animals, but no jeans?* I wondered, picking the lilies out and styling my hair into two messy braids. Nothing like the twin's work, but it'll have to do.

Speaking of which, the twins regarded me quietly as I moved around the room like a mouse. Perhaps they thought I'd gone mad. Perhaps I had.

"My lady!" Both shouted as I stormed down the hall.

I ran as fast as I could, past the elven guards and court servants whose eyes followed me until I vanished from sight. I found myself encircled by the eleven heartless statues outside. The dragons looked down at me with narrowed eyes, or so I imagined. I shuddered and slowly took a step back.

"Going somewhere?" I nearly screamed when an unexpected voice came from behind me.

I whirled around to find Caz riding his flame horse, dressed in silver and black. Fiery red eyes bored into me for a moment, and then the dark horse bowed his head. Startled, I looked back at Caz, having forgotten the question he had asked.

Caz raised a brow and shook his head. "Quite a show you put on tonight. No one disrespects the king and lives to tell the tale."

"You're here to scold me then?" I stared at him, daring him.

He smiled and looked away. "No. That's not my job," Caz said with a sigh. "Besides, it won't be of any use. You're too hardheaded."

I nodded, unsure of what else to do. "Then why are you here?"

"To tell you that the king's right. You should understand that your father is the ruler of Summer. As the king of Solmark, he shouldn't attend to less important matters—"

My blood boiled and I couldn't control my temper. "Then you're here to tell me that we shouldn't do anything, is that right? Should I do as your dear king says and forget about my mother as well?" I snarled, cutting him off before he said another foolish word.

Caz sighed. "As I was saying, this affair should not be attended by the rulers or the nobles, so I propose we take matters into our own hands. Surely you won't be missed in the court. Neither will I."

My face lit up with excitement. Finally, someone understood just how important she was to me. And of all people, I never expected serious Caz to understand me. The moment I opened my mouth, I was cut off by him.

"That is if you're not too busy screaming out your lungs. I'll gladly accompany you on this journey, as I've made a promise to your mother to protect you and stay beside you. Always."

"But… won't we be in trouble for this?" I wondered.

"They'll have to catch us first," Caz said with a smile. The moonlight danced around him, and his eyes sparkled like diamonds.

"However," Caz dismounted briskly and came face to face with me. "I want you to understand that this journey isn't just about finding your mother. You must learn the way of fire if you're going to defeat the last Shadow. I will teach you everything you need to know, but you'll have to promise me you'll learn. You'll have to promise me you'll try, princess."

I recoiled at the thought of having to face a shadow myself, let alone fight one. I had no intention of claiming the Faye Throne, so why would I? Nevertheless, I needed every advantage I could get.

"I'll try… on condition that you take me to the Pixiehouse by dawn," I said as I crossed my arms, hoping I was convincing enough. "And no questions about whom I'm meeting."

Caz's eyes widened and the dark horse snorted in disbelief. "Pixiehouse? You…you've been there before? The Pixiehouse?" He narrowed his eyes.

I didn't understand what all the fuss was about. "Does it make a difference? I'm hoping to meet someone there. Will you take me, or should I find someone else?"

Caz groaned as he raked his fingers through his hair. He slowly shook his head and then held his hand out for me.

"As you wish. We'll have to leave now if you want to meet your *someone* by dawn."

I realized what he said and blushed, even though I knew it was nothing like what he thought. Caz waited patiently until I placed my hand in his and we shook on the deal.

We mounted the dark horse and rode off into the darkness. I turned to look at the Solmark Court one last time before the trees buried it out of sight.

CHAPTER 7
DEVIL'S DEAL

THE NIGHT FLEW by in a blur thanks to my overactive imagination. I thought of every possible scenario for what could happen next. Some were plausible, while others were ridiculous. What if I didn't reach an agreement with Lucien? What would I do if he refused to help me? What would Caz do if he found out how I first met Lucien? What could I possibly tell him? *Oh hey, this is the man that tried to kill me in the mortal realm?* I wouldn't be surprised if Caz attacked him then and there. No, I simply can't tell him how I met Lucien. Certainly not when Caz's only concern is my safety.

Before I could think of any excuses, dawn broke, painting the horizon with a beautiful yellow tint. The dark horse came to a halt, and I realized we had arrived at the Pixiehouse. As I took in the sight, I understood why my request to go there surprised Caz so.

The Pixiehouse was infested with elves dancing around each other, wearing barely any clothes on their backs. They laughed, danced, and kissed.

"See your friend anywhere?" Caz murmured, as he

helped me down. I hardly heard him over the din of the crowd.

Friend? Over my dead body, I thought as I scanned the outside for a soon-to-be-dead raven thing, but I couldn't find him anywhere.

"Should we look inside the Pixiehouse?" Caz suggested.

I nodded. No sooner did Caz take a step forward then I grabbed his wrist to stop him. "Actually…I really think I should go alone," I stammered, "the…uh…person I'm meeting may not be comfortable if we both go in."

Caz wasn't convinced. The dark horse wasn't either. Their eyebrows furrowed in suspicion, and I didn't blame them.

Ignoring them, I walked to the Pixiehouse entrance. My stomach twisted with each step, and finally contracted into a nervous ball as I pushed open the door. The inside was painted red with black flowers dangling from the ceiling, far less dull, but still far too crowded. Elves and other fairy creatures played games and gambled while others tested their strength in private duels.

I stood there watching two goblins arm wrestle for a pixie trapped in a golden cage. The goblin with giant biceps easily won, tearing his opponent's arm in the blink of an eye. Other fairies applauded as the winner snatched the cage from the table and lifted it above his head, much like a trophy. The poor pixie squealed in protest, but no one seemed to care. And the other goblin's cry faded with the cheering.

My heart skipped a beat as two strange hands rested on my shoulder. I flinched away, almost tripping over the goblin's arm when two fauns caught me and pulled me back to my feet. The fauns had hairy goat legs and hooves that danced around me in circles. They spun faster and faster until I could no longer see their features, only the horns that were protruding from their heads and the tail wrapped around their bodies. A hot cloud of smoke arose, obscuring my vision and making my mind increasingly fuzzy. Their hands continued to pull and release my braids, causing me to lose balance.

"Enough!" I shouted and silence descended on the Pixiehouse. All eyes were on me, and the fauns were gone. I felt like a complete idiot. All the predators, gamblers, champions, and bartenders stopped to judge the little crazy elf. I regretted leaving Caz behind, but it was no use now.

"Carrots!" Lucien matched my volume. Fortunately, I was free of their critical stares. When I turned around, I found the raven resting on a pile of pillows, wings spread, and five female elves hovering over him the way bees hover over flowers. Spore slept soundlessly in his lap. "Fancy seeing you here," he said sarcastically. I clenched my fists and ran over to him as the conversations and games resumed.

Seeing him reduced to shambles, the fear he once held over me vanished. If anything, his current state makes me want to punch him right in the guts for all he'd done to me. "Why don't you join us? The more the merrier," he giggled.

I glared at him in disgust.

"You sure are the life of the party," Lucien sighed and clapped twice for the elves to go away.

"Tell me, what do you know about my mother, devil?" I asked as soon as his entertainment left.

"*Devil?* Easy now, Carrots," Lucien grinned, gesturing for

me to sit beside him. I snatched one of the pillows and sat across from him, crossing my arms and legs.

"Are you going to tell me what you saw, or should I guess?"

He *tsked* and shoved his coal hair away from his eyes. "I just happened to…" Lucien struggled to find the right word, "Borrow. Yes, I happened to borrow something when I saw the Spring guards riding alongside your mother when they were confronted by the Darklings."

The Darklings! Lord Damien was right in assuming they were responsible for the attack. I recalled the unfriendly nobility's conversation in the Faye Throne room.

"Very entertaining creatures by the way, you should meet them someday," he went on, "if they got a hold of something, they never let it go."

So much for getting my hopes up. "You don't happen to know where they went…do you?"

"Carrots…I know where everyone goes," Lucien put both his hands behind his head. "Sure, the Darklings can be difficult to track for anyone, especially someone like you, but nothing ever hides from me. All you have to do is trust me," he winked.

"Trust *you?*" I winced. "Did you forget that you tried to kill me the first time we met?"

A corner of his mouth lifted. "You won't need to worry about that anymore, Carrots. I'll only fight you if you choose to fight me."

"Really? Well, that's a relief," I gave a false smile. "So, what's your price?" I asked, glaring at him.

"A favor for a favor," Lucien said as he leaned forward, waking up Spore by doing so. "I'll be your guide to find the

Darklings and your mother. In return, I'd request a favor from you at the appropriate time. Have we got a deal?" Lucien grinned and extended his pinky towards me.

I hesitated, narrowing my eyes. Lucien let out a loud sigh. "Don't worry, I won't ask for your hand in marriage. I'm confident you'll beg for it yourself."

I rolled my eyes, knowing that I didn't have much of a choice. "Fine," I said as I wrapped my pinky finger around his to seal the deal.

Lucien took my hand and pulled me up to my feet. "Take this," he said, handing Spore to me. "It's a good idea to have a snack for the road, Carrots."

"He's my friend. And stop calling me that!" I snapped as we left the Pixiehouse.

Outside, Caz was far too preoccupied, surrounded by the entertainment crew. Though he didn't seem to appreciate the attention.

"Look who's here! If it isn't the infamous bastard of Lord Damien," Lucien said, his voice was loud enough to silence the crowds. "Now, shouldn't you be back at the Solmark Court to defend your Spring Queen?" his voice went up an octave.

I glared at Lucien to shut him up, but he went on. "To my knowledge, Solmark is one queen short."

Caz stormed towards us, his face flushed with rage as his eyes darkened. He angrily grabbed Lucien's collar, pulling him closer. "What was a scum like you doing in Solmark?" Caz gritted out.

"What you should've done," Lucien replied calmly, "keeping an eye on your queen."

Caz raised his clenched fist and went for a strike at Lucien, though he didn't flinch one bit.

"Caz, stop it!" I shouted, catching his wrist before he went too far. "That's enough. Come to your senses. Both of you." Although no one made a move, their eyes were pinned on each other. "Lucien will help us find my mother," I said.

"What?" Caz growled, shifting his dark eyes on me. I resisted the urge to run away and hide forever.

I sighed, knowing this wasn't going to be easy. "We made a deal, Caz."

"*You what?*" Caz stepped closer to me, scaring even Spore, who shrank slighly in my arms. "You made a deal with this *vile* criminal? Have you lost your mind, princess?"

"Only Lucien knows where these Darklings—these *things* could be. I need him just as much as I need you, Caz," I said, glad my voice didn't tremble as much as my heart. "We should take matters into our own hands, isn't that what you said?"

"*We,*" Caz replied, his voice soft yet threatening. "You and me."

"I understand if you don't want to help me anymore," I sighed, hoping that wasn't true. "I won't hold it against you, Caz."

"No, you wouldn't," the roaring waves in his eyes abruptly stopped, "but I would."

Guilt grabbed a hold of me. I may have made things easier for myself, but I've also made things much more diffi-cult for Caz. "I don't like it either, but I've found a way. It might seem insane and dangerous, but that's alright. I have you, Caz. I trust you to keep us safe." His eyes went soft in response. "So, please, trust me on this. We don't have much time," I added.

Caz jerked his head away from me. I didn't have to look at Lucien to notice how entertained he was. I sucked in a breath, fighting the desire to punch him in his smug face for nearly costing me Caz.

Lucien stiffened. "My dearest ones, I hate to put an end to this lovely argument of yours, but we've got company."

Caz and Lucien gazed ahead of us, as if they could see beyond the hundreds of trunks and thousands of branches. "Solmark guards," Caz muttered as he took my hand in his. "We have to get out of here, princess."

"Follow me," Lucien said, spreading his wings and flying away.

We followed Lucien for several minutes before the Solmark guards vanished from sight, but their horses' gallops were still audible. Suddenly, the dark horse came to a halt as we found ourselves on the edge of a forest cliff.

Lucien landed, sending a surge of wind our way. "The Vileforest is just below; they can't follow us there. Have you made up your mind, Damien's bastard?" he drew nearer. "Or should we wait for the king's guards to take her back to court?"

Caz didn't respond. I looked back and found him glaring at me with his glinting eyes. This close, I could see my reflection in his eyes. Embarrassed, I averted my gaze.

"Fine," Caz sighed, "take us to the Darklings."

I shivered, gazing down the steep drop. My legs trembled uncontrollably to match my heart. Spore took one look down at the distance we'd have to fall, then fainted in my arms. A freezing breeze surged, stabbing my face like a stack of needles. Screams and hisses drifted out of the darkness, but I couldn't see anything past the gray clouds. If by a miracle I would survive this fall, I wouldn't know what to expect in the eerie darkness below.

Caz patted the dark horse gently as he whispered his goodbyes. I could swear I saw the dark horse shooting me a look of hatred. Perhaps he understood that Caz would be going with me instead. I wasn't sure before, but now I'm certain that the dark horse most likely hates my very existence. A few moments later, the dark horse rode away with glassy eyes, leaving a trail of ashes behind.

"Don't worry," Lucien said as he placed a hand on my shoulder and held my unconscious friend with the other. "You won't die if you know how to fly," he teased with a wink before he flew down the cliff screaming with excitement.

God, it's a good day to be a bird.

"Are you sure about this, princess?" Caz asked.

"Y-yes," I tried to sound brave, but I knew I wasn't fooling anyone. Caz turned me around so that I'd face him instead. With a hand wrapped around my waist and the other on the back of my head, he pulled me closer.

"W-what are you doing?" I stammered, struggling to break free from his grip. "Let go, you fool."

A muscle twitched in his jaw as he held my gaze. "Stop fighting. It's the only way, princess. Unless you're experienced at flying or ready to forfeit your life, don't let go."

I wasn't ready to sign my death warrant, so I let him press me against his chest, and together, we jumped.

Both my head and my heart were thudding wildly, and I couldn't help but think I was falling to my death. I felt like we were stuck in a loop, with the same images playing over and over again, making me wonder if I was dreaming it all.

Subconsciously, my fingers dug deeper into Caz's back, and he tightened his grip around me. I buried my face into his chest, trying to make the life-flashing images disappear.

After what felt like an eternity, the ringing in my ears slowed, and I could finally breathe again. I opened my eyes slowly, expecting to see angels with musical instruments floating around me. Instead, I met Caz's glowing eyes on top of me. I might have enjoyed the moment a lot more if we weren't in such sinister darkness.

"Are you hurt, princess?" Caz demanded, his eyes darting around me to see if I was well.

"I-I don't think so," I shook my head, shivering. Caz breathed a sigh of relief and pulled me to my feet. I tried to stand on my own, but everything got hazy. The dark forest swayed from side to side, making it harder to stay conscious. Several moments blurred out of memory and the next thing I know I was back in his arms.

His lips were moving, but I couldn't hear a thing. I frowned, trying to read his lips then remembered how bad I was at it. There was no use. Caz grasped my shoulders and shook me so hard until I gained my consciousness again.

"Are you all right, princess?" he asked, his hands cradling my face, though not too gently.

A frown line appeared between his brows as he poked

my forehead. "Still there?" Caz asked with a faint smile. My face must've been funny enough to make him smile.

I wanted to answer, but I couldn't. I watched the smile fade from his lips as a look of awe crossed his face, drawing him even closer.

Twigs snapped from a distance, and Caz took a few steps back, shoving his hands in his pockets.

Lucien glared at Caz then back at me. "Well…miracles do happen. Who knew carrots could fly," he grinned. "Any idea when we'll eat this thing?" He asked, raising Spore like a plastic bag. "I'm starving, you know."

"We won't!" I protested, grabbing the creature from him and clutching it like a baby. "Spore is my friend, not your snack."

"*Spore? Friend?*" He mocked, but didn't get a reaction out of me. Lucien straightened. "Oh, you were serious? Okay… I'm starting to question your sanity," he added.

I ignored him again, partly because I too had been questioning my sanity the moment I got here, but mainly because I had no time for all that.

"Where are we going now?" I asked, hoping the Darklings weren't too far away or that we wouldn't have to jump off another cliff, because God knows I can only handle a limited amount of that. Once was already too much

"Carrots, unless the Great Whisperers allow us to, we won't be going anywhere," Lucien replied, leaning against a tree.

"The Great Whisperers?" Caz asked. "Why would we need permission from the dryads to go anywhere?"

Dryads? *Do nymphs of oak trees actually exist?* Of all things fairy, I didn't know why I found the idea of dryads unbelievable. I'd read about nature spirits before, but no amount of reading could ever truly prepare me for *talking trees*.

Lucien chuckled and tilted his head. "Do you think a Solmark heir and a Damien's bastard would be welcomed here, pretty boy? One whisper is all it takes to send the nastiest of fae on a royal hunt," he said, stepping away from the tree. "You and carrots here wouldn't last a minute. Now, I suggest we get them on our side to avoid unnecessary hardship."

Caz's gaze met mine, and I knew he wanted me to make the final call. All of a sudden, I remembered the Fateteller's words about how increasingly difficult decision-making will become frequent on my uncalled-for adventure. I nodded, despite my discomfort. If there's one thing I remember from the books I've read, it's that dryads are benevolent creatures. I prayed to all the gods the authors were telling the truth. Otherwise, we'd be in for a world of trouble.

Under the gloomy clouds, we walked more cautiously than usual, trying not to attract unfriendly faces. With Lucien in the lead and Caz behind me, I've managed not to scream every time the wind blew the leafy tree branches in my face. Time passed at a snail's pace as Lucien entertained us with his tales of improbable adventures. As if gore, stealing, and burglary were good topics to discuss while traveling through a real-life nightmare. None of us thought so, except Spore who giggled at every word Lucien said. I wasn't sure if he thought it was actually funny, or that he was simply bored of the silence.

Caz and I groaned in protest as Lucien started a new robbery tale.

"What's the matter?" Lucien sounded offended. "I'm only trying to kill time."

"The only thing you're killing is us," Caz replied with a serious face, and I couldn't help but giggle uncontrollably.

"You think *that's* funny, Carrots?" Lucien asked as we arrived at the Great Whisperers' home. The dryads lived in a colossal, twisted oak tree with branches reaching as far as the sky allowed. Pixies and will-o'-the-wisps wrapped around like Christmas lights on a balsam fir.

Lucien swallowed a lump in his throat and dropped to his knees as if the oak tree were sacred. "Oh, Great whisperers," he announced, "forgive this wicked soul and let us enjoy a glass of elderberry wine." Lucien cried out, dramatically throwing his hands in the air.

A spooky green smog emerged from the oak tree, filling the air with a fresh mint scent, and whirling around until four figures appeared out of nowhere. The smog slowly disappeared, replaced with beautiful dryads. They had green skin, blonde hair with green strands, and bright green eyes that were enough to illuminate the forest. Three identical triplets stood behind the tallest dryad with slightly sharper features, and tree leaves stuck out of her neat and straight hair. With a looming presence, as if she owned the forest itself, I wondered if she was the dryads' leader. She leaned towards Lucien, lifting his chin with a skinny finger. "No," she said so simply. She had the ability to steal the hearts of many with her voice alone.

"How about a cup of tea, Aurora?" Lucien grinned. "So, we can talk about our indifferences in a sober manner."

"You dare?" Aurora crossed her arms. "If you had your way, you'd be talking to a ghost right now," she spat.

Lucien jumped to his feet. "I was hoping we'd gotten past that, sweetheart."

"Oh, forgive me if I don't praise you for attempting to steal our heart in exchange for a hundred golden coins, and enticing dozens of fairies to follow your lead."

Lucien laughed nervously, taking a couple of steps back. "Sweetheart, I would never do that," he said firmly. "To make you feel any better, I had intended to sell it for twice as much."

"How kind of you," Aurora jerked her head in our direction. "Oh, and you've brought company too," she smirked and drifted toward me. "I've heard whispers about you, *rightful heir*, or should I say, spoiled princess. Long before you arrived. You see, the wind began to sing of Solmark's Princess the moment you were born. And ever since your birth, it wouldn't shut up about you."

I didn't understand why, but I sensed jealousy in her voice, her words, and her eyes. As Aurora drew closer, a blazing sword, as hot and bright as the sun, stood between us. "That's close enough," Caz's voice was thick with authority. Once again, he held the flaming weapon as if it didn't burn him at all.

"Ah, the good seed of Lord Damien," Aurora *tsk-tsked* and shook her head. "A bastard who isn't afraid of his rulers' wrath. How unfortunate of you to remain in service of the scandalous queen."

"Stop it," I gritted out. "Do not speak of my mother in vain."

Aurora applauded in a silly manner. "Forgive me, Your Highness," she paused and looked me up and down, "but I find it impossible to believe that you will defeat the last shapeshifting Shadow. A fey who lived in the mortal realm like you simply cannot win the Sea of Flames battle. In fact, I think you will be Solmark's first defeated heir. What a sight you'll become."

Aurora had an angel's face and a devil's soul. A dangerous combination that could easily lure the greatest of rulers to their downfall. I ignored all the signs and stepped closer to the dryad. "You must keep quiet about us being here. That's an order," I gazed straight into her eyes and watched as her brows furrowed. I didn't look, but I was sure Caz had the same expression on his face.

"I don't *have* to do anything for you, princess," Aurora replied, crossing her arms, and tilting her head.

"Oh, but you do," I inched forward, and she jerked back. "I don't know, I'm just a spoiled princess who gets whatever she wants. Imagine if I announced a reward of a thousand golden coins for your heart; how many hunters do you think would compete for that sum? How many greedy, starving faeries does your forest have?" I tried to sound as confident as possible, and it seemed to work. Pursing her lips, Aurora swallowed hard, and I knew I was getting to her. "Why don't you ask the wind for an answer." Her lips started to move, but I wasn't going to give her a chance to think. "Or you could do as I've ordered and keep quiet."

I hated playing the princess card, but I had no other choice. The wordsmith's comment echoed in my head. Unlike other fairies, my tongue isn't bound to tell the truth. Aurora didn't need to know that. She looked back at the triplets and found them under Lucien's wings, nodding furiously as they cuddled him.

She blew out her cheeks and straightened. "As you wish, *princess*," she hissed.

Caz and I watched as Aurora walked away, ordering her sisters to stay away from Lucien and later smacking him on the head. I found that hilarious and strangely satisfying.

"You know, you could sell iron to a fay, princess," Caz murmured. An amused, soft smile spread across his face then vanished as Lucien staggered toward us.

"Never anger a dryad, that's what I say," Lucien growled, scratching his head. "Oh, no. This is bad," he said, gazing up at the sky.

Lightning sizzled, and for a split second, I could see the forest in its entirety. Encroaching tree limbs obscured the sky. Spider webs shimmered like chandeliers before blending back with the darkness. A roar of thunder shook the ground as the gravel-grey clouds threatened to rain.

"We have to get out of here," Lucien said emphatically, and I couldn't agree more.

Without warning, the Vileforest dropped a couple dozen degrees, sending a cruel breeze whipping through the trees. Twigs fell like snow over our heads and hisses and growls echoed through the forest. Fortunately, we made it inside a cavern before the merciless rain started.

Mosses and liverworts decorated the gloomy cavern. My nose was filled with the scent of sweat and rotten plants. As we ambled deeper into the unknown, humidity provided some warmth, but not nearly enough to stop my shivering. Water dripped from the ceiling onto the wet stones, and a few landed on my scalp. The cavern barely passed for shelter, but it was far preferable to freezing to death in the rain.

"Make yourselves comfortable," Lucien said as he sank to his knees. "We'll be here for a while."

CHAPTER 8
WHISPERS IN THE STORM

Terrible rain continued outside, drawing more and more unpleasant growls that turned into screams and faded with the storm. We stared in silence at the crackling fire Caz had created by simply gesturing with his hand. I wondered if I would ever be able to control fire the way he does. Warmth spread over every inch of my body, and I surrendered to its dreamlike embrace. Spore stacked pebbles near the fire, gurgling happily as he finished building the world's shortest tower. He yawned and waddled over to me, resting his face on my lap.

I watched as our shadows danced across the liverworts-covered walls, morphing into strange shapes with each spark of fire. I looked down and found Caz studying me carefully. He realized I was staring back and straightened, turning his gaze to Lucien instead.

"How far away are the Darklings?" Caz asked, sounding awfully bored, probably from being trapped in a cavern and all.

Lucien jerked upright, eager to speak with anyone about

anything out of sheer boredom. "Not how far, pretty boy," he said with a devilish grin that stretched from ear to ear, "but how *high*."

I didn't understand a word Lucien had said, and neither did Caz for a brief moment, before his eyes widened in surprise. The shock that crossed his face made my stomach twist in fear.

"The Mountain of Ruins?" Caz asked, scowling.

Lucien nodded. "Your people didn't quite give them a choice."

Everything was clear as mud to me. "What exactly is the Mountain of Ruins?" I inquired, though part of me wished I hadn't.

The mossy stone walls could have answered by the time either of them spoke. Caz and Lucien kept quiet as if I'd asked them to reveal their darkest secrets to me. "Caz!" My voice rose in authority.

"That's…" Caz hesitated. "The Mountain of the Ruins belongs only to Vironnos."

Vironnos. That name had completely slipped my mind. What I thought was a dream quickly turned into a nightmare. My warmth fled, and I shivered once more. If I want to rescue my mother, I must risk encountering the last Shadow, Vironnos. No, I would have to *defeat* him.

Aurora's words gnawed at me, and worse, the wicked queen's vision showed up uninvited.

I have offered you mercy and you refused it. Remember that when your heart will be torn out between the flames of the Summer and the Shadows. As your blood turns cold, your memories will fade. You'll drown into the Nothingness, lost forever and forgotten, that is the alternative.

Her menacing laugh played in the back of my head like a sickening record that made me want to rip my ears out. With a jolt, my wandering mind returned to the present.

I'm in a muddle trying to figure out what to do next. A million questions caught in my throat, yet somehow, I managed to mumble one out. "I don't get it. Why would the Darklings abduct my mother? What could they possibly want from her?" I asked.

Caz and Lucien shared a quick glance at each other, both waiting for the other to answer.

"They don't want her," Caz said, looking at me strangely. "They want you, princess."

"The Darklings are Shadow worshipers," Lucien broke in, stretching his legs out in front of him. "You'd understand if they had a grudge against you. After all, you're destined to battle Vironnos on the bloody night."

"We shouldn't worry about that now," Caz said, shooting a glare at Lucien. "First, we have to find the Darklings without drawing attention to ourselves. Then we'll decide what to do next.

"In the meantime, princess, you must unleash your innate power and learn to master it. We must hope for the best and prepare for the worst." His solemn voice implied that we had no time to waste.

I closed my eyes, trying to calm myself, when a sudden thought crossed my mind, and it terrified me. *What if I don't have any powers?* Silent lightning flickered ceaselessly through my eyelids, a welcomed distraction to say the least.

The night grew still as death. The sound of rain died away, and I found myself alone in the cavern. I looked around for Caz and Lucien, but they were nowhere to be found. Spore had also vanished, and I feared the worst. The fire crackled in the center, drawing me closer to its warmth. *At least the fire's still waiting for me,* I thought, oddly unbothered by the fact that they abandoned me in this eerie sanctuary. Outside, the wind howled through the trees, a haunting voice whispering my name in the pitch-black night.

I shuddered as smoke made its way inside the cavern, quickly reaching my feet. A figure emerged from the smoke, stepping closer with each beat of my heart.

I leaped back, my heart stammered in my chest, and a scream welled up in my throat. Caz's fire sparked ferociously as the lean figure came to light. To my utter surprise, I stood face to face with an exact clone of myself.

"Don't fret, living one," she said, kneeling to the ground. "You've made the right decision when you refused the queen's proposal, if you had, you wouldn't still be here," the Fateteller mused. "Which would've made the matter of payment considerably more difficult. Although," she paused to look at me with a poisonous glare, "you are already off to a dangerous start."

"Why are you here? What do you want from me?"

"I ought to be asking you that question, living one. You've summoned me here yourself."

I frowned at her, and she sighed. "The question, living one. What question do you have for me?"

"O-oh," I stammered, for a moment I forgot about the questions I had. "I actually have a few—"

The Fateteller cut me off before I could continue. "It appears that you don't listen very well. I can only answer one question, living one. Now get on with it," she said as she snapped her fingers and gravity forced me down on my knees.

Moments passed as I racked my brain for the right question to ask, but I couldn't really settle on one. "I got it!" I shouted, though the Fateteller didn't share my enthusiasm. "Do I have any special powers?" I needed an answer. I needed to know if I'd be able to defend myself when the time came. I still didn't want to fight Vironnos, but it wouldn't hurt to know if I had a chance. Nothing seemed to matter more.

The Fateteller cocked an eyebrow at me and shook her head. "What nonsense. You're the daughter of Spring and Summer, dear, of course. You'll have unmatched powers. How else would you be able to defeat the last Shadow?"

A burst of relief surged through me. A feeling I haven't experienced in a long time.

"Careful now," she went on, "the Solmark Court desires your demise. With a new secret edict, you'll find yourself in greater danger than ever. It's time you learn to use your unfathomable powers. Make no mistake, a queen without power is a queen without a crown."

She grinned, motioning for the fire to erupt into flames, hiding her from sight. "Until next time, living one."

When I awoke, I found Spore playing with my braid, twisting, and pulling at it like a rope. With a jerk, I sat up and looked around to find Caz sitting at the cavern's edge, looking out as the last few drops of rain fell to the ground. I breathed a sigh of relief. "Where's Lucien?" I asked, glad to see Caz hadn't abandoned me.

"He went hunting," Caz explained without looking back at me. "That vile thing can't go a day without threatening innocent creatures."

"Innocent?" I asked, sitting down beside him. "I thought the Vileforest was home to iniquitous fairies. That's what my mother had told me anyway."

"Iniquitous, yes," Caz agreed, lowering his head to look me in the eyes. "But innocent in comparison to him. Bringing Lucien with us was a mistake," he whispered.

There it was. Somehow, I knew Caz would never trust Lucien, let alone allow him to help us. I wanted to challenge him, but there was nothing I could say in favor of Lucien. Nothing came to my mind. Caz was right in every way, and I hated it. "He promised to find the Darklings. We need his help, Caz." I reminded him, and myself.

"And what did you promise him, princess?" he asked, sounding concerned and slightly angry.

I licked my lips and murmured, "It doesn't matter." I must've sounded ridiculous. Perhaps I've dug my own grave with this deal, but I didn't have much of a choice.

"Do you trust him?"

I didn't answer at first. I couldn't. Making a deal with Lucien didn't exactly mean that I trusted him. Despite his assurances that he would not harm me, he did attempt to do so once. That is something I would never tell Caz. A heavy burden of regret weighed me down. "I was drowning in despair, and Lucien offered to help," I whispered, feeling guilty for hiding something from him. Caz was the only one who my mother trusted, and I couldn't even tell him the truth. "But I don't know if I do," I finally answered, my eyes welling up with tears.

Caz regarded me with sympathy. He placed a hand on my head and inclined his head to mine. "That's fine, princess," Caz reassured me as he pulled me upright. His eyes flickered with an emotion I couldn't place. "Nevertheless, you can't go on like this. Do you at least trust *me*, princess?"

I froze. My senses spun with the gust and my face flushed crimson. "I-I do," stammering, I watched as a radiant smile stretched across his face and a faint crinkle appeared at the corners of his eyes. Caz still held my hand, gently pressing tighter before releasing it completely.

"You're getting married?" someone yelped, jerking us back to reality.

Caz groaned, shooting Lucien a dangerous glare, and saying something impolite.

"And without my blessings? You two are phonies!" Lucien whined, dragging three dead rabbits behind him. He set them on a stone near the cavern and turned to finish his act. "I expected something like this from the pretty boy here, but *you*," he said, shaking his head, the way I imagined fathers would do. "Carrots, you disappoint me."

I rolled my eyes. "What's this?" I asked, pointing to his stack of prey.

"That's food, Carrots," he said, obvious to my concern. "And not the type to cuddle and call friend," he gestured to Spore, who was clutching my leg.

I bit my lip hard, concealing a curse. I don't know how he manages to say something idiotic every time he opens his mouth. One of these days I'll lose my patience with him and it won't be pretty.

"When do we leave?" Caz asked, watching us with visible irritation.

"Now," Lucien replied. "Unless you two phonies want to plan your wedding event here, it's better to leave the Vileforest as soon as possible."

"We're leaving for the Mountain of Ruins *right now?*" I shrieked, shuddering as I imagined the monster we'd have to face.

"Oh yeah," Lucien said, nodding slowly, "right after we enter the Enchanted Abyss, summon the Banshee, find the portal to the Icymark region, intrude Icymark, endanger ourselves, possibly start a war, and then we'll deliver Your Highness to the Mountain of Ruins. So, if that sounds like we're leaving for the Mountain of Ruins right now, then yes, we're leaving right now."

Strike one, my mind whispered.

"I'm afraid no one is going anywhere," an old voice spoke, standing behind a trunk. "Ain't that right boys?"

Twigs snapped, the trees rustled from one side of the forest, and goblins appeared everywhere. Hideous short creatures with yellow crooked teeth held their glass spears close to their chests as they strolled toward us. They wore vicious grins on their faces that stretched their bulging noses wider.

My chest tightened with fear. *Did the dryads betray us?*

Caz drew me behind him as he held his flaming sword in defense. "Stay back, princess," he warned. "Things might get ugly."

Lucien reached into his back and pulled free a black

crystal dagger, flipping it in his hands as if it weren't a lethal weapon. "Now that's how I like to start my mornings," he grinned.

"No need for violence, boys," their leader, I assumed, said. "We don't intend to hurt Princess Alexandra. We only want to take her back to the Solmark Court, by order of the King."

"Since when do the goblins of Vileforest follow the Solmark King's orders?" Caz inquired, raising his sword.

The goblins snarled altogether. "Since your king promised a chest full of gold to anyone who brings her back. Now, hand over the princess, boy."

"Funny," another malicious voice came from the tree-tops, frightening the goblins back. "His queen promised us more to bring the bastard alive." The trees trembled as a herd of redcaps fell to the muddy ground like heavy rain. Their shaggy beards as tall as them flapped in the wind. The redcaps wielded scythes that could cut through bones simply by looking at them. "And *much* more for the princess dead," the biggest one said, pointing at me with his clawed finger.

I cringed with fear, hiding behind Caz as a shield. The words of the Fateteller suddenly came to mind. *The Solmark Court desires my demise. No. Queen Rose,* I thought. *That must be her secret edict. Generous of her to put a ransom on my head.*

"Walk away now," Caz ordered, "and you may leave with your limbs intact."

The redcaps stood their ground. "Your offer is as good as a broken promise, lad," the redcap said with a sneer.

Caz's sword flared with anger as if it reacted to his emotions, his wrath. The once frigid forest could suddenly melt from the rising heat. Afraid of his mere shadow, I was glad he was on my side.

The redcap flinched. His eyes darted around the forest, searching for a way out. He gave a lopsided grin as his eyes shifted to Lucien. "Half the gold," he announced. "What say you, Lucien?"

Lucien grimaced, revealing his sharp teeth. His expression hardened as he gave me a once-over. I was trembling like a leaf as I watched his golden eyes dim with desire. "Nah," Lucien replied, looking up at the redcaps. "She's worth more. Besides, no amount of gold would persuade me to forego this fight."

With a snarl, the redcaps and goblins charged towards me. Caz and Lucien whirled in opposite directions, each ready to fight a herd of foes on their own.

The sound of glass shattering filled the air as Lucien evaded the goblins' strikes with ease. Dashing through them, his dagger thrusting faster than the eye can see, leaving stacks of dead goblins behind. His wings carried him in the air, forcing three goblins to bump into each other and causing another to trip over their bodies.

"Come on, weaklings," Lucien mocked as he landed, "I've seen rabbits fight better than you."

They charged again, hissing, and swaying their swords at him. Lucien continued to move through them like a flash, sending some goblins flying high in the air and then dropping dead. Only a few remained, but he wasn't going to end this fast. Not until he was completely satisfied.

Caz, on the other hand, lunged forward and sliced through the redcaps' necks with his flaming sword. The dead were reduced to ashes and scattered across the field before being carried away by the wind. He moved swiftly through the herd, not a single scythe reached him. He was unstoppable. The savages decided to swarm over Caz like ants. One moment I could see him, and another he disappeared beneath the mountain redcaps. Enough to crush him to death.

"Caz!" I screamed, unable to see any trace of him.

More redcaps scurried over him, crushing my hope of ever seeing him again. The wind stopped howling and everything slowed down. The redcaps let out one last scream before Caz erupted in flames. The scorching wind knocked me down before I could see what happened next. When I lifted my head, I found Caz standing alone, panting in a field of embers. The redcaps had vanished, leaving only their filthy scythes behind, and their threat had become a thing of the past.

A screech made my heart jump. I turned and found Lucien over a goblin's body, sheathing his dagger. "A little warning wouldn't hurt, pretty boy," he said, as he stepped forward.

"Are you hurt, princess?" Caz murmured, pulling me upright.

I was at a loss for words. I now have more enemies than ever before thanks to the Solmark Queen. Perhaps having Caz and Lucien with me should have made me feel safer, but it didn't. I despised how I felt. I stood in the corner, a pitiful princess, while the guards fought to protect me. I can't be weak, not when I have to *save my* mother. I had to be strong. If I had any powers, this was the time to find and use them.

"Princess?" Caz ran a hand over my face, drawing my attention back to him.

That's right; if anyone could help me, it would be him. "Teach me the way of fire," I demanded, looking Caz in the eyes. And to my surprise, Caz shook his head once, almost denying my request. He dropped his hand and began to walk away, dragging Spore to his feet.

Dazed, I stared at him, unable to make sense of his behavior. "You told me I have to learn the way of fire if I was going to defeat the last Shadow. What changed?" I asked.

"Nothing has changed," Caz said calmly. "But I don't think you're ready, princess. You can only use your given powers once you accept who you are."

"Who am I?" I frowned, trying to understand his words, but I couldn't. "What do you mean?"

The sky darkened unexpectedly, drenching the forest in an eerie mood. Lucien looked up at the clouds and sighed. "We should start moving," he suggested. "The Enchanted Abyss is four days away and we can't afford to waste more time. The longer we stay in one place the more enemies we'll attract. And with the ransom of the king and queen, I'm sure we'll attract more without even trying."

We marched steadily through the shadows, rarely pausing for a breather without Caz and Lucien arguing over something completely insignificant. I couldn't do much thinking thanks to Lucien's storytelling that had us all begging for our ends to come sooner. My mind felt clouded with Caz's words; I needed to accept who I am or else I wouldn't be able to use my powers, but what could he possibly mean by that? What exactly must I accept? The overhanging branches snagged my hair, and I hissed in pain. I looked ahead at the vine-infested tunnel and sighed. I couldn't decide whether the sharp needle-like vines that stabbed me everywhere or Lucien's rambling would kill me first.

I was certain it was nighttime by the time we crossed the tunnel, despite the fact that there had been no sign of the sun all day. Drained from walking for hours in the darkness, we collapsed on a log, and my shoulders sagged with exhaustion.

The sound of water flowing over my gasping for air was barely audible to me. The cold wind burned my scars with each breeze, and I winced from the pain. We were quiet, listening to the swishing sound of the leaves when Lucien decided it was time to break the silence.

"Tell me, Carrots," Lucien began, "how do you find Everlynia?"

At least it wasn't another tale of his life, I reasoned. I lifted my shoulders in a shrug. "I find it…" I paused, trying to come up with a word that could describe this place. The place where one can experience all emotions at once, see unnatural colors, hear strange voices, and dream of strange people claiming to have answers, only to cause more questions. "Exceptional," I said nervously. "I never imagined such a place existed, even though I spent most of my time fantasizing about the most unusual worlds where I could be considered...*normal*," I fought back tears, "but once again, I find myself an outcast."

Lucien narrowed his eyes. "What are you talking about, an *outcast?* You're home, Carrots. Everlynia is where you belong."

My heart sank at the prospect of spending the rest of my life in a fairy world. *No, I don't want this. I don't want this nightmare to last.* "That's not true," I protested, as Spore whimpered at my tone. "I'm not one of you, and I don't belong here."

I felt Caz's gaze on my back, stabbing me harder than a knife. No sooner did I turn my head that he got up and stormed off without a single word, vanishing into the night.

Lucien blew out his cheeks. "That was cruel," he said, shaking his head, "even for me."

"I don't understand," I murmured, looking back at Caz's trail. "Have I offended him?"

He exchanged a glance with Spore before raising a brow at me. "Just him? You've offended Everlynia in its entirety, *promised one*. You really don't understand just who you are, do you?"

"Why is that anyone's concern?" I asked, throwing up my hands. "No one knew of my existence before, and now everyone acts like I owe them something. It's not like I asked to be here," I paused, shooting a venomous glare at Lucien. "It's all your fault, you know."

"Oh, go ahead, blame me for saving your ungrateful soul."

"*Saving me?*" I cried as he flapped his wings. "Because of you, I'm stranded here listening to fairy creatures tell me I should be someone I'm not. No one even noticed me before, but now everyone expects the world from me."

Lucien's face was solemn for a change, his golden eyes fixed with wild intensity. "Perhaps you *are* the person they'd like you to be. Perhaps you've always been that way. If you want to survive Everlynia, you must accept your fate.

There's no point in trying to be someone else. They won't accept the alternative," a painful smile crossed his face for a moment, and I realized he was talking about himself. "I didn't learn that on my own, Carrots," he whispered.

While his words swirled around in my head, I realized what Caz meant by accepting who I was. *What have I done?* My chest constricted. *You have to make this right, Lexi. You must accept this nightmare isn't going to end, not soon at least.* I rose from the log and began walking towards the waterfall sound.

"Where are you going now?" Lucien asked, scowling.

"To find Caz," I said, without looking back.

I weaved my way through the trees, following Caz's trail as will-o'-the-wisps guided my path. Their burning blue bodies drifted through the cold air, always one step ahead of me. The sound of water bubbling against the rocks surrounded me as I ventured deeper into the forest.

The waterfall glowed in the darkness, and the room was filled with a bright aquarium-blue hue. Alien fairies the size of sardines, with long, shimmering fins, swam around in the crystal clear water. A few of them sat up on the floating rocks, softly humming along with the burbling of the stream. Their soothing voices replaced all my worries with serenity. I drew closer, breaking small branches under my boot and announcing my presence to the fish fairies. They hurried back into the water and hid beneath the rocks.

"Finding new ways to intrude?" Caz asked in a calm voice, leaning against a tree as more will-o'-the-wisps lingered around him.

Ignoring his comment, I walked up to him and watched as surprise painted his face. He tensed and moved forward, closing the gap between us. For the first time since meeting him, his nearness did not affect me.

"Caz," I murmured, unsure of what to say next. "You may not know this, but I learned about my father and Everlynia for the first time that night we left the mortal world. My mother didn't think that I would want to know, and I don't imagine that she would've ever told me if it hadn't been for that incident. Although she was right, I doubted her at first. Not long after we came here, I lost her. I left nothing behind in the mortal world, but I lost *everything* here in Everlynia," my eyes quickly filled with tears.

"Alexandra—" Caz whispered my name for the first time. His expression was one of sympathy.

"I *will* find my mother, as I am ready to find myself," I interrupted, clenching my fists to keep them from shivering, "and I will need your help to do so. As a princess, I'll decide what I'll do henceforth. Right now, my duty is to find my mother."

Caz looked down at me, confused. "So," I took in a deep breath. "I, Princess Alexandra of Solmark, rightful heir to the Faye Throne, daughter of Spring and Summer, command you to teach me the way of fire as you've suggested before." My heart flared as I spoke those words, and I felt as if a long-dormant part of myself awoke. A missing piece that somehow completes me.

Caz's eyes widened in disbelief, a corner of his mouth pulled up slightly, revealing a hidden dimple I never noticed until now. He leaned back and quickly dropped to one knee, bowing his head.

"As you wish, Your Highness," Caz said in a soft, contained voice.

CHAPTER 9

THE WAY OF FIRE

Using fire was nothing like I had imagined. I'm not sure why I thought anything about this would be *easy*. Partly because I've seen Caz manipulate fire with ease, as if it weren't the most powerful element to exist, but mainly because I felt something change inside of me when I accepted who I was. I expected it would come naturally to me, as a part of me I never knew I had awakened. Instead, I found myself fighting for my life in the middle of the forest since the morning, trying to figure out what Caz was talking about. "Fire must first be ignited within your heart," he told me over and over again, but his words did not make any sense to me. I feared the day would pass with nothing but exhaustion, headache, and nausea.

I closed my eyes for the millionth time, trying to envision my heart on fire; I could feel something beginning inside of me, but it vanished quickly as I couldn't go any further. I opened my eyes again, groaning, and looked at Caz who was patiently waiting for me.

"Why can't I get it right?" I cried, pulling my knees to my chest and burying my face in the middle.

"You're scared, princess," Caz sighed as he placed a hand on my shoulder, kneeling beside me. "Your heart is prepared, but your mind denies what you've become. Fire cannot harm you. Summer fairies are immune to its effect. You must get past that, or your powers will remain restrained," he explained. "Now, try again. This time let your mind wander."

I took a deep breath and closed my eyes again. Fire was all I could think of, and with the image in my head, my heart flared. *Focus, Lexi. Don't be scared. It won't hurt you*, I convinced myself. It took a few moments for a spark to ignite a flame in the back of my mind, drawing me into a dark oblivion I'd never experienced. The candle-sized flame danced calmly and steadily to the sound of my heartbeats until it grew with each heartbeat. Warmth overtook me, and for a moment, I wasn't afraid of its beauty. But when it flickered violently, I jerked away, afraid it would consume me.

"This isn't working," Caz whispered to himself. He took my hand, pulled me up to my feet, and didn't let go. "Let me show you," he said as he brought my hand up to his chest and drew me closer to him.

I flinched as I felt his heart beating under my palm, making my own thud wildly.

Caz closed his eyes, and I followed his lead. The sounds of the trees and the wind howling faded as I found myself in the same oblivion, quiet and dark. The echoes of his heartbeats filled the space like a piece of relaxing classical music. A small flame burned brightly as it moved freely with the music, alive and dangerous. I felt its power like it was my own. The flame crackled and flickered with ease, following Caz's command. It grew large enough to devour a forest, then it shrank back until it became as small as a matchstick.

"Can you feel it, princess?" Caz's voice came from everywhere to put out the flame. "Fire can be as wild as the Vileforest, and as serene as a summer breeze. Once it is ignited within you, it will follow your command."

I glanced back at Caz. That was the most Caz could do to help me overcome my fear. I straightened and pushed my hair back, ready to try again.

I must do this right. I refuse to be the powerless princess that needs saving in every fairy tale. I must learn to control Summer's power, for my mom, for Caz, and for myself. *Magic flows like the wind in Everlynia,* Caz explained. It's time I made it part of my life.

The sky had darkened unexpectedly, indicating that it was nighttime. Ignoring everything around me, I shut my eyes and let myself sink into oblivion. *This is it,* I told myself as the candle flame flickered in the darkness. My heart sank into an eternal calmness that felt like a silent river, carelessly flowing with the wind. The fire blazed as my heart picked up the pace, but it was in no way daunting. It soon poured into a peaceful river of flames that stretched as far as the oblivion ran. Without saying a word, the river raged into captivating waves that rose and fell furiously. Colorful hues of orange, yellow, red, and blue spread across the void, and my heart pounded with excitement.

I watched the river flow for a few more moments before it shrank back into the tiny flame, then extinguished as a cold breeze touched my face.

"I did it!" I threw my hands in the air—then I collapsed from the nausea that suddenly washed over me.

Caz caught me just as I was about to fall over the dried leaves field, almost as if he was expecting it. "Yes, you did it," he murmured, unimpressed. He held me in his arms and pulled us both up. My stomach grumbled and I struggled to stay awake.

"Is…this supposed to happen?" I murmured, unsure whether he heard me. But his grip on me tightened, and I knew he did.

"This was your first time, princess. The way of fire is anything but effortless. You will be exhausted at first, but in time your body will adapt to your power," Caz explained. He let out an irritated sigh as I struggled to hold myself in his arms. "Now, are you feeling better?" he asked, annoyed.

Nausea gradually faded, and I nodded, my head still heavy with pressure. "I think so—"

I couldn't finish my sentence when Caz released me from his grip and I fell to my face, cursing. "What's your problem?" I groaned as I rolled onto my side and pushed myself up. Twigs and dead leaves stuck to my pinafore, and I cursed once more.

"You said you were feeling better, and I take no pleasure in holding you any longer than I have to, princess," Caz replied, glaring at me over his shoulder.

"Oh, Caz, please hold me just a little longer. There's nothing I desire more," I mocked as I smoothed down my pinafore.

"I don't care for your desires, princess," Caz blinked at me, taking it seriously.

I narrowed my eyes. "Arrogant fool," I whispered, tailing close behind him.

We walked quietly through the forest, savoring our last moments of peace before having to face Lucien again. Leaving him alone with Spore for hours must've driven him insane by now. My mind was still foggy, and I wasn't in the least ready for Lucien's chat time.

"Finally," Lucien said, leaping to his feet, and dragging Spore with him. I was relieved he didn't decide to eat him out of boredom. "I've been waiting for you two. How about a duel, pretty boy?" Lucien asked, his tone solemn for a change.

"Stay back," Caz warned, shoving him out of the way. It would undoubtedly be the end of the world if they ever got along. "I'll take first watch," Caz announced. His eyes flicked back and forth between us. "I advise you to rest, princess; you will be busy tomorrow. I bid you good-night."

Oh great, more training, I shivered with exhaustion. As if today wasn't enough.

"Good night to you too!" Lucien called back, knowing very well those words weren't intended for him, but Caz was already out of view. "What's the matter with him?" he murmured to me. "Weird, I get the sense that he doesn't like me."

No kidding. I scowled at him.

"Anyway, how'd the training go, Carrots? You think you can try to kill me?" he asked, almost hoping I'd say yes. He wanted a fight *and* he's asking for it. I frowned in sympathy.

Dropping to the ground, I felt my limbs becoming numb. "Trust me, I would if I could," I told him, watching his face brighten with hope as if I'd confessed my love for him.

"That's the spirit," he grinned, leaning down beside me as Spore staggered over to me and slept in my lap.

Since I have ignited the fire within my heart, the warmth never faded. As I wondered whether this strange sensation would ever go away, I felt myself drifting into a fitful sleep.

~

"Mercy, my lord!" A female centaur pleaded, dropping to the floor. Her long hair covered her wet face as the half-woman and half-horse cried.

I recognized the floor, the dragon sculptures, and the crystal walls. This was the Faye Throne. My stomach twisted with fear. *Why am I back here? Is this another vision?* I wondered.

"You tried to harm our queen and you dare ask for mercy? Your execution will be held at dawn. Unless…you speak the truth here in the presence of the Solmark King and Queen, the high nobles, and the witnesses before you. You have been a loyal servant to Her Majesty until now. Tell everyone who wishes Lady Helia harm, and your life shall be spared," the wordsmith said as he stood on the throne's edge.

Startled, I looked up and met my mother's eyes. She looked…young. The Queen of Solmark sat up on the throne. Her face twisted into a mask of hate and fret. I wanted to run to her, but my feet were pinned. I couldn't speak or move. I was a mere shadow in the court.

"I can't," the centaur whispered. Her words were barely

audible through her sobbing. "Lady Helia, I wish you no ill will, but you must believe me. I don't remember why——"

The centaur trembled uncontrollably. As she lifted her head, the audience gasped. Her once-pale skin darkened, and her eyes welled up with tears of blood. Her maniacal laughter shook the throne room.

"The witch?" The nobles whispered under their breath, leaning forward in their chairs.

"The prophecy shall come to pass," a maleficent voice spoke through the centaur, pointing at the Solmark Queen. "Blood for blood," she snickered.

The centaur jerked back to her normal self, confused, and lost in the crowd's gaze. "W-what? What happened?" her lips twitched in panic.

"We've heard enough. Escort her to the dungeon, and prepare for her execution at dawn," the wordsmith gestured for the guards to do so.

"No," she murmured with a shake of her head, "Your Majesty please don't let them kill me! Your Majesty…" her voice disappeared as the guards dragged her out of the throne room.

The scene abruptly changed, and I found myself surrounded by filthy, stained walls. The air was thick with sweat, blood, and death. I gagged as I ventured deeper, screams and cries became louder with each step.

"Your Majesty, you shouldn't be here. It's not safe for you," someone said standing behind me. I turned to find two elven guards walking behind the Solmark Queen. Their faces were white as paper, a mask of terror.

"Where is she?" my mother asked in a low commanding voice, that made my blood run cold.

"T-there, Your Majesty," one guard stammered.

She walked down the dim hallway and stopped a few feet away from me. Her eyes widened in shock. "What have you seen?" she asked.

The hairs on my neck stood up. *Can she see me?* I opened my mouth to call for her, but words froze in my throat.

"The future of Solmark," the maleficent voice spoke near my ear, and I jumped with fear. Filthy hands brushed against the wooden bars of the cage as a blurry figure stood behind it. Her black cloak trailed behind her. I looked down to find the centaur lying lifeless on the cold ground. "The ruin that'll come," she said. Though I couldn't see her face, I knew she had a predatory grin on her face. One that made the Solmark Queen cower back.

"Am I in any way the cause of this fate?" my mother asked.

"Not the Solmark Queen…but the Solmark *Heir*," the figure leaned forward. "The promise of Solmark."

"My child?" my mother murmured in a voice coated with fear. "What have you seen? Tell me at once!" she raged.

The figure sank gracefully to her knees. "Death," she whispered. "I'm afraid the prophecy of death will come with your daughter. Defeated on the battleground she will be. Blinded by hate and the smoke of the sea. The fate of your firstborn is sealed. Remain in Solmark and you shall see."

My mother took in a sharp breath. "My daughter? That's impossible. That can't be!" She was on the verge of tears. "She…she's the first daughter of Spring and Summer. Her powers will be——"

"A curse," the figure finished. "The Summer Guardian may have been victorious once upon a time, but the last

Shadow will shift the game of power. Your daughter will bring nothing but destruction and chaos."

The queen clutched at her chest and sank to her knees. Her crown tumbled off her head, blood covering it as it rolled away from the queen. "You're wrong," she said, trembling as she pressed a hand on her belly. "That cannot be her fate."

"The prophecy does not lie, Your Majesty," the figure said in a low voice. "Isn't that right, princess?" She lifted her head and red eyes gazed directly at me. I gasped and leaped away. "Princess? Princess? Princess?"

"Princess?"

Caz's voice broke through the darkness, and I stared blankly into his face. "Bad dreams? Thought it would take a miracle to wake you up," he said with a sigh.

"Huh?" A dense cloud formed inside my head. *I-I had a dream but...what was it about?* I couldn't recall, but I knew it was important.

"Come on, princess, we have some training to do."

Oh, right. I groaned as I sat up.

And I thought igniting the fire within my heart was a difficult task. Of course, that was only the beginning of the torture; the crux of the matter is that I must channel my inner strength into a powerful weapon. *Bringing the fire to life,* Caz had called it. As lovely as it may sound, it was an uphill battle for my mind. Caz on the other hand, thought it was as simple as drawing your next breath. *Typical of him,* I thought.

"Princess," Caz said with a snap of his fingers to get my

attention. "If you can imagine it, you can create it," he said. "You must clear your mind and focus on this. If you face an enemy, you can be certain that they will not wait for you to take your time deciding how to fight them."

He's right. God, I hate it when he's right. *All you have to do is imagine it, dammit.* I shook my head and tried again. Closing my eyes, the flame ignited almost instantly. *A sword,* my mind whispered. My palms heated quickly, and I opened my eyes to a flaming sword in my grip. It wasn't as ferocious as Caz's, but it was there. My lips curled into a smile. *There's something there!* I attempted to raise my sword, but it vanished as soon as my hand was lifted. Nothing was left—nothing but the smoke and embers that twisted through the air.

Caz nodded at the edge of my vision. "That's better," he said simply. "I see you can command fire, but you have trouble controlling it. Without you, the fire could never be ignited. And without fire, you could never defend yourself like a true Summer heir," he said, pressing a hand against my chest. My heart bounced under his touch, and my cheeks flamed. "Your power knows what you want, princess. Let it control you and it'll ruin you. Ignore it and it'll cease to exist. Work with it and it'll grow to become part of you. The answer is clear. It is what *you* choose to do. Try again," Caz said, folding his arms.

I did. This time I gripped the hilt of my sword and a thin, sharp blade stretched before me. *Okay, now concentrate, Lexi. Do not ignore it, but don't let it consume you.* I swung my sword, and it flared up in the breeze.

"Good," Caz said, "now, use it to defend yourself."

"How would I—" I lifted my head as Caz drew his

flaming sword. Raging flames danced with the wind. "Oh, you're serious," my voice nearly trembled.

He circled me slowly, waiting for me to swing first. I clutched the hilt and jabbed at him with my sword, but I was slow. Caz blocked it with great strength, I almost let go of my weapon. Almost. I jabbed again and again and again, my heart raged with each try. My insides felt like they would combust.

"Any time soon, princess," Caz mocked. A flash of fire, and he was suddenly behind me. I leaped back and evaded a weak hit. "If you were my enemy, you'd be dead by now."

My body shook with rage. Caz had disappeared. My eyes darted around the dim forest. My sword erupted and I whirled quickly, blocking a stronger hit. Caz grinned and disappeared again. My shoulders pulled back and I lunged, stabbing at him before his figure sword made a threat. Caz jumped back, but I couldn't let him escape again. I lunged and struck as Caz slid aside. "Is that all you got?" His movements slowed and I was enraged. *Does he take me for a joke?*

My blade moved faster than my hand to where I thought it would fly away. *That's not good.* I pulled back, my ragged breath slowing as I tried to take back control. My hand shook as the sword flickered as if it had a mind of its own. *Shut up and stop, dammit!* My mind called for the sword to stop, and it did. I took a step forward and felt the ground beneath me melting slowly, and then it hit me.

I clenched my jaw, meeting his gaze with something sharp, something that promised pain. He took it as an invitation, just as I had hoped. A flicker of amusement crossed his face before he lunged. I stepped away in time, watching his boots slide against the slippery ground. His balance wavered. With all my strength, I shoved him.

Caz fell to the ground and a fresh patch of leaves rained over us.

With my sword to his throat, I rendered him motionless. His eyes widened in disbelief. I enjoyed it so much, I thought I'd pass out from satisfaction. "If you weren't my friend," I whispered, "you'd be dead by now."

A slow smile spread across his face. "Pity," he murmured, leaning into the blazing sword. My powers threatened to vanish. Caz noticed it, too. His dimples surfaced, those disgustingly pleasant dimples. He knew exactly what he was doing. Worse, it worked.

My focus splintered.

His hands found my shoulder. A sharp twist, a blur of motion, and suddenly, the world flipped. Pain rattled through my head as I staggered, looking up at him.

Caz hovered over me, strands of his hair lightly brushed the skin of my forehead. "Only if *you* were my friend," he whispered, his breath warm against my cheeks. Silence stretched between us. His glinting eyes—unreadable— flicked to my lips and lingered for a moment. Two. A shiver ran through my body as he pulled away, outstretching his hand and yanking me to my feet.

"You did well today, princess," Caz murmured, looking away as he buried a hand in his hair. "For a beginner anyway," he went on, an octave higher.

I sighed. That was as much of a praise as I would get from him.

The next two days flew by in the blink of an eye. I spent

my mornings practicing fire magic with Caz. Every time I thought I knew everything there was to know about Summer's abilities, I was proven wrong the hard way. Our evenings were spent strolling through the Vileforest until our feet cried out for help and intrusive thoughts of killing Lucien to stop the yapping took over. Telling Lucien to stop would only provoke him to dig into his past for gory tales. And there were plenty of them.

Our nights always ended in pointless arguments and near-duals between Caz and Lucien. I stopped them at first, but I grew tired of wasting words on two headstrong lunatics though it amazed me how Spore remained calm with all of the back-and-forth cursing. I slept right through them just fine. If the shouts stopped, I sometimes wake up startled in the middle of the night, thinking one of them had finally murdered the other.

I had asked Caz many questions as we wandered deeper into the forest. Could my powers be taken away by force? Can I pass my powers on to someone else? What happens if I stop using Summer power? He scowled at almost all of them but answered them nonetheless. We both knew if we risked shutting up, Lucien would indulge us with a *fascinating* tale almost immediately.

Lucien groaned and looked back at me. "Don't you have a question for me, Carrots?" he asked, a hint of jealousy in his tone.

"Yes," I nodded enthusiastically, "when will we arrive?" I needed to know how much more pain I would have to endure.

"Soon," Lucien rolled his eyes and turned away.

"Oh, like *soon* soon? Or yesterday's soon?" I wanted to ask, but I knew he wouldn't answer.

"Caz?" I slowed down to walk beside him.

"Hmm?"

"Do all Summer fairies have powers? I don't recall seeing anyone besides you with a flaming sword in the Solmark Court."

Caz shook his head. "Generally, only the rulers of Solmark would inherit the Summer power. However, all Summer fairies are indeed immune to its effects."

"Oh," I frowned, "then why do you have Summer power? You're not a ruler of Solmark…are you?"

"No," Caz sighed heavily as he looked down, suddenly not having the energy to say anything. "I'm…I'm just unfortunately cursed," he stammered.

I've never seen this side of Caz before. This sorrowful, hollow Caz. Strange how *I* felt a flame igniting within *his* heart. Even stranger, my heart did the same without a second thought. As if my heart could suddenly act as it pleases without my mind telling it what to do.

I placed a hand on his shoulder, but Caz flinched away. For a brief moment, a wounded expression crossed his face, but it vanished as quickly as he straightened. The old Caz was back in the blink of an eye. He paused, motioning for me to walk in front of him. He made it clear that he wanted to be left alone. So, I obeyed, feeling a little hurt.

Silence mocked me and regret gnawed at me. Somehow this silence that I craved before made me uncomfortable. We must've walked a great distance for my legs to tremble like jelly.

"We're here," Lucien's voice came to the rescue. I never thought I'd want to hear him again.

Alarmed, I stepped beside Lucien. A great dark Abyss stretched out before me.

"The Enchanted Abyss," I whispered as Caz joined us at the edge, crossing his arms.

"We're here."

CHAPTER 10

THE ENCHANTED ABYSS

AT THE BRINK of the Enchanted Abyss, I gazed down at a narrow pitch-black hole. There was no sign of life down there, at least none that I could see. I pushed a few rocks beneath my feet and waited for a sound, but there was nothing. Exactly how deep the Enchanted Abyss was, I did not know. My stomach flipped. *Was this going to be another near-death experience?* I wondered.

Lucien whistled softly to himself. "I must say, I'm a little terrified." Great. Now *Lucien* is terrified. Just how screwed are we?

"You know what they say: those who are brave enough to enter the Enchanted Abyss are the real winners. Oh, wait…no. Never mind, I think they were losers."

"So," I said, trying to hide the fear in my voice, "what now? Do we jump?"

"Oh no, Carrots," Lucien replied, for a moment I thought he was serious. I assumed there was an odd task we must complete first. Who knows, perhaps we'll need to make a sacrifice. I was still in Everlynia after all, and my erratic thoughts were never stilled. "No, we can just sit back and wait. I'm sure that way we would *magically* find ourselves in the Enchanted Abyss. What do you think?"

I should've known better. I smacked him and he straightened, rubbing his shoulder as if I had hurt him. I wished I had.

Lucien slumped his shoulders. "Fine," he sighed, "we'll jump straight into the Enchanted Abyss. Everyone makes it through the fall, but there is no assurance that we will land in the same location. With that being said, it shouldn't be so hard to find each other…I think. Just scream if you're in trouble."

"Anything we should be aware of?" Caz beat me to the question.

"Nothing in particular. As long as you don't fall into traps, that is." Lucien answered.

My breath caught in my throat. "What happens if we do fall into a trap?" I asked, not really wanting to hear the answer.

Lucien shrugged. "One of many things," he said, "you could be enslaved, served as a meal, or put up for auction if you're lucky. After all, the Enchanted Abyss is nothing but a huge, bizarre Market. Just…try not to get captured. Got it, Carrots?"

No pressure. I bobbed my head.

Lucien inhaled deeply. "Well fellas and…fungi, this is it. I'll see you all at the Market. Embrace the challenge and try not to miss me too much," Lucien smirked. He spread his wings and dove in head first.

Spore hugged me tightly as he whimpered. Caz nodded when I turned to face him. There was no going back.

Together, we leaped into the bottomless darkness of the Enchanted Abyss.

The blustery wind whipped through my hair, clothes, and face, forcing me to close my eyes and sink into agony. Even when I tried to open them, I couldn't see anything. My stomach clenched and my heart hammered against my ribs, feeling like it could break them. Enchanting music slowly began to vibrate in my ears, consuming me whole. Countless herbs and spices, as well as blood, smoke, and wax, filled my nose in a single breath. A thousand different voices spoke all at once, shouting and bargaining for goods, deals, contracts, and promises. As the volume of chaos increased, I thought I'd lose hearing.

After a lifetime of falling, a beam of warm light shone through my eyelids, and I opened them with hope, only to regret that decision instantly. Soft silk slipped against my skin, and then flying fabric of various colors entangled me, wrapping around my body like a mummy, and I landed on something hard. Laughter erupted, and that was the last thing I heard before everything went black.

Low voices spoke above my head, but I was too weak to move, too weak to open my eyes. Exhaustion lured me into oblivion, and all I wanted to do was…nothing.

"Elves. I haven't caught one in a long time. It would be a waste to kill this one," someone said.

"Aye, it's worth more alive than dead," another agreed. "How many gold coins do you think we'll be able to get?"

"No less than five hundred I'd say," the first replied, "if

we're lucky, some moron would fight for her. Then we'll have the satisfaction of death as well as gold. To fight against Titan…only a fool would take that risk." Their laughter faded with their footsteps.

I awoke to the sound of applause gradually finding my ears. My head felt like a heavy rock as I attempted to open my eyes. My vision blurred, and I wiped my eyelids to focus. Staring at a swaying cage, I jerked up to find myself still covered in rainbow cloths. Under the piles of sheets, something crawled up my stomach. I barely contained a scream as Spore emerged from beneath the fabric, his wide eyes fixed on me.

I breathed a sigh of relief. Floating candles entered my cage like fireflies, and my eyes widened with alarm. *That's right. I'm in the enchanted Abyss and…* I groaned as I remembered Lucien's warning, *trapped.* All kinds of creatures surrounded me like I was a museum exhibit. I looked past them to observe my surroundings and hoped I'd find Caz. The Vileforest is considered radiant in comparison to this. The Abyss Market was as dark as the depths of the ocean, with millions of flaming candles glowing with pride. There were stalls scattered about in every inch of the Market selling all kinds of various goods. *How long have I been out?*

"There you are!" shouted a familiar voice, making my heart skip a beat. "I thought I wouldn't see you again. Oh, and look!" I turned my head to stare at Lucien, throwing his hands in the air and scaring a few trolls back. "Falling into a trap! You did the one thing I told you not to, Carrots. Why is it that no one listens to me?" he complained to Spore.

"Lucien!" I walked over to him and hauled him by his

collar, slamming his chest against the thin wooden bars. "What happened?"

"Oh, and you have the audacity to ask *me* questions. Bold of you, Carrots. You know, this reminds me of a tale I suppose I could tell you—"

"Not now, Lucien," I hurried on before he began. "Where's Caz?"

Lucien lifted his shoulder in a half-shrug. "He wouldn't be able to do anything anyway. Once you're trapped, you're considered the servant of your master...unless you're sold off or won as a prize by someone else," he explained.

My shoulders sagged as I let go of Lucien. I hid my face with my hands.

"Don't fret, no one is going to buy you anyway, trust me," Lucien grinned.

"One hundred golden pieces!" A goblin shouted, stepping forward.

"Two hundred!" Another one shouted.

Lucien snickered. "Idiots don't know they're buying trouble."

I ignored his statement, though it was true. Spore tapped my thigh. "Shroom," he said, holding a candle with both hands.

I scowled at him, trying to figure out what he wanted when it hit me like a train. *Right! I'm no longer powerless. If only I could free myself from here*—I closed my eyes and struggled to concentrate through all of the bidding shouts. My heart knew what I wanted, and a flame ignited within a second. *Good, now all I have to do is imagine a sword.* Heat began to take over my body and flowed to my palms. *That's it*, I opened my eyes only to find a small tear-shaped flame above my finger. Not even enough to light a birthday candle.

"Woah!" Lucien cowered back from the cage. "Careful now, Carrots, you might kill someone with that," he teased, and I wished he was within reach so I could smack him or maybe pluck out his feathers.

Strike two, my mind whispered.

"Seriously, the candles could do more damage than you," he said.

My brows knitted in a frown. "I don't understand," I whispered in despair, "Why couldn't I do it?"

"This cage reeks of magic. Your master must've done something to conceal his hunts' powers. Otherwise, you would've broken out of it using your Summer power," Lucien gave a lucid explanation.

Great, the first time I needed to use my Summer power, it wasn't available. I wish I had inherited a fire gun instead. I shook my head to focus. If I couldn't use my powers, I needed to find another way to escape this. *Now think!*

"Two thousand," The crowd gasped in surprise as a tall woman called out. She emerged from the masses, her long coal hair gliding around her. Her face was pale and beautiful. Her red gown brushed the ground as she walked gracefully.

"Leannan Sidhe," Lucien murmured, "tough luck, Carrots. Leannan Sidhe is known to collect pretty things, but girls never make it alive."

"Two thousand!" The goblin, whose trap I had help-lessly fallen into, announced to the crowd. Silence fell over everyone, no one dared to bid higher than Leannan Sidhe, who smirked and turned her cold gaze at me, taking my breath away. "Does anyone object?" The goblin asked. No answer.

The goblin's sickening grin stretched as he reached out to shake her hand. The auction had ended, and I was on my way to being sold to Leannan Sidhe. Panic made my heart race, but I swallowed my fear. I refused to show them how scared I was. And it didn't matter a bit, I wouldn't surrender to this fate. Right before their hands shook, a voice called from a distance.

"I object," Caz said, walking past the trolls and goblins. His eyes flashed to me, and he bowed his head. My chest leaped with excitement, but I refused to show that either.

"What offer do you make, lad?" the goblin asked. "Have you more gold?"

"No," Caz replied, and the goblin's eyebrows shot up. "For your servant, I'll offer the ultimate sacrifice," Caz said, and the goblin shook his hand without a second thought. The crowd cheered Caz as he climbed the stairs and stood beside my cage, head raised high.

"Blood! Blood! Blood!" The crowd screamed over and over again until the goblin raised his fist to make them stop. The sickening grin never left his face. More fairies gathered around to watch the "ultimate sacrifice," Caz had offered.

"What exactly did he offer?" I asked Lucien, who stood speechless. Astonished.

"His life," Lucien murmured. "Caz must fight a warrior chosen by the master. If he wins, he'll take you as a prize, but if he loses the fight, that will be the end of him. Never knew pretty boy cared so much for you, Carrots."

No, please don't do this! I glanced up at Caz, but he made no effort to look at me. As though he knew I wouldn't be pleased with his reckless offer.

"Let it be known that this lad will face off against my best warrior, Titan. If he wins, he shall have the girl and the little creature. If he loses…" the goblin's grin widened, "he will die, and the girl will remain as my servant. You still want to do this, lad?"

I ran to him before he could answer. "Caz, please stop this before it's too late," I told him. Still, he didn't look in my direction. "Caz, I can find another way out. I know I can. If you would just—"

"I'll fight your warrior," Caz interrupted, nodding to the goblin. My words made no difference to him. *I* made no difference to him. I knew this wasn't the time, I stomped back to the other side of the cage as my heart burst into flames.

The fairies cheered and demanded blood. Outside the cage, the curtains shook as an enormous giant appeared, the ground shuddering with each step. Titan was at least three times the size of Caz, but he had one less eye. He held a stone axe in one hand, and a troll's head in the other. The head shattered into pieces with one clench of his fist, and the crowd yelled furiously for more.

"One last thing," the goblin had everyone's attention, "powers are not allowed for this fight," he announced to my displeasure. Caz's face remained expressionless.

"That's not good," Lucien whispered.

A nearby boggart giggled uncontrollably. "Titan will finish him in no time," he laughed.

"Really?" Lucien turned to face the ugly boggart. "I bet the lad will defeat Titan," Lucien held out his hand.

The boggart snorted. "I'll bet you twenty golden coins that lad will be dead meat by the end of the duel," he said as he shook Lucien's hand. I couldn't believe Lucien was betting now of all times, but what's more impossible is that he was betting on Caz winning this fight.

"You're quite irrational, Lucien. This isn't the time!" I gritted out as disbelief took hold of me.

Lucien smirked, bringing a finger to his lips. "There's always time for fun, Carrots. Besides, we could use some gold in the Market," Lucien sounded sure of the outcome.

"Now, let the fight begin!" The goblin announced and the applause filled the air.

Titan charged towards Caz with great force, leaving destruction wherever he stepped. Caz leaped out of the way, dodging the giant's stone axe. Reaching down to his boots, he pulled out a couple of daggers I never knew he had. "Let's dance," Caz whispered.

The giant growled and charged again, moving slowly with the weapon he carried. Caz lunged, a quick stab in the calf, and the giant fell to one knee with a scream that made my cage sway. Dust fell like snow over my head. Titan struggled to stand, blood pooling from his left leg, but somehow, he managed to gather his strength and ran with great speed directly at Caz.

Caz leaped forward, barely avoiding Titan's blow and a flying candle careening over his head. "I WILL KILL YOU!" The bloodthirsty giant snarled.

"Well then, you better keep your eye on me," Caz said with a grin.

The giant pounced, raising his axe above his head and snapping it forward, missing Caz by only an inch. His axe sliced through the rocks and sent candles flying at him, bringing him closer to landing a hit on Caz with each strike.

Caz flew straight at the giant, closing the gap between them, and my heart screamed. My throat tightened as life moved in slow motion. *You're just as useless as before*, the voice inside me spoke. I clenched my fists, feeling my nails dig into my flesh. Caz was fighting for me again and there was nothing I could do. Once again, I was the helpless princess waiting to be rescued.

A screech rang in my ear, and I flinched back to the fighting before me. Titan's axe was buried into Caz's shoulder as he cut at his face. The crowd gasped as Caz landed on his knees a few feet in front of my cage, blood seeping down his fingers. With Titan's back to us, I feared he'd turn around and finish Caz off with a final blow. Now that Caz was injured, there's nothing stopping the giant from winning the fight. For the longest time, the giant stood motionless, and then he fell on his back, cracking the ground and sending a cloud of dust over the fairies watching.

Everyone became still as the grave. Caz stood up with a low grunt. Past him, the cloud of dust faded, revealing the dead giant, a dagger sunk deep into his chest and the second in his eye. It was over. Caz had defeated Titan.

The cheers of the crowd showered over us like heavy rain. The cage door creaked open by itself, as though it was waiting for Caz to step inside. As though it knew he won. Caz approached slowly, extending his hand to me. He breathed heavily and steadily, waiting for me to take his hand. I did. Standing up, the blanket of cloths slid to my feet and Spore staggered out of the cage like a bird.

The boggart cursed behind me as he handed Lucien a

bag of coins. He'd lost his wager, and as I predicted, Lucien knew the outcome before the fight even started.

I glanced at Caz's shoulder as he walked away and winced. It amazes me how he's standing firmly without showing an ounce of pain. Was it arrogance? Pridefulness? I didn't know. All I knew was that I was free. And once again, saved by him.

We strode across the Enchanted Abyss, following Lucien as he guided us towards the Market's Inn. Caz had insisted on going straight to the Banshee, but he was quickly over-ruled. I promised Caz that if he wouldn't rest tonight, I'd make Lucien repeat all of his endless tales and even bribe him to sing for us. That was enough to convince him to give in. Caz could deny the pain he was in, but his tired face couldn't hide it. It's not every day that he gets to kill a giant.

Dead plants and dried pixies waved at our faces as we walked by the stalls. Everyone tried to sell us things all at once. I could barely hear myself thinking through their shouts. We made it to the Market's Inn by some miracle, and when I looked up, I was not surprised to see that all of the windows were broken. Flies, candles, and smoke entered and exited the rooms as they pleased. This Market might provide many things, but privacy isn't one of them. A gnome sat behind a wrecked desk, his head tilted back, and his feet crossed on the desk. An old book served as a blind-fold over his eyes. Snoring greeted us as we approached the world's most unimpressive hotel.

Lucien slammed his hand on the desk and the gnome jolted with a curse. "Hello Skunky, I haven't seen you in a long time. How have you been?" Lucien grinned.

"Fine until I saw your face," the gnome growled, eyes

drifting to us as he sat upright. "What's this now? Haven't I told you not to come here anymore? You even brought friends."

"Come now," Lucien tossed ten golden coins in the air, one after another and the gnome snatched them right away. "Don't be stubborn Skunky, I know you miss me."

"Not you, but your gold, lunatic," the gnome sneered as he shoved the coins in his pocket and opened a creaking door. "Your room is on the far left. It will already be crowded with all of you, so don't bring any more guests tonight. I'll be keeping an eye on you, Lucien. You brought five nymphs with you the last time you came here, and I found the room in shambles. This time, there will be none of that. Eh?" The gnome raised a brow at Lucien.

Lucien smiled innocently, though he knew he wasn't fooling anyone. "I'll try, Skunky," he said with a wink.

The room wasn't as total garbage as I'd imagined. Yes, there were spiderwebs, dirty couches, two broken beds, and a hole in the wall that made me see unfathomable sights of our neighbors, but I had managed to expect worse. Lucien dived on the couch, spreading his wings like a butterfly. Spore ran up to the bed, jumping on it as if it were a trampoline.

"Need an invitation, pretty boy?" Lucien asked with a grin that never faded.

"How are you feeling, Caz?" I asked.

"I'm fine," Caz replied, coming off the doorframe. "Don't worry about me, princess."

"How could I not? Caz, you're bleeding!"

Lucien groaned. "Seriously, Carrots, he's a fae. He'll be

better than before in no time. All he needs is to rest, you'll see."

"He's right, princess," Caz agreed.

Lucien stood, raising a brow at me as he looked back and forth between Caz and me. "Well," he said finally, "I'd love to stay here longer, but I must be somewhere to meet my old friends. Oh, and I'll take your friend with me, Carrots," he said as he caught Spore in his hands. "He'll help me attract new company. Try not to have too much fun without me," he waved at the door before closing it behind him.

When I turned around, Caz was shirtless on the bed. A drop of blood slowly trailed down his stomach and his abs contracted with every painful breath he took. I realized I'd been staring for too long, but I didn't want to look away. When I looked up and noticed his eyes on me, I whirled around with embarrassment. Caz let out a low grunt as he attempted to clean his wound with a white cloth, only to make a mess of it.

"Let me help you," I said as Caz glanced up at me. He hesitated, ready to argue, but I didn't give him time. "I'm the reason you're hurt, Caz. The least I can do is help clean your wound," I stepped closer, meeting his eyes.

Caz nodded once and handed me the cloth while straightening his back. I sat on the edge of the bed. This close, I saw my reflection in his blood. He winced as I wiped the blood around his wound. Somehow, I felt his pain too, and hated myself for it. *It's all because of you*, that voice spoke again to remind me of my weakness. To remind me that I could have all the power in the world and still be a powerless fool who needed saving.

I pressed down hard on his shoulder, letting my rage get the best of me as I wrapped the bandage around his wound. "You didn't have to fight for me," I finally said, allowing my thoughts to speak for themselves. "You didn't have to get yourself hurt because of me." I had no right to say that, but I wanted him to understand that he was under no obligation to put his life in danger for me.

Caz flinched. His gaze came up to me, a scorching glare that stole my breath away. "If you weren't so naïve, princess, you'd realize that I didn't have much of a choice," he snapped, eyes blazing with rage.

I stood up to face him again. "Offering your life shouldn't be a choice either, Caz. If you had given me a chance, we could've found another way out. You don't have to risk your life just to keep a promise you made to my mother!"

"Of all stupid things to say," Caz murmured as he rose from the bed, an intimidating figure looming over me. "Do you take promises lightly, princess?"

His words strangled my throat. I only wanted to ease his stress, but somehow, I've wronged him. Twice. I stood my ground despite my mind telling me to flee. "If it endangers you, you shouldn't have to put up with it, I'm sure my mother would understand—"

"You're asking me to break my promise?" Caz asked, and the candles around him reacted violently to his sudden calmness. "Tell me, princess, would you abandon your mother? Would you turn around and forget about her simply because you found yourself in danger? And you *will* find yourself in danger. So, tell me right now if you wish to return to the Solmark Court."

I shook my head. "I want to save my mother," I said quietly as Caz nodded and sat back down. "And I want to do it without losing any one of you," I admitted. "I don't want to lose any of my friends."

Friends. Perhaps I said it too soon. Was Caz truly my friend? Was Lucien my friend? I didn't know, but I knew I hated the idea of losing them.

Caz looked up at me with a confused expression and…*was that a blush?* I wondered, but he dug his face into the pillow before I could tell. When he lifted his face, the cold Caz was back. "Be careful who you call friend, princess," he gave me yet another lesson.

Seriously? I was trying to be polite to him, and all he could think of was more lessons? I was speechless.

"As I recall, I still need to rest. You'll have to excuse me if I no longer want to hear your babbling," he said, burying his face in the pillow and dismissing me with a wave.

On another note, I wasn't entirely speechless. "And you'll have to excuse me if I ever called you my friend, you arrogant fool!" I stormed out of the room feeling the need to shout at the top of my lungs. *No, that wasn't what I needed,* I realized as I walked down the hallway, meeting the snorting gnome at the desk. I needed something else.

"You!" I pounded my hand on the desk to wake him up. The gnome jerked awake, cursing as he fell from the chair.

"Lunatic!" he shouted, "what do you want from me?"

"Where's Lucien?" I asked.

The gnome spat. "Lucien…even his company is as irritating as he is. He's at the darn barn."

"Take me to him," I commanded, forgetting that he had no idea who I was.

The gnome yawned. "I don't provide traveling services to customers. You gotta pay for that kind of favor, and I see you carry no gold."

I clenched my fists, and he raised a brow to my show of temper. "Lucien will pay you," I gritted out, but he didn't move. I sighed, "I promise."

I trailed behind the angry gnome as he trotted across the Market. My temper flared as Caz's words came back unexpectedly. Why did I bother worrying about him in the first place? I should have known better. I couldn't decide whether I was more upset by Caz's careless offer or by my own weakness.

The gnome snarled. "There is your guy."

The barn was a bigger version of the Pixiehouse, with deadlier duals and bigger hunts as prizes. The gamblers duped each other with tricks, which quickly escalated into fights. Everything was the same as the Pixiehouse, but a hundred times more chaotic.

Lucien sat at the drink table with Spore in his lap and six nymphs around him, laughing and getting to know him. When Lucien saw me approaching with the gnome who extended his hand without saying anything, he frowned.

"Pay him," I told Lucien as I sat next to him, slamming my hand on the wood to get the barn keeper's attention for tealoxica.

"With the gold you deemed irrational, Carrots?" Lucien mocked as he pulled a golden coin which the gnome snatched from his grasp in the blink of an eye.

"You tell your friends to stop bothering me. Lunatics!" he shouted as he left the barn.

"What did you do to Skunky?" Lucien turned to me

with a proud look on his face. "And I thought he hated me the most."

The barn keeper slammed a shot glass on the table which I drank in a gulp. The Enchanted Abyss' tealoxica wasn't nearly as good as I recalled. It must've been mixed with water for it did nothing to ease my temper.

Lucien shared an appraising look with Spore. "Does the pretty boy know you're here, Carrots?" he asked, tilting his head.

"Seeking his approval?" I asked, crossing my arms. "Not so vile of you, Lucien. You'd have to do better if you want a duel with him."

Lucien grinned at the prospect of a duel between himself and Caz. "Very well," he said, smirking as the barn keeper replaced the empty shot glass with another.

Tealoxica was a total flop. I hadn't intended to talk about Caz, but by the third glass, I couldn't stop myself from jabbering.

"You know," I flung my fourth glass, spilling half of it on the floor. The nymph in Lucien's arms rolled her eyes at me and walked away from Lucien, cursing.

Lucien sighed, as I interrupted his flirting for the hundredth time this evening. "What?" he asked, not seeming interested.

"He's rude and unrefined. A trouble, that man is," I said with a hic.

"Yeah," Lucien rested his chin on his palm, admiring the nymphs from afar. "That's why they call him Cold Caz."

"Oh?" I reached for Lucien's glass, but he took it before I could. "He's much more than that. He's a *cruel, cruel* man," I paused, then started to giggle, slamming my hand on the bar table. "That's right! Cruel Caz, that's what they should call him!"

"Carrots," Lucien whispered as he held my flying wrist. "As much as I agree with you on this, I need you to stop right now. You're making me lose my charm. Look over there, you see those beautiful nymphs glaring our way?" I nodded, waving to them but they gave me a hateful glare and continued to whisper among themselves. "Yeah, I'm kinda here for *them*."

I giggled. "Well, you could've said something sooner, silly," I rose from my chair, feeling the world spinning around me. "Hey, girls!" I shouted with a hic, making everyone pause momentarily. Lucien put a hand over my mouth, but I bit and shoved him away. "This fine gentleman…raven thing…would very much like your company. I must warn you, he does talk an awful lot. He's not so kind, but he is funny!"

"Shut up!" Lucien murmured as laughter filled the barn.

"Oh, he tells stories and jokes. They're bearable most of the time. He doesn't have a good reputation, but manners… well…no, he doesn't have that either."

Lucien blew out his cheeks. "I hope you're going somewhere with this, Carrots," he whispered as he chugged his drink.

I put my arm around Lucien, barely recognizing him. Everything became blurry, dreamlike. Suddenly, I was on the verge of a blackout. "But there's something good in him.

Granted I don't know what it is, but I know it's there." I felt Lucien's shock as I said those words, and then he sobered up and backed away from me.

Someone caught me as I began to fall forward, pulling me with great force. I slapped the hands that were tightly wrapped around my waist like snakes, as if doing so would make them disappear. "Bad, bad snakes."

"Princess?" A soft, worried voice spoke. I glanced up and found him.

"Oh, look!" I said as I whirled around to face him, almost tripping over the swaying floor. "Cruel Caz is here! I've been looking everywhere for you." I stole a glass of tealoxica from a passing floating tray. Maybe it wasn't floating because whoever carried it said something very rude to me. Caz snatched the glass from my hand and slammed it on the table.

"Are you drunk?" he asked. It was only then when I realized why tealoxica wasn't working. It wasn't tealoxica after all.

"You *will* pay for this," Caz told Lucien as he took my wrist and walked me out of the barn.

"Good night to you too!" Lucien called out. I waved back to him and Spore, nestling in his lab. It struck me as odd that they were relieved to see me leave. *Who was I waving to?* I tried to recall, but my mind refused to work the way I wanted it to.

I looked around at the hive of sellers that had swarmed us like flies. I couldn't focus on what they were selling, and when I did, they multiplied like rabbits, further perplexing me. There was an interval, and I was dragged into a narrow alley, away from the noisy sellers and the aroma of spices.

With my back against the cold stones, I thought I would collapse from the nausea, but Caz's arms pinned me to the wall.

"What were you thinking? Getting yourself drunk in the Enchanted Abyss? Tell me, do you have a death wish, princess?" Caz's voice was trembling. I didn't have to be sober to notice he wasn't so much angry as he was worried.

I shook my head and got a sample of the headache I'd experience the next day. "I'm not drunk…you're drunk," I said as I pressed a finger to his chest.

Caz caught my falling hand and tightened his grasp. "Why are you doing this? What are you so desperately trying to prove?"

"That I'm not weak!" I replied too quickly. Warm tears spilled over my cheeks, strangely comforting. *What the hell are you saying?* That sober voice whispered. I ignored it completely. "You know I'm not powerless. You know I am capable of saving myself, yet you…you underestimate me. And I'm sick of it."

Caz stood motionless, taking in what my intoxicated self had told him. His wild eyes softened. He wasn't afraid to share his expression, knowing full well that I wouldn't remember anything from that night. His expression was one of *interest*. I knew it. I've read about it in many novels to know it was true. I felt it like an electric shock that sent me closer to oblivion. His hand wiped a tear from my cheek as his lips curled into a soft smile. "I don't think you're weak," he whispered and wiped yet another tear.

I slapped his hand away. "I know!" I closed my eyes, struggling to stay awake. "Had I tried a bit harder," I said, my loud voice echoing in the empty alley, "I would've had you the last time we fought. But…” I couldn't help but close my eyes again, this time for longer. The top of my head hit against his chest. “Your damn…dumplings? No…what's that word?” I raised my head to find him smiling down at me. “Dimples! Dimples are a tricky thing, I'm telling you.”

That was the last thing I said that night before collapsing in his arms.

“You have me without even trying, princess,” I imagined someone whispering in my ear. And with that, I was welcomed into oblivion.

CHAPTER 11
BANSHEE

I HAD the same nightmare that night. Standing in front of the dark figure and the queen of Solmark for the second time was unsettling. The queen clutched at her chest and sank to her knees. The same way she did before. Her golden crown was painted with blood as it fell to the ground. "You're wrong," she cried, pressing a hand to her belly. "That cannot be her fate."

"The prophecy does not lie, Your Majesty," the witch whispered, reaching for the crown. "But," the golden crown corroded against her fingers, "with a great sacrifice, there is a way to save your heir from destruction."

"My daughter could be saved? Why haven't you said something sooner?"

"Do not succumb to the temptation my queen. You haven't heard my price yet," the witch sneered.

My mother stared at the rusted crown between the witch's hands and swallowed her uneasiness. "Whatever the cost may be," she murmured, "for my daughter's sake, I will pay it."

No! I wanted to scream, but my voice stuck in my throat.

The witch shattered the crown in her hand, turning it into a cloud of glittering dust. "To change the prophecy, you must give up your throne—power for power," she said, as the wall sconces erupted in a blaze. There was a blinding flash, and I awoke to a heavy weight on my chest. Unfortunately, the memories of that nightmare remained intact this time.

Spore tilted his head as his giant eyes regarded me strangely. As though I'd awoken from a coma. My head felt heavy as a boulder. Perhaps I had awoken from a coma. I don't remember anything. Where was I? I sat up, my gaze fixed on the raven boy with his arms crossed, and staring at me.

"How are you feeling, Carrots?" Lucien asked in a tone that was anything but concerned.

"My head hurts," I replied.

"Oh, does it?" Lucien sat on the edge of my bed. "Strange. I wonder why," he raised a brow that he usually serves with an evil smirk. I frowned at his expression, then gasped as a fragment of my memory suddenly flashed back. I was sure my face matched the color of my hair. "Nice to know fairy wine doesn't kill you," Lucien grinned. Embarrassed, I buried myself under the cover, hoping I would disappear.

The door creaked open, and I jerked up. Caz stared daggers at Lucien before turning his gaze to me. "Here," he said, handing me a Borrelglas of tealoxica. "Drink this—"

I didn't need encouragement. For the third time, tealoxica's magic had not let me down. The awful hangover was gone within a short minutes. As I drank the last of the magic beverage, Caz's scolding glare awaited me like bad news.

He took the empty Borrelglas and set it on a broken table in the middle of the room. "You shouldn't have drunk last night, princess," Caz said calmly.

"I didn't mean to," I muttered, barely audible. "I thought it was tealoxica. I wouldn't have gone there if you hadn't been so cruel to me."

"I wouldn't have been cruel to you if you hadn't provoked me to."

"I wouldn't have provoked you if you hadn't made such an unreasonable offer," I raised my voice to match his.

Caz clenched his jaw and pursed his lips to stop himself from arguing any longer. I could play that game forever if he wanted. And he was aware of it. "What do you remember anyway?" he asked to change the subject. Oddly, I felt he was worried. As though there was something he was afraid I'd remember.

Lucien gulped down his glass of wine in the corner, bored of our little arguments.

"I don't remember much," I admitted, trying to recall the last memory before I went all out with the fairy wine. "A nymph," I said, as a memory finally came to my mind, "she smacked Lucien across the face after he whispered something in her ear. I remember her calling him pathetic as she left."

Lucien spat out his drink. "*That's* what you remember, Carrots?" he sounded offended. "Since your memory works so miraculously all of a sudden, do me a favor and find the pieces to my dignity you were so eager to shatter last night."

"What?" I scowled at him. Nothing about insulting Lucien came to mind. Though I reckon it was fun.

"Stop it, both of you. We've wasted enough time already," Caz said, taking off the white tunic that came with the room reservation and garbed himself back in silver and black. I noticed Caz's injury had healed faster than I'd imagined. Only a faint scar remained from his wound. "Don't we have somewhere to be, princess?"

The Frozen Pond of Secrets was our next destination. Meant to be the centerpiece that connects the Vileforest to Icymark. *The only way to open the portal to the Icymark region is to summon the Banshee,* Lucien had told us when we left the hostel.

Deep inside the Enchanted Abyss, we found a hidden underground tunnel that led us straight into an eerily quiet clearing. Icicle chandeliers hung from the ceiling. Some were large enough to reach the ground. In the center, lay a frozen pond so clear that one could see their reflection perfectly in it, like a mirror. My reflection stared back, motionless, and cold. I shivered like a leaf in the winter wind when I saw that look.

"So," I began, my voice echoing from everywhere. The piercing cold filled my lungs with every breath. "How do we summon the Banshee?"

Lucien sobered. "That's the easy part. Place your hand on the frozen pond and tell it your darkest secret."

I laughed. "Is this a joke? You'd want me to tell it my darkest secret so you could hear it. I'm not a fool, Lucien."

He sighed and rolled his eyes. "You don't have to say it aloud, Carrots. You only need to *think* about it. Only then will the Banshee grace us with her presence."

"What if I don't have a dark secret?"

"Nonsense. Everyone has a secret."

What is mine? I wondered, shifting my gaze to Caz. He regarded me solemnly as if he could see what I was hiding from him. In truth, I've kept a lot of things from Caz, including my first meeting with Lucien, the Fateteller's deal, and my recent haunting nightmares. Surely one of those would be fit to summon the Banshee. I placed my hand on the frozen pond, feeling the ice crawling up like it was in my blood. At that rate, it would reach my heart in no time. I hurried on with the Fateteller's deal. To me, that was the most disturbing. *I only ask for payment after I've delivered my help,* the Fateteller's words echoed in my head. *What could she possibly want from me?* I thought as my body trembled from her effect. After something fell from the ceiling, I opened my eyes. An icicle fell onto the pond and there was no Banshee around.

"That's it?" Lucien asked, "That's your darkest secret? Tell me, is the Frozen Pond of Secrets a joke to you?"

I didn't understand. How *dark* must the secrets be? A few more icicles fell, and my eyes darted back to the pond, where Spore hovered over.

"Oh, look. Even the little one has a darker secret than you," Lucien mocked.

Seriously? What secret could Spore possibly have that's better than the Fateteller? "Why don't you try it yourself?"

Lucien cracked his knuckles and stepped towards the pond. "Gladly," he said as he placed his hand on its surface.

His wings spread wide and the ground underneath me trembled. I took a few steps back, a flaming sword forming in my hand without thinking. Caz stepped closer to me, his sword drawn.

More icicles fell over us like spears, piercing the frozen pond until it cracked. Water rose from beneath the ice, melting it away like a dying promise. A whirlpool formed in the center, sucking all the icicles in like a vacuum. From it, the Banshee appeared as a figure of smoke, like a ghost.

Goosebumps ran over my body as glowing blue eyes met mine. Mirthless laughter rang throughout the Frozen Pond of Secrets and back. "This should be interesting," the Banshee said. She was neither alive nor dead. Something in the middle. "You want an entrance to Icymark, heir of Solmark?" She asked, floating towards me like the wind and my sword vanished as easily as it appeared. "Why?" Somehow, I wasn't surprised she knew who I was.

"My friends and I need to get to the Mountain of Ruins," I said.

She spun around me once. "You want the moon to bleed earlier, why?"

My face twisted slightly. "You're wrong. I don't intend to fight the last Shadow any day sooner than expected. I don't intend to fight Vironnos at all."

The Banshee froze. Blue eyes darted back and forth between Caz and Lucien, who turned their faces away from mine. The Banshee laughed again; this time it was a cruel laugh. "How ignorant of you, heir of Solmark. Your *friends* have hidden the truth from you."

Caz turned his face away when I looked at him. He wasn't at all like himself. "What truth?" I asked the Banshee who took an interest in my naivety. Rather, foolishness. "What truth?" I repeated my question, raising my voice louder.

"Your presence on the Mountain of Ruins will only fuel the long-awaited battle. When the real form of the Shadow meets his rival, the moon will bleed for a sacrifice. For a noble-born heart. Yours or Vironnos', the debt will be paid."

My fear spiked. *The prophecy of death*, the witch's words whispered in my head.

You're a fool for thinking you could escape destiny, my inner voice mocked me.

You're Solmark's promise. The only one who can save Everlynia from destruction, the wordsmith's voice was next.

The Sea of Flames battle may only have one victor. You could become an heir to the Faye Throne…or a useless dead elf, there's no in-between. Rose's was the worst.

Drowning in my own thoughts, I was yearning for a way out. My mother's voice somehow found me, *whatever the cost may be…for my daughter's sake I will pay it.* Those words pushed me deeper into the darkest part of my mind.

"Shame," the Banshee whispered, her voice pulling me out of my river of thoughts. "You might as well be powerless, for it is hard to prevail over a waning prophecy."

More insults. The fear in my heart became tainted with fury, igniting ferociously. A sword deadlier than before raged in my hand as I raised it to the Banshee's chest. The tip of my blade inches from her heart. "I will not have my strength questioned by the dead," I said, watching her eyes widen in dismay. "Insult me again and find out how much Summer power I've got in me."

Caz put a hand on my shoulder, and the rush of adrenaline faded away with my next breath. I lowered my sword.

"That's much better," the Banshee said with a smile. "Now, heir of Solmark, if you wish to enter Icymark, the three of you will each answer a different question. Answering truthfully will open the portal. Those are the terms. Will you abide by the terms of this agreement?"

Our faces were drained of blood. Caz and Lucien appeared ghostly and distressed. I didn't hold it against them. No one knows what the Banshee will ask of us, naturally we think of the worst question she could ask. And the Banshee, despite not being a mind reader, saw right through us.

"Good," she said, floating over to Lucien first. This was the first time I'd seen Lucien alarmed. "Why does the wicked Lucien wish to accompany the heir of Solmark on this mission?"

"To uphold my end of the deal. I'm her guide to find the Darklings and save the exiled queen," Lucien said, relief crossing over his face. Perhaps there were worse questions to ask him.

"The treacherous queen. Thoughtful of you to help her, given the risk you'll encounter. You will be despised no matter what you do, *Lucien*," the Banshee sneered before vanishing, only to reappear beside Caz. He was next.

"Caz, son of Lord Damien. Blessed with the power of Summer," the Banshee murmured. Caz grimaced at the mention of Summer's power. "There's so much regret within you. I need to know…what do you regret the most?"

Sadness lingered in his eyes, stripping him of light. There was one thing he regretted the most, and even for someone like Caz, it was difficult to admit. The air grew warmer the longer he waited, melting icicles from the ceiling that dripped quietly onto the ground, eventually falling and shattering into millions of pieces. Wavy strands covered his eyes as Caz dipped his head. His lips trembled as he spoke. "Killing my mother," he whispered, voice strangled with woe.

I shuddered when I heard his regret. I never expected the honorable Caz to do something so heinous. I couldn't fathom why he did it.

"She paid the cost," the Banshee said, whirling around him. "You needn't mind the past. If you're not careful, son of Lord Damien, your heart will betray you once again."

The ground shook as a glowing gateway emerged from the pond. If I squinted hard enough, I could see the Icymark from where I was standing. Bright and frigid.

I caught a glimpse of the glowing blue eyes studying me out of the corner of my eye. I stood my ground, determined not to flinch away. Though my heart raced faster than I wanted it to.

"You're next, heir of Solmark," the Banshee murmured, tilting my chin up. A smirk stretched from ear to ear, and I knew this wasn't going to be easy. "Tell me," she said, floating behind me so I could see the portal again. And the field of snow on the other side. "What did you whisper to the Frozen Pond of Secrets?"

I felt as though my soul curled into a ball. A small gasp escaped, betraying the mask I'd put on. My answer was all that stood between us and Icymark. The *truth*. Caz and Lucien had done their part, and it was now up to me. Anything I say that isn't the truth would violate the terms of the agreement, and we'd have wasted our time. I hoped the Fateteller wouldn't mind me sharing our little secret. She never warned against it anyway.

So, I told the Banshee and everyone who stood in the Frozen Pond of Secrets the truth. Grateful I chose that secret in the first place. The word *shock* might as well be written on Caz's face as he glared at me, speechless.

"A deal with a Fateteller will do you no good, heir of Solmark," the Banshee warned, "remember this when you are lost."

The Banshee grinned, pleased that she had ripped information from each of us to satisfy her curiosity. "Well then," she said, clapping her hands. "Off you go. Fate awaits each of you." The Banshee gave us one last look of grim triumph before we entered the glowing portal.

CHAPTER 12

ICYMARK

A WHITE BLANKET of snow covered the field around us. Icymark resembled an icy desert in its emptiness. The occasional savage breeze pushed us back and nearly knocked me over by the fifth wave before it finally calmed. In the frigid weather, the sun, which I had almost forgotten existed, provided very little warmth. This was beyond my expectations. The wind screeched as it whipped through the trees, humming a forbidden song of death.

I paused to take in the view of Icymark before returning my attention to Caz, Lucien and Spore, who had rolled around into a snowball. I swallowed, meeting Caz's sharp gaze. He knew about the Fateteller's deal now, and he hadn't said anything since we passed through the portal. Even *I* knew it was a risk, I had no choice. Without the Fateteller, I would have been tempted by Rose's proposal. It wasn't only me that felt exposed, the Banshee had taken part of each of us. Caz, in particular, I assumed.

"What's the plan?" I asked.

Lucien flapped his wings to get the snow out before

answering my question. "To get to the Mountain of Ruins, *unnoticed*," he said. "We can't risk being discovered in Icymark," he added.

"Why not?"

"Because we're intruders, Carrots. They won't justify your noble actions of saving an exiled queen. The Icymark rulers are aware that she was exiled for a reason."

Caz nodded. "Your unexpected appearance here means war. Many rules agreed upon by both regions would be broken if they found the heir to the Faye Throne wandering their region as she pleased. That much is certain," Caz explained.

Snow crunched beneath Lucien's feet as he stepped closer. "Lucky for you two, I know someone who can help us cross Icymark unseen."

Bullets of ice sliced through our skin with each gust as we traveled further into Icymark. It pained me to know I could end my suffering, but Caz had warned me not to use my Summer power. *It will attract Winterguards,* he reasoned. Though I couldn't see a single guard within hailing distance. We appeared to be the first to inhibit Icymark, at least to me. We've walked a long way and haven't seen the slightest hint of life.

Frozen skeletal trees were sprinkled evenly across the field of snow. If it weren't for the frostbite, which only made me think of pain, I would have thought it was beautiful.

Caz stopped suddenly, and I peered over his shoulder to see what he was looking at. There was smoke further down, indicating that we had arrived at the first of Icymark's settlements.

Lucien kicked the door open and walked inside. "Knock knock," he called out. Far too late for that. There were empty tables inside the warm, cozy restaurant filled with the scent of burning wood. I walked in, followed by Caz and Spore, snow trailing behind us on the clean floor.

An older fae, with green strands of hair tangled around his crooked horn, slammed his head against the table and groaned as he watched Lucien approaching him. I didn't hold it against him. Lucien had that kind of effect on everyone. "What now?"

"I've tried to stay away as you've suggested, but I always find myself drawn to you. Have you put a spell on me, Alvin?" Lucien grinned.

Alvin sighed heavily. "If I could cast spells, you wouldn't be in my presence right now, Lucien." He gestured, and two small goblins emerged from the kitchen with brooms, cleaning the snow trail we'd left behind. "Why are you here, Lucien? The Winterguards haven't stopped looking for you since you killed two of them. There's a generous prize on your head, and there are many who need that silver."

Caz shook his head. "Is there a place where you're not wanted?" Caz asked through his teeth.

"Only the ones I've never been to," Lucien replied proudly, turning his head back to Alvin. "I don't want trouble. Not this time. I've come to collect my debt."

Alvin went still for a moment. Then he smiled. "You know about my hidden passages?"

Lucien matched his smile and nodded. "Yes, now show us the way."

Alvin's lips stretched wider. "No," he said simply. "I'm only in debt to you, Lucien. Not your friends. What have they got to offer me?" His eyes shifted to Caz and me.

I gave no expression. "We don't have time to waste. You know what you want. Tell us what it is."

Alvin stood, both hands planted on the table. "You're different, my lady. I can sense your emotions. You have so many for a true fairy." His smile faded, and his expression became dangerous. "I want your ability to love."

He must've felt my uneasiness as the corner of his mouth quirked up. Fairies did not care for love or emotions; I've learned that much. His eyes hinted at curiosity, and I knew my ability to love wasn't what he truly wanted. Alvin wasn't surprised when I refused to give it away.

"I knew it," Alvin whispered, walking closer to me before Caz stopped him with a dagger placed on his throat. Alvin narrowed his eyes. "You and your guard," he shot Caz a quick glance, "did not come from the Vileforest. You came from Solmark."

"You're clever, but you still haven't asked for what you truly want. Do you mean to keep us waiting until you figure it out, or is that just a game of yours?" I asked, drawing closer to him. Though every bone in my body screamed for me to back away.

He shook his head. "No, my lady. I know what I want." He leaned forward, meeting the sharp edge of Caz's dagger. A single drop of blood stained his pale skin. Ice-blue eyes pinned me with a prying look. "Information," he said. "Who are you, really?"

It felt strange to think it. To say it. To believe it. "I'm the heir of Solmark."

. . .

Back to the darkness we went. Alvin had led us to a passage beneath the ground and given us a burning torch. "Be on guard, heir of Solmark." Alvin had advised. Or warned. I couldn't read his face in the darkness, but his smirk wasn't inviting.

The underground tunnel echoed our footsteps, our breaths, and—at least to me—my thoughts. To my surprise, the tunnel wasn't a labyrinth. Just a straight passage that I had hoped would take us right to where we wanted. To Icymark's periphery. Away from the Winterguards and the rulers of Icymark.

"Do you trust him?" Caz asked after a few hours of walking.

Lucien clicked his tongue. "I trust no one. I wouldn't be able to uphold my reputation if I did."

I took in a shaky breath as Caz's hand wrapped against my ribs, drawing me closer to him with force. My eyes searched for an explanation in Caz's face, but I didn't find any. His eyes gave nothing. I sensed his worry—and my heart began to thump wildly. Caz trusted Alvin as much as he trusted Lucien. Not at all.

We strode through the tunnel, our fear growing as several minutes flashed by. We had anticipated walking for days until we reached the end of the path, but the light ahead suggested otherwise. *This can't be right*, I thought.

I clearly remembered Alvin's words and wondered why I hadn't paid attention at the time. *You know about my hidden passages?* Not passage. He paid his debt in his own deceptive way.

Lucien whirled to face us, his hollow eyes confirmed my worry. Without hesitation, we tried to turn back but were stopped by a stone wall. We were trapped, and there was only one way out: straight ahead. To whatever awaited us there.

Lucien cursed, but he wasn't angry. He was amazed. "Tricked the trickster," he murmured.

The torch burned out, and the tunnel began to tilt beneath our feet. More and more until it turned into a slide, forcing us to the bottom. I screamed my way down until we plunged into a bed of snow, then flew high above. Caz, Lucien, Spore, and I were crammed into a trap net, dangling from a tall, frozen tree.

Caz tried reaching for his dagger, but a flying arrow warned him not to do so.

"There's your guy," Alvin said, which didn't surprise us. We looked down, and to our displeasure, we were surrounded by silver-clad guards. Winterguards. I counted a dozen.

One of the guards handed Alvin a bag of coins. "Fifty for him alive," he said, eyes never leaving Lucien.

"*What?*" Lucien shrieked. Caz winced at his high-pitched voice. "Only fifty? Is that what I'm worth to you, Gil? After killing two of your guards, you deem me unworthy?"

Of course, that was what Lucien was concerned with. Not the fact that Alvin betrayed him, or that we're trapped, or that our plan of crossing Icymark unnoticed had failed miserably. Not even the possible war Caz had warned us about. No, it was the price at which he was sold.

"No need to rush, Lucien," Gil took Alvin's place after

he'd run off with the prize bag, long white hair whipping in the wind. "Once I deliver the intruders of Solmark to our queen, you and I will have all the time to settle our debt. I promise you I'll show you just how much you're worth to me." Gil said, sounding a lot like Lucien himself. They shared the same brain cell, so it seemed.

"Oh, that's good," Lucien said, sounding genuinely relieved. "I thought you were still a coward."

Gil laughed without humor. "Me? A coward? Come down here and I'll show you who's the coward."

"Free me and we'll see," Lucien refuted.

"Girls! We get it, you both can fight," I said, bored with them both. "Can we get down now?"

Another arrow and we dropped to the snow below. I cursed as Caz pulled me up. "Are you mad?" I fixed Gil with a poisonous stare. "How dare you trap me like a rabbit and then release me like one? Don't you have any idea who I am?"

Caz shared my false show of rage, though I could feel him trying hard not to break character. I noticed something different about him since we left the Enchanted Abyss. I felt as though something had changed.

Gil stepped back, his gaze searching his friends for an answer. I may have had a little too much fun watching him get scared because my next words were insults and threats. "Did the rulers of Icymark put a sword in the hands of every simpleton they found, or just you?" I asked. Lucien chuckled.

Gil opened his mouth to speak, then closed it again. "Don't have the guts to answer? Very well, I'll report this to your queen once I meet her."

He blinked, then frowned. "You're a Solmark intruder, why would the queen even *want* to listen to you?"

"Intruder? Call me that again and I'll have your head for it, simpleton," I warned as I loomed closer. "Your queen invited me herself," I searched my mind, begging it to remember the name of the event Caz had mentioned before. "I'm here for the Seasons Celebration."

Gil's frown deepened. "You mean the Seasons Gathering?"

Dammit. "And now you dare correct her highness? How many offenses must my princess charge you with before you learn your place?" Caz rescued me.

"*You* are the princess of Solmark? The one we heard about?" Gil asked.

I gave a cold nod. "The one and only."

Gil glanced sharply at Lucien. "And why is he with you?"

"I'm their guide," Lucien answered in my stead. "Is that a problem?"

Gil pointed to Spore, not even bothering to ask.

"He's my friend," I said, "you'll carry him yourself on the way to the Icymark Court. He's not very friendly, so I advise you not to anger him." I almost laughed, imagining Spore getting angry at anyone. "Ready the horses at once, simpleton. We don't have all day."

I watched as the Winterguards scampered off to carry out my orders. A smile of triumph stretched on my face, and I felt as though I'd won the lottery. At the same time, the thought of being in the Icymark Court made my stomach sink. Caz studied me carefully. I waited, expecting him to chastise me. "If you're going to tell me how foolish I am, you needn't bother," I told him.

Caz surprised me with a smile and a nod of affirmation. "I suppose I won't then," he murmured, though he looked like he wanted to say something entirely different.

I rode with Caz. Spore with Gil. And Lucien insisted on flying instead. With the wind on our side, riding proved easier than ever. The Icymark territory was the total opposite of Solmark. There were no roses of various colors, no fountains of gold, and no fairies in sight. Icymark looked almost abandoned, a monochrome landscape. The temperature dropped with each breath. I was grateful for Caz's proximity; his body radiated heat like the sun. However, the closer we got to the court, the less impact he had.

We approached a wall of ice taller than Mount Everest. My neck ached from looking at it. I wondered if the wall extended all the way to heaven.

"Open the gates!" Gil announced, and a gate that blended in with the wall slowly lifted.

More Winterguards stood beyond the gate, making me wonder if Icymark was at war. They most certainly outnumber Solmark's guards. Something was missing—I took a good look at each and every one of them, which only confirmed my suspicion.

"They're all Winter?" I asked Caz. He nodded. "But…I thought Icymark was ruled by Winter *and* Autumn."

He nodded again. "*Was*," he said, "but they lost their right to rule centuries ago. Winter and Autumn were destined to unite, but the prince of Autumn betrayed Icymark by declaring his love to another during one of the Seasons Gathering."

I swallowed. "Who?"

Caz's eyes met mine. "Your mother," he said.

Several heartbeats later, we arrived at a glass castle. The Icymark Court. I would have been relieved that there were no dragon statues outside, but fear overrode all other feelings. I had no doubt that the queen I must endure despises my mother, and I have no doubt that she feels the same way about me.

I looked up at the court of iced glass and questioned whether I would ever survive. I then noticed something. Within the court's windows, a shadow shifted. Glowing red eyes were fixed on me. Before I could gasp, it vanished.

The gazes of the Icymark subjects were just as sharp and wicked as I walked the halls of the court and was led straight to the Fae Throne room. As I stepped inside, there were murmurs, then silence filled the air. Icicles dangled from the ceiling of the throne room, sharp as knives. One shout is all it would take to send them stabbing into our flesh, I imagined. Unlike the Solmark Court, this one is covered with silver paint that spilled from the walls to the metallic floor.

Gil handed Spore to Caz, then turned around and knelt. *The queen,* I thought. Her ice throne was so high up that I didn't notice it at first. Caz brushed his fingers against my back, and we bowed.

"Long live the queen of Icymark," Caz and Gil spoke in unison.

The queen of Icymark lived up to her name. She was as beautiful as a pearl in an oyster. As graceful as a Winter night. And as dangerous as an ice storm. Her hair, a river of milk, ended at her feet. A diamond crown bent colorful lights over her head. Her violet eyes pierced my soul as Gil gestured to me.

"Your Majesty, this is—"

"Yes. The daughter of the exiled queen," she said quietly, as though she was talking to herself. "The usurper."

"Princess Alexandra is not a usurper. She's the daughter of King Alrick. The only rightful heir to the Faye Throne," Caz said, stepping to my side.

The queen smiled. "Yes, I can see that, son of Lord Damien. But as we all know, the wind sometimes whispers hateful lies. I'm afraid that was all we heard in Icymark." She turned her gaze at me. "You came for the Seasons Gathering?"

I nodded.

She laughed. "Does the king of Solmark have no regard for his daughter's life?" she mocked, and the crowd shook with laughter. "Sending you away with a bastard and a crea-ture of the Vileforest," she added, glancing at Lucien, who had walked inside, delighted at the mention of him. "He must *really* care for you. Shouldn't he be concerned?"

"Should I?" I asked. My voice was all it took for the laughter to die out.

The queen's face twisted. I might've imagined her shadow becoming larger with rage. The courtroom dropped below freezing. I felt my blood thicken in my veins. "You should," she said, "if you're smart."

Caz waited for me to handle her threat. When I didn't, he stepped closer to the throne. "Queen Eira, the Seasons Gathering is an act of peace, not war."

"I never said it wasn't, son of Lord Damien. I'm simply cautioning your next queen."

I realized I wasn't bound to silence. "Threatening me isn't an act of peace either."

The queen gave a nod of agreement. "That is true, but…" she paused, offering a wicked smile. "If the heir of Solmark was discovered dead in the Vileforest wouldn't that be due to her father's neglect? King Alrick chose to send you away with a killer and a well-known dissembler. He gave you nothing, but a small mushroom that even my hounds wouldn't see fit to hunt, let alone eat. Surely, he must've known the consequences of doing so. A deserved ending for the misfortunate heir, wouldn't you agree?" She rested her hand on her cheek. "*That* was a threat, heir of Solmark."

I grinned at the now-angry queen. "I've heard better threats," I said, and a few guards stiffened. "None of which I cared for, though you're welcome to speculate. I will tell you what I've told others before you," I took another step towards her, "my ending is not yours to decide, Queen Eira."

"It was a joke, Your Highness. My mother didn't mean it," a gentle voice spoke. As footsteps entered the throne room, the fae creatures bowed in respect. When I turned around, a tall figure towered over me. The untied bottom part of his silver hair was buried beneath his long white cloak, which rested on his shoulders. Above his left shoulder, a snow-white raven cawed softly.

He took my hand, bringing it closer to his lips, and placed a gentle kiss. "Princess Alexandra," he murmured my name. His violet eyes were full of amusement. "Will you ever forgive me?"

I swallowed. "What for?"

Caz and Lucien tensed as his cold hand brushed against

my cheek and lifted my chin. "For nearly two decades I have doubted the wind when it spoke of your beauty. I thought the whispers were exaggerated a little, but now I realize I was completely wrong. They haven't exaggerated enough," he said for all to hear.

He bowed, and so did his guards. "I'm Prince Cillian, heir to the Fae Throne of Icymark. We are truly grateful to have you and your companions as our honored guests, my lady."

I returned his polite nod. "Show the princess and her companions to their chambers. I'm sure they're tired from their journey," he ordered and offered a wink before I left the throne room with a female Winter elf named Selene, followed by Caz and Lucien.

Selene showed us to our chambers as Cillian ordered. Caz and Lucien's chambers were next to mine, which was a relief. A rush of cold wind blinded me as she opened the door. I looked around wildly, beautiful crystal chandeliers lined the ceiling of the room. A white bed sat against the far wall. Everything else was glazed in silver. A leafless tree was planted in the center, its ice-coated branches reaching the length of the room. *A symbol of death*, I thought.

"Should I draw a bath for you, my lady?" Selene asked. I nodded.

After the bath, the Winter elf dressed me in a grey gown that was too tight for my liking. Selene unbranded my hair and shoved my curls back, leaving my chest barely covered. She reached for a box on the dressing table and pulled something out. A wire crown. She watched my worried reflection in the mirror and beamed. "Prince Cillian wishes you to wear this to the dinner, my lady," she said as she placed it on my head, not waiting for an answer. As though his wishes were commands.

When I opened the door, Caz was standing outside with Spore in his hand, ready to knock. He froze, eyes surveying the length of my body. Twice. The fabric clung to my body, and I felt completely naked before him, even though I wasn't. Caz, on the other hand, wasn't dressed in Winter attire. Which oddly made me feel guilty. "Don't," I said to cut him off, "don't tell me how ridiculous I look. I already know."

His dimples appeared. "I couldn't even if I wanted to, princess." As his dimples continued to amaze me and his eyes lingered a little too long on my lips, I quickly turned around, hiding my flushed face.

Only then did Lucien appear, hair soaking wet. He whistled at the sight of me.

I rolled my eyes at him. "You're late," I said.

"Oh, *will you ever forgive me,*" he mocked, impersonating Prince Cillian. He didn't have to say the words, but I knew he hated Cillian. "Has the plan changed, Carrots? Are we going to dress up and have a tea party with the prince now?"

I frowned at his comment. "You're blaming me? Was I the one tricked by Alvin?"

"Hey, I lost a debt to that."

"Princess," Caz said, and I turned back to face him. "The Seasons Gathering is in two days; if we wait until then, there's no doubt King Alrick will take you back with him when it's over. He'll take you by force if necessary."

My lips were set in a hard line. "There's no way I'd let that happen. We didn't come all this way just to return empty-handed." I glanced at Caz and Lucien, who both agreed for the first time. Even Spore nodded.

"Then we'll have to flee Icymark before then," Caz said, his glance trailing from Lucien to me.

I wrapped my hands around myself, not from the cold, but from the worrisome thoughts that crept into my mind as we made our way to the dining hall. *What if we couldn't?*

CHAPTER 13
SHADOW AND REGRET

THE DINING HALL DOORS OPENED, revealing a magnificently long table in the center, covered with hundreds of different types of main dishes and sweets. Enough to feed every living creature in Everlynia. Far in the corner, Winter elves played classical music to ease the tension. Queen Eira sat at the head of the dining table, regarding me with disdain as if my presence ruined her whole evening. After bowing to the queen of Icymark and receiving a simple nod in return, Prince Cillian motioned for me to sit next to him, and I did.

"Winter suits you, my princess," he said, as he placed a soft kiss on my hand.

I shivered from his proximity, and offered a smile, hoping it was enough to make him let go of my hand. Thankfully, it was. Caz sat back in his chair, avoiding my eyes.

The queen lifted her chin, and the servants placed plates already full of mouth-watering food in front of us.

We ate in silence for the first part, just as I had hoped.

Then the queen indulged us with her memories of my mother. One hateful memory at a time, until my bites of food stuck in my throat. I expected the prince to say something, but he was busy throwing venomously sweet smirks at Caz when he glared at him for too long.

"Your mother was never fit to be a queen; we all knew that. Lady Helia was more of a…savage. She wasn't a wise woman, but she was rather daring. Too daring in fact. A dangerous quality for a ruler," Queen Eira said as she sipped her fairy wine again. "At one of the Seasons Gatherings, she had too much to drink and embarrassed all of us by making a fool of herself. I recall her being unable to lift her weight and when she did, she stood on the dining table, daring the rulers to a duel."

I forced myself to swallow the bite. "Fascinating," I said, trying my best to sound interested enough. "And was this before or after the famous love declaration?" I asked, and Lucien choked on his drink.

Then there was silence.

The queen could have frozen me if she truly wanted to, and I know she wanted to. But she smirked instead. "You're just as daring as her," she said quietly, "good. I'm looking forward to seeing where that'll take you." She smirked again, this time it was more of a threat. She excused herself not long after she finished her glass.

With her gone, I could finally breathe again.

"Try this, my princess," Cillian said, offering a ruby chocolate.

I popped it in my mouth, and the delightful flavor bloomed a smile on my face. "This is the best sweet I've had in a while," I said. sinking back into my chair. Cillian leaned in, his breath warm against my ear.

"Not nearly as sweet as you, my princess," he whispered in my ears. When he pulled away, I dared to look at Caz and Lucien. Both were equally uncomfortable, but Caz did a better job of hiding it. Lucien excused himself next, stealing a bottle of fairy wine with him as he left.

"Caz," Cillian said, crossing his legs. "I've heard you can wield Summer power, is that true?"

This time, Caz wasn't hiding his uneasiness. "Yes, Your Highness."

"A power so strong, you must be very lucky."

Caz didn't answer.

"What was the name of that working girl your father had an affair with?" Cillian asked, clicking his tongue as he tried to remember. "Ah, Emilia. She was a fine elf. A pity she died because of you."

If a look could kill, Cillian would've been dead by now. Thankfully, Prince Cillian did not care for Caz's hateful gaze. "Some say they were perfect for each other. After all, that is what love is all about. To find someone who completes you. Isn't that right, Caz?"

Caz looked down. "It isn't," he answered.

"How so?" Cillian asked quickly, as though he'd expected what Caz would say.

Caz looked back at him; his eyes were drained of emotions. "When in love, one does not find their other half; they simply lose half of themselves to be with someone else. And until it's all over, they won't know which half they lost. Love is a war that'll always end in defeat."

It never occurred to me that Caz thought of love as war. And worse, something about that made me less comfortable. "What an awful thing to say," Cillian said. "Not at all what your parents thought.

"The wind used to sing songs about them. Such a sweet love story they had—until you came along." Caz bobbed his head, unable to meet my gaze anymore. As though he was guilty. Suddenly I remembered Caz's greatest regret—*Killing my mother, he said.* "Tell me," Cillian continued, oblivious to his silence. "Was it worth it?" he asked. "Are *you* worth it?"

Caz's chair creaked as he stood. His chest rose and fell faster than usual. "No," he answered quietly as he left the dining hall.

I stood too. "I haven't properly thanked you for having us as your guest of honor, Prince. We truly appreciate your generosity," I said, "If you'll excuse me—"

"Not so fast." Before I could take a single step, Cillian grabbed my wrist. "My princess," he said softly, towering over me. "I'm afraid I must warn you of the danger that surrounds you."

"What?"

"Caz," he said, and I lifted my eyebrows in surprise. "Before you cast your suspicions on me, please allow me to explain."

Prince Cillian walked me to the Garden of Hope, where a giant living oak tree encased by glass glowed like diamonds in the dark. I looked up to see the moon and stars shining brighter than I'd ever seen them. Cillian led me to a stone bench and kneeled in front of me, gently tucking a rose from the hundreds scattered around behind my ear. His silver hair shimmered blue from the moonlight. His expression was pained, grim even. He sat close to me, his knee bumped into mine.

"My princess," he murmured, voice filled with worry. "Do you trust him?"

"Who?" I asked, confused about who he could be referring to. "Lucien?"

"No, your guard," Cillian replied, looking around in paranoia

I trusted Caz with my life. He never did anything to prove he was a danger to me, so what made Prince Cillian think he was? "Yes," I answered, wanting to hear his reasons for asking.

"Caz is a killer, princess. You shouldn't trust him. He killed to wield Summer power, and he will no doubt do the same to earn yours."

I frowned. "Caz has Summer power, you said so yourself. Why would he want mine?"

Prince Cillian gripped both of my wrists. "Don't be foolish, princess. It's not your Summer power he wants." He shook his head slowly. "Caz wants your Spring power. Your ability to create life, control nature, and move mountains. He wants it all to himself."

"What?" My voice was faint, and my heart skipped several beats. *You're the first daughter of Spring and Summer, Lady Alexandra. You're Solmark's promise.* The wordsmith's words found me. Still, I couldn't get my head around the idea of Caz betraying me. *Why hadn't he mentioned my Spring power?*

Prince Cillian stared at me with his wide eyes. "He didn't tell you?" he asked. "And you trust him?"

I didn't answer this time. *I* didn't know the answer. I was desperate for power. Desperate to save my mother. Desperate to save myself. Caz knew the whole time and didn't tell me. Why? Now, I was desperate for answers. I rose from the bench, stumbling away from the prince.

"He lied to you, princess. Caz is using you." Cillian lessened his grip on my wrist "Ask him yourself if you don't believe me."

I freed myself from his grasp and inched closer to read him. "Why are you telling me this? You're the prince of Icymark, why would I trust you?"

Prince Cillian looked down at me, running a finger down my cheek. "I'm nothing like my mother and you're not like your father." His finger pressed against my lips. "Together, we are the rulers of Everlynia. The future. Let us not make the mistake of limiting our desires."

I took a step back, breaking the tension between us. Prince Cillian dropped his hand. "I-I must retire to my chamber," I stammered, taking another step. "I appreciate your concern, prince."

He smiled softly and nodded, and I could feel his eyes bore through me as I walked away.

I trotted through the halls, making my way to find Caz. I needed him to answer my questions. To explain why he kept my Spring power hidden from me. To know if I could trust him. I took another turn and—the hall where the chambers were had vanished. A dark, narrow path had taken its place. I heard footsteps and my heart leaped.

The moonlight bathed the hall, but it wasn't enough. A figure stood in the corner, hiding completely by the shadow. "Is someone there?" I called out in the darkness, "step into the light."

He did. He wore a hooded cape that hid his body completely. Half of his face was hidden behind a mask, revealing only his glowing red eyes. The same ones that fixed me with a predatory look that day I stepped foot into the Icymark Court.

"I have a message for you, Princess Alexandra," his voice was shrill.

"Who are you?"

"A messenger."

Was he sent by the queen to frighten me? I wondered.

"I was not sent by the Icymark Queen, Princess Alexandra," he answered, reading my mind like an open book. "I'm here on orders from the Darklings."

Darklings. That word stole the air from my lungs, leaving me suffocated. Cold sweat coated my neck. "What do they want?"

"You're running out of time, Princess Alexandra. The moon will soon bleed for a sacrifice, as it has done for centuries. The blood curse may only break if the rulers join to undo their mistakes. The last Shadow offers you a promised beginning. You may choose to fight and die or break the curse once and for all. We wish you no harm, princess."

That made me lose my temper. "You abduct my mother, and you dare speak of promises?"

"Your mother is an honored guest of ours." He stepped

back into the darkness. "We will be waiting," he said before vanishing into the shadows.

I was left speechless in the hallway, forgetting everything that mattered for a moment. The Darklings sent someone not only to warn me but also to give me a chance to survive. To break the blood curse. *Why would they want that? It doesn't make sense—*

"Princess?" I whirled around at the familiar voice. "What are you doing here alone?" Caz asked, eyes squinting with concern.

I wanted to tell him everything, but then, I remembered Cillian's words. "I was looking for you."

Caz straightened, taking my hand in his and leading me back to my chamber. He shut the door and looked at me with an unreadable expression. "What do you want to know?" He was convinced that Prince Cillian had told me many things about him that he should have told me himself.

"You knew I have Spring power and you didn't tell me, why?"

He wasn't at all surprised by that question. Caz sighed. "I didn't want the knowledge of Spring power to distract you or cause you to lose focus on your training. I could only teach you the way of fire, and I wanted to do my best."

"Is that all?"

He didn't look away. "What else is there?"

I took a step toward him, another. "You tell me. Do you want the power for yourself, Caz? You told me once that powers can be taken away."

Caz recoiled from me as his eyes widened. "You think I'd do that to you?" His face became clouded with betrayal. "Don't you trust me, princess?"

I'd never seen Caz so hurt before. I didn't answer.

He stilled, his eyes never leaving mine. "I've seen what powers can do, princess, and if I could give it all away for what it had cost me, I would. When I was a child, I'd return home with new scars every day, hiding whatever I could, knowing that I was more of a burden than a son to my mother," he said, voice dangerously low. As though he's forcing himself to speak, to remember. "She wouldn't say it, of course, but in my heart, I knew it was true. So, I'd wish upon every star that I'd be invincible. Until one day when the stars listened, and I had awoken thinking I had everything I ever wanted, only to find the cost of my power was the only person I cared for. She was lifeless in my father's arms. That was the first time I met him, and he made sure to remind me what I'd done for a long while after."

Silence hung in the air, heavy with the burden of his guilt. "I learned two things that day," he continued with a fragile voice, "powers are a dangerous curse, and wishes may only come true when one no longer wants them. I had everything and nothing at all." He forced a weak smile. "You shouldn't worry, princess. Power is the last thing I want. Of that, you can be certain."

I hated the way he stared at me with his hollow eyes. "I'm so sorry, Caz." I held his hand, not knowing what else to do, but Caz flinched at my touch.

"Is there anything else Cillian wanted you to know, princess?" He said in a harsh tone. He backed towards the door, not wanting to spend a moment longer in this room than he had to. My audience with him was over, and I didn't have the time to tell him about the Darklings' message.

"No," I murmured. "And Caz…" I said as he opened

the door. He stopped but didn't turn back to face me. "I do trust you. I always have."

"Is that all, princess?"

"One more thing," I said, approaching him. His gleaming eyes made it ten times harder on me, but I did it anyway. I reached up to gently stroke his cheek. This time, he didn't flinch. Caz froze, watching me closely with surprise. My eyes met his, and the world fell to pieces beneath my feet. "You are worthy, Caz," I whispered, feeling his face warm up against my fingers. "I need you to know that." I finally pulled away, relieved that he didn't say anything because I couldn't hear him over my own heartbeat anyway.

Caz nodded after a long pause, then closed the door behind him.

As I lay in bed, I could still feel his skin on my fingers, soft and warm. I shook my head to forget about it, even for a moment. I watched the leafless branches that stretched like claws over my head, and I thought about everything that had happened so far, wondering where it all went wrong. One thing is for certain: the more I knew, the more there was to know. My thoughts slipped away as easily as they came, and I did too.

For the last time, I stood in the darkest corner of the dungeon. I watched as the same scenes replayed, expecting to wake up at any moment. But this time, I didn't.

"To change the prophecy, you must give up your throne, Queen Helia," the witch said, "you must betray your king."

The queen lifted her head to glance straight at the witch. "You cannot ask this of me," she begged.

The witch rose. "You've already betrayed the crown once, my queen, have you forgotten?" Though her face was blurry, she smirked mirthlessly. "You weren't so shaken when you asked me to curse a noble's son years ago. You knew the curse of power would take a living, yet you weren't concerned. You hoped Damien himself would die, didn't you? Why are you afraid now?"

My heart jolted from my chest and my stomach churned as I gaped at the Solmark Queen. My mother. I blinked, stunned. *My mother did this? Caz's greatest regret stemmed from my mother's actions?*

You think your mother is a saint? I never imagined Queen Rose was right about her.

"Lord Damien was a threat to us all," the queen reasoned, "but I never meant for you to curse his bastard. I suppose it's my fault I wasn't clear with you. I do regret what I've done, and I will not have you deceive me again, witch."

"I cannot deceive you this time, my queen. Give up your rule and your daughter shall survive the blood curse. Power for power, that is the cost to alter your daughter's fate."

My mother stood up slowly. Her gown was drenched in blood and dust from the dungeon. "What do you see?" she whispered.

The witch grinned. "I see your daughter taking her place on the throne. In a court of darkness, she will not be alone. Joined by the Shadow, the blood curse will be broken. And the game of powers will finally begin."

A moment later, the dungeon crumbled away. In a void,

I stood rigid with disbelief. "Why?" I whispered, my choked voice filling the space. "Why did you show me this?"

"There are no rules to the game of powers, living one," the Fateteller said, "some cheat, steal, kill, and betray. Whatever it takes them to earn power, and they'll do much worse to keep them."

I faced the Fateteller. The clone of me. "Like my mother did?" I asked through my teeth.

"On the contrary," she replied with a lazy smirk. "Your mother gave up her power, her right to rule for your sake. And what have you done for her, living one?" The Fateteller was now surrounded by clouds of smoke. "She's not a saint, but she has saved you from a perilous prophecy. The rest is entirely up to you."

"Perhaps she should have feared what I'd become."

"She will," the Fateteller said, "but she will not be the only one. Be warned, living one; there are others who crave more power and will deceive you into the darkness if you aren't careful." She started fading away but I still had so many questions

"Will I see you again?" I didn't know why I felt the need to ask that question. It was as if my mind spoke for me.

She gave one last faint smile before fading completely out of my sight. "That is up to you, living one." Her voice was all that remained.

I awoke gasping for air, feeling suffocated beneath my blankets. The thunderous branches above my head reminded me of where I was, and I hurried out of bed.

Not long after, Selene informed me of Prince Cillian's invitation to a private council meeting. It seemed strange for the heir of Icymark to invite me, not only an outsider but a rival in the eyes of many, to a private meeting. Once again, it was more of a request than an invitation.

I couldn't imagine what Prince Cillian's intentions were, but it didn't matter much to me. We had agreed to flee Icymark before the Seasons Gathering, and a small private meeting wasn't going to change that.

This is the last time, I told myself as I stripped off my nightgown and changed into another Winter gown. This one did cover every inch of my body up to my neck, but it was equally scandalous as the last one. Tight-fitting, the black velvet glued from my throat and down to my knees made breathing difficult. Silver crystals made their way from the loose fabric on the floor to my bust in lightning patterns.

Selene reached for the crown, but she met my gaze in the mirror as she picked it up. "I can do without the crown," I said.

She put it back slowly, pursing her lips. "Isn't my lady scared of him?" She asked quietly as she removed the pins from my hair and let the curls fall to my back.

"Who would I be scared of?"

"Prince Cillian," she said, smoothing my curls with her long fingers.

I turned in my chair, gazing up at Selene. "And why would I be scared of Prince Cillian?"

She stumbled back, face white with fear. "I-I'm sorry, my lady," Selene stammered. She dropped the pins on the dressing table, a few fell to the floor as she moved carelessly, but she didn't notice. "I didn't mean to say that. Please forgive me, my lady."

She turned to walk away but stopped as I called her name, voice rising in authority. "Why did you say that?" I asked.

She turned, fingers trembling. "Because," she murmured, "Prince Cillian…wants you to be his queen, my lady."

CHAPTER 14
ESCAPING THE PRINCE

I WAS COMPLETELY TAKEN ABACK by her response. *Me? A bride?* I almost laughed at that ridiculous thought. I just couldn't imagine that was what Prince Cillian truly wanted. He had indeed offered nothing but kindness thus far, but that didn't mean he was interested. Besides, the rules of Everlynia forbid such a union. It was unthinkable. Impossible.

I brushed her comment off and walked past her to open the door, only to be astonished by the cramped halls. Dozens of trolls, goblins, and redcaps stood around, watching others decorate the halls from end to end. New curtains, chandeliers, and rugs replaced the old ones. Ladders were placed against the towering windows in the hall, where servants worked tirelessly, scrubbing every inch of the glass. A group of kobolds rushed in to sweep the floor as dirt fell from the ceiling.

There were so many creatures in the hall that I barely noticed Caz stepping beside me. "The preparation for

Seasons Gathering has begun," he whispered, eyes darting about the hall.

From his proximity, my pulse refused to slow down. His voice brought back the memories of last night, and my fingers yearning for his touch. Though I couldn't bring myself to look at him, I felt his eyes pinned on me like I was the only one standing there. And it might as well have been just us in the hall.

I swallowed hard and gathered whatever strength I had at the moment to face him. "When do we leave?" I whispered, careful not to let anyone hear our plan to escape.

Caz fell into step beside me. "Aren't you a little busy with the Winter Prince to be asking that question, princess?" There was a hint of jealousy in his voice, something I never expected. Certainly not from Caz. What's strange is that it made me *feel* something. Like I was special.

I frowned at him, and he finally relented. "If it pleases you, I'm not at all looking forward to spending time with him." I had no idea why I said that.

"It pleases me," he murmured. His dimples greeted me as I spared him a glance, and regretted it as I felt my face burn.

We were away from everyone when we stopped to gaze out the frosted window. Outside, hundreds of carriages pulled up to the gates and the Winter nobles stood in line to greet the Autumn guests. Caz had informed me that despite Autumn's absence of authority over Icymark, they were still expected at the Seasons Gathering as they are one of the Seasonal courts.

I stared at Caz, who still hadn't answered my question.

He leaned against the wall of glass, crossing his arms.

"We leave tonight," he said, "but first I'll have to find Lucien and your little friend."

I grimaced, ready to ask a question that Caz answered right away. "He took your friend with him last night, but they haven't returned yet." I frowned. "Don't worry, princess, I'll look for them."

"It's not that," I said with a sigh and turned to watch more guests arrive. Caz uncrossed his arms to rest a hand on my shoulder. "I've been feeling terrible since this morning," I said. "I can't help but think something awful will happen tonight. What if..." I looked down at my shaking hands. "What if we won't make it out of Icymark? What if we're stuck here forever? What if something happens to any of you? I can't watch you get hurt again, Caz. I can't possibly let you wound yourself for me—"

"Princess," he cupped my face with his hands to focus my attention on him. "No one will get hurt," he whispered, lifting my head so we were eye to eye. "And we will get out of here. Tonight," he amended. "We're not alone. I will look out for you, and you look out for me," he whispered. His warm breath brushed my cheek. Then, he pulled me in for a hug, and I surrendered to him, wrapping my arms around his neck. Caz did not let go of me until my breathing was normal again.

Through the glass, I saw the white raven on a branch near the window. His white eyes were on us for a long time, then he flew away.

Caz had left to find Lucien and Spore, and I walked alone to the private council room. At the door, awaited the Winter Prince. He grinned and bowed his head as he saw me from a distance. I did the same.

"You look divine, my princess," he said, eyeing my every step.

He took my arm in his as he walked beside me. "Thank you, that is very kind of you, Prince Cillian."

He stopped, pulling me far too close. "Say that again," he whispered.

Outside the council room, Winter and Autumn nobles glared daggers at us as they awaited the Winter Prince. I swallowed and looked away. "Thank you—"

"Not that," he said. "Say my name. I want to hear you say it, my princess."

"Prince Cillian," I said loudly and pushed myself away, "we shouldn't keep your guests waiting any longer."

"Certainly not," Queen Eira's voice sounded like a blizzard. For once, I was thankful she was here. We walked inside the council room, and everyone took their seats. I sat next to Prince Cillian, everyone's eyes were pinned on me and worst of them all the was the Queen's.

No one questioned why I was there, though I had hoped someone would. It would've been a legitimate reason to excuse myself from a dull political meeting. It was more of a one-sided meeting, as the Autumn rarely shared their insights and when they did, they were often interrupted by the queen or one of her nobles.

"The last topic on the agenda involves the Darklings," the Winter General said, making my heart skip a beat. "They've been seen infiltrating the Icymark region repeatedly in the last few weeks. In particular, the Autumn region." Everyone shifted their gaze to the Autumn General. It was then that I realized he had been staring at me the entire meeting. I flushed.

"The Darklings often intrude wherever they like," he replied, brushing his long chestnut hair back, revealing a mark that ran from the middle of his forehead down to his cheek. "Is that a surprise now?"

The queen leaned forward. "Are you saying you have nothing to do with the Darklings?"

The Autumn General nodded. "Strange," Queen Eira said, "considering you've betrayed Icymark once, why not do it again?"

"I've never betrayed Icymark, my lady," he said. "I've only been honest. A quality you don't possess."

The queen sneered. "And where has honesty gotten you, General Jora? You lost your right to rule the moment you chose to be *honest*," she spat.

I quickly turned my head to get a better look at him. General Jora. He was the Autumn Prince that confessed his love to my mother. He smiled at me with a wink and turned to answer the queen. "And I'd lose it again," he said. "I'd lose it a thousand times if I had to. You have forgotten who I am, my lady." He stood, his deep brown cloak moving luxuriously as he sauntered over to the queen. "I am Autumn. Liberated as the wind, why should my heart be held hostage for the sake of that headpiece you're wearing?"

"Isn't it obvious, General Jora? We give up cheap senti-ments for power. Rulers don't have the luxury to have it all. In power, we found our freedom." Queen Eira said, reaching for her wine glass.

"You're mistaken, my lady. Freedom is freedom, no power on Everlynia can change that." He sighed, bored with the conversation. "Is this meeting over, my lady?"

"It is," Queen Eira announced. She was the first to walk out of the council room, followed by her angry Winter nobles. It wasn't until she was gone that the room temperature finally returned to something tolerable.

Prince Cillian moved to the corner of the room after Gil whispered something in his ear during the meeting. I couldn't hear what they were discussing, but surely it was important enough for the heir of Icymark to excuse himself from the politics and agendas.

I remained in my seat, waiting for Cillian to finish his conversation with Gil so I could properly excuse myself. I imagine it would be considered impolite to leave without thanking the host for the invitation. Even if the invitation reeked of alternative motives.

"You're as beautiful as your mother, princess," General Jora whispered, taking a seat next to me.

I smiled. "Thank you, Prince Jora."

He scrunched up his face. "I'm no longer a prince." I began to apologize, but he didn't let me. "It's alright, princess," he said, "I knew I wasn't meant to be a prince."

I turned in my chair, puzzled, but hesitant to ask him the question. General Jora cocked his head, waiting, as though he knew I was going to ask him a question. "How did you know you weren't meant to be a prince?" I asked.

He didn't take long to answer. "I knew because I didn't deserve my princess. Fate is a cruel thing," he said, "but I've learned to accept it. Do you know why?" I shook my head. "Because there is no escaping it, but…" he paused, glancing at Prince Cillian and Gil who were still deep in conversation. "I believe you already know that, princess. So, why are you here?"

He knew. General Jora knew I wasn't here for private meetings or the Seasons Gathering, and he wasn't trying to hide it. There was no point in lying to him. "I want to save my mother," I told him, hoping his loyalty to her was enough to keep him quiet.

He gave me a sidelong glance and rubbed his chin. For a moment I thought he wasn't pleased to hear that, but he nodded. "And what do you need?"

"I need to get out of here before the Seasons Gathering."

"And the proper gear, I assume?" His smile widened as he studied my dress.

I nodded, sharing his enthusiasm. "Very well, I'll see to it that you have what you need. Until then, do not succumb to dangerous desires, princess."

I didn't know what to say to that. General Jora stood, pulling me to my feet as Cillian approached us.

"I see you've already made yourself comfortable, General Jora." Prince Cillian's face was emotionless, as was his tone.

General Jora bowed his head. "We were just talking about Lady Helia." He didn't lie but didn't say the full truth either. "How delightful and remarkable she was." He turned to me as he said those words.

"So I've heard," Cillian said, taking my hand in his and leading me out. I turned to smile one last time at General Jora, and he winked at me once again.

When I thanked Prince Cillian for the invitation, he

shook his head and told me that our time together wasn't over yet, so excusing myself was out of the question. Faeries in the hall parted as we ambled by. Winterguards trailed the prince and me everywhere we went. At each turn, two new guards joined our procession, adding to the train.

After endless hallways and turns, we finally arrived where Prince Cillian wanted. The Fae Throne. Cillian directed his guards to stand outside so that no Winterguards, servants, nobles, or the queen were present in the throne room. Only us, and the pointed, glittering icicles above our heads. Dread swirled in my stomach as Prince Cillian sat on the frozen throne, chin held high.

"Do you know why you're here, my princess?" he asked, his voice raised as if the room were filled with faeries. My heart nearly stopped. *Does the prince know of the escape plan? Does he know why I am really in Icymark?* I buried my fear deep inside, and acted the part of Summer's Princess, like I was meant to be here.

I clenched my hands together, stepping towards the throne. Even walking up the steps to stand closer to the heir of Icymark. "No," I answered calmly. "Why am I here?"

"I'm giving you this chance to tell me, my princess."

I didn't back away. No, that would imply I was hiding something. And I had a lot to hide. "Why don't you tell me what you want to know, Prince Cillian? And I'll answer you."

His face couldn't hide how pleased he was to hear his name on my lips. "Very well," he said, rising slowly and taking a few steps towards me. His hands were at my waist, and he pulled me closer to him. With his lips against my ear, he whispered the question, "Why do you want to start a war?"

I stiffened, perhaps he did know I wasn't here for the Seasons Gathering. I managed to pull myself away from him, but he was still too close.

"You're not here for the Seasons Gathering," He murmured, eyes locked on my lips.

I didn't answer, which only made his wicked smile grow wider. "You couldn't have been sent here by King Alrick to start a war. No, he's far too strict to break the rules of Everlynia. Which means," he said as he leaned in closer. His lips were only inches from mine. "You, my princess, desire war."

His grip tightened on my waist, surely leaving a bruise in its wake. He relaxed slightly as I winced. "You have no idea what your desire does to me. Finally," he gently pumped his cold forehead against mine, "an heir with the desire to rule more than one region."

"What?"

"Wed me," he proposed, "and I'll give you all that you desire. And more." His lips trailed what was exposed of my neck and over the velvet.

I pushed him away, startling him. A fire ignited in my heart, and I was ready to burn the place down. He knew it. "Are you mad?" I wanted to scream at him. Selene was right. The Fateteller was right. General Jora was right. I was the fool for assuming he didn't want anything. "The rules you mentioned earlier forbid this union. You're aware of that," I reminded him.

"And what about intruding Icymark, princess? Do the rules allow that?" He tried to take a step forward, but I stumbled back. "Answer me."

I took a deep breath. "I came to save my mother," I said, watching his eyes soften a little.

"And how do you intend to face an army of Darklings on your own? How do you intend to defeat Virronos?" He pointed to the window. "Look outside, princess." I did, watching an army of Winter, hungry for battle, for war. "I can offer you my army, princess."

"You think the rulers will allow that? You think your mother, the queen, will let you break rules agreed upon centuries ago?"

He sneered. "And who could stop us? Your father? My mother? We'll have the powers of Spring, Summer, and Winter. We will rule Everlynia, and those who oppose us will face our wrath." He sat back on the throne. "Once we rule, your mother will be pardoned of all crimes. The last Shadow will no longer be a threat to you. We'll make new rules, banish whoever opposes us, and eliminate whoever gets in our way. We will be unstoppable, Alexandra."

Prince Cillian was blinded by power. He was a monster. I needed to leave the throne room and get away from him because if I stayed any longer, I would fall into his trap. The Fateteller warned me not to be deceived by power, and here I am, actually considering his offer.

I needed to find Caz and tell him, but Cillian wasn't going to let me leave without an answer. I felt his ice gaze on me and realized I'd been silent for too long. I held my head high, as if the heir of Icymark was beneath me. He did not like it one bit. "Give me time," I said as we locked eyes. "I need to properly consider your proposal."

Cillian slammed his fists on the throne, his silver head turned away from me. The room had become far too cold for me to bear. His rage caused fresh frost to cover the walls and floor. Finally, he spoke. "You have until sunset, princess," he said quietly and gestured for me to leave.

I left, followed by four Winterguards who made sure I went straight to my chamber. They remained at my door even then. Walking over to the balcony, I sighed. The sun was high in the sky, mocking me as I stood helplessly watching it for a long time.

I heard voices at the door, then a knock. I dashed over, hoping it was Caz. As I flung open the door, Selene bowed. The guards stood at the door, refusing to leave us alone. That was Cillian's order no doubt.

"The proper gear you requested, my lady," Selene said, setting the bag she was holding on an empty chair. I didn't let the guards see my smile when Selene said *proper gear*. "Is there anything else you require, my lady?"

I shook my head. "No, thank you, Selene."

She bowed and left my chamber, closing the door behind her. I hurried to the bag and opened it. I didn't scream, but I gasped loud enough to make the little critters cover their ears.

"Quiet, you fool," the angry critter whispered, still covering his ears.

"Don't call her that!" The lady protested, "She's a princess."

"A fool one."

"Max? Rue?" I never thought I'd see the squirrels in my dream again. I frowned at the dressed critters. "What are you doing here?"

"The ginger remembers. What a surprise," Max said,

waving his tail. "And her head is still intact I see. I didn't think you'd make it this far in Everlynia."

Rue climbed up the bag and placed her little hand on my thumb. "General Jora sent us to help you flee the Icymark Court."

"Of course, we wouldn't have had to do that if you hadn't been so careless," Max added. "Here," he handed me a letter the size of him.

I snatched it, almost tearing the letter as I opened it and read aloud. With each sentence, my voice comes closer to a whisper.

Princess,

I'm writing to inform you of some rumors I've heard from the Autumn breeze.

The Winter Prince has ordered that the company you came with be detained.

Beneath hope lies a secret lair. There, you will find your friends.

You must act quickly before night falls and Summer arrives.

Overwhelmed by despair, I sank onto my bed and groaned. "My friends are in danger, and I can't even leave the damn chamber. Could I be more useless?" Rue jumped on top of me, pulling at my curls. I felt a sharp pain in my thigh and sat up, wincing. "Ow! That hurts," I told Max who stuck his needle sword into me.

"We have to leave now," Max said, pulling my finger with both hands.

He clung to the bed sheets after I pushed him over. "I

can't!" I snapped. I returned my attentionto the bag and pulled out a long tailcoat, pants, and leather boots. I wished General Jora was here so I could express my gratitude. I hurriedly removed the stifling dress behind the dressing screen, finally able to breathe properly.

"But…princess…we must leave, now," Rue muttered.

"I'm not leaving without my friends," I said, putting on my boots.

"You fool," Max grumbled, "I'll buy you new friends."

I glanced down at them, braiding my hair back. "I'm not leaving without my friends," I repeated. In the mirror, I saw my reflection and giggled. My appearance was a mix of a warrior and a spy. Two things I never thought I'd resemble.

Max and Rue climbed up my coat and stood on my shoulders. "We don't have time, princess," Rue reasoned. I looked out the balcony at the slowly approaching twilight and sighed. A shudder crept up my body as I remembered Prince Cillian and his ridiculous proposal.

"You're right," I told her, and they nodded. "We should find them soon."

"And how do you propose we do that, princess?" she asked, "do you know where we could find your friends."

I sighed, rereading the letter over and over again. "Beneath hope lies a lair room," I said quietly, not sure what any of that meant.

Max sneered. "Hope? Ridiculous! This place doesn't know what hope is. Icymark Court is the symbol of death. We're wasting our time."

A symbol? I thought, my mind racing. "That's it!" I turned to Max and Rue, both sharing a strange expression.

"Beneath hope lies a secret lair. The Garden of Hope is the only place in the Icymark Court that serves as a symbol of hope. We must hurry!" I tossed the letter into the fire.

The Winterguards might let me leave the chamber without being interrogated. When pigs fly, that is. I cursed my fear of heights as I stood on the balcony, gazing down at the snowbank hundreds of feet below. This should be easy, I told myself. I survived jumping the cliff to the Vileforest. *Yes, but Caz was there,* that voice reminded me. I shook my head to ignore it. I also survived falling into the Enchanted Abyss. *You got yourself trapped,* another reminder. It doesn't matter; I ought to find my friends. *We're not alone. I will look out for you, and you look out for me,* Caz had told me. I'm not going to let them down. I promised him.

With that in mind, and the well-dressed critters clutching my hair tight, I jumped. I drifted

with the wind until I landed on the snow. And, as I had hoped, I survived. I made my way back into the court, thankful for the crowdedness that came with the Seasons Gathering. I borrowed a silver coat from a servant passing by, who was too occupied to notice. I snuck through the halls unnoticed by the Winterguards.

Several hallways later, I was close to the Garden of Hope, watching the oak tree from afar. Two Winterguards were stationed at the glass entrance. I gave a subdued wail.

"So, it's true what they say," Max whispered, "follow the ginger and you're doomed. Aren't I right, Rue?—Rue?"

Rue was already at the entrance, making a useful distraction for us. She picked at their capes and made them follow her down the hall. *Genius Rue!* I made sure the guards were out of sight before I made my way into the Garden of Hope.

I searched the area for a hidden entrance, but I couldn't find any. There was nothing but glass walls and the glowing oak tree. *This isn't right; it must be here.* My gaze flitted across the garden before settling on the stone bench. There was no way the bench could be pushed or slid over because it was incorporated into the garden. Only one other option remained, so I lifted the bench top, which cracked open to reveal a set of stone stairs below. As I made my way down, Winterguards caught my eye, and hurriedly went to warn the others.

Aware that time was ticking away before the Winter Prince received the news, I harnessed my Summer power to lighten hundreds of candle flames throughout the lair. I reached the first door, opened it, and nearly fell thousands of feet below. My heart was still racing when I went further, encountering several doors along the way, but they all led nowhere. I called for Caz and Lucien and heard faint voices far below.

CHAPTER 15
PROMISES OF THE PAST

When I reached the basement, there were three doors. Caz and Lucien's voices seemed to be coming from all of them, which was impossible. I heard footsteps high above and knew I was running out of time. So, I opened the first door and nearly passed out while Max screamed. The room was filled with hissing snakes falling from the roof and onto the ground. I quickly shut the door before they attacked.

"Ugly things. I don't ever want to see that again," Max said as I hurried to the second one expecting to find spiders and roaches, but the room was empty. We both breathed a sigh of relief. They had to be in the last one. I kicked the door open and there I found Caz, Lucien, and Spore dangling by their feet in a dark room, wreathed in strange, glowing mist. My Summer power vanished as I stepped inside. It had to be the same magic that prevented me from using my Summer power in the Enchanted Abyss. That explains why Caz was helplessly hanging from the ceiling.

"To be saved by Carrots...oh, the humiliation," Lucien

whispered, though his voice echoed loud. He sounded very drunk.

Max cut the ropes with his needle sword, and they fell to the stone floor. "Caz!" I ran towards him, to see if he was alright. To my relief, he was unharmed, as were the others. "Prince Cillian—"

"I know, princess," he murmured, gently pulling me closer. "Did he hurt you?"

I shook my head. I noticed how unusually silent Lucien was and glanced at him. He snorted. "How long have I been out?" Lucien asked, wrinkling his nose. "And who's this?" He picked Max up by his waistcoat.

"Put me down, you fool. I'm a knight! This is what you wanted to save, ginger? An elf, a mushroom, and a bird? They're everywhere! You should've told me before I bothered coming with you."

"We don't have time for this," I told them. "We have to get out of here, now, before the Solmark rulers arrive."

"*Why?*" Lucien protested as we climbed the stairs. "And here I was planning a possible future with—"

"Shut up," Caz cut him off. He never liked him sober, never mind drunk.

Lucien grabbed my arm and dragged me over to him. "Do you think he doesn't like me?" He thought he was whispering in my ears, but his voice was louder with every word.

By some miracle, we made it out of the lair undiscovered. It was already sunset outside. My stomach twisted with fear of Prince Cillian seeking me out for an answer. There were no Winterguards at the entrance. I wondered if they were still chasing after Rue, but the halls were clear too. I wasn't sure what to make of it, so we kept sneaking into the empty halls until we were almost at the exit.

Something was wrong, we all knew that much. There were no Winterguards around to question or stop us. Not even servants. *Is everyone in the Fae Throne room?* I wondered if the Solmark guests had already arrived. Despite our apprehension, we prowled towards the exit, only to be stopped by an army of Winterguards. They blocked our path but made no move to attack us. The white raven cawed above our heads, making me jump.

"Leaving so soon, my princess?" Prince Cillian's voice was cold and sinister, drawing his raven to him. He was dressed in sapphire velvet with grey thorn patterns from head to toe. A silver crown, matching the thorns, rested on his brows. "I thought we had a proposal to settle, wouldn't you agree?"

Caz looked puzzled, eyes locked onto me. "You know my answer, Prince Cillian," I replied.

"Don't be so hasty, my princess," he said, raising a gloved hand to wave to his Winterguards surrounding us, "things have changed, and I'm afraid not for the better," he added.

"You can't force me into this union," I reminded him.

"And I don't intend you," he said to my surprise. "But, you see, but I can't let you go either. *You've* been promised to me. Promises aren't easily broken."

I turned to Caz hoping he knew about the promise Cillian mentioned, but he seemed as perplexed as I was. "I have no knowledge of that promise, and I don't believe it's true."

Cillian sneered. "You never asked your mother for the

reason for her exile, my princess?" When his eyes shifted to Caz and Lucien, he laughed as though he'd told a joke. "My, it seems Lady Helia had everyone fooled," Cillian said, and Lucien laughed at that.

I felt sick. My mother told me she'd been exiled for conspiring with an enemy, but she never said she wasn't guilty. I remembered the witch asking my mother to betray her king. Is that why she did it? No, it doesn't matter. She had betrayed us all. She had cursed Caz, used me as a pawn, and manipulated my future to her advantage.

"Regardless of what my mother promised you, I will never be yours. I promise you that." My voice shook a little, but it didn't make my words any less real.

Cillian placed a hand over his chest as if I had shot a bolt through his heart. "Am I so undeserving of you, my princess?"

"Yes," Lucien answered, still very drunk. Prince Cillian scowled at him, before turning his attention back to me.

"Nonetheless." Prince Cillian stepped closer, as did Caz. "A promise cannot be broken, but…" he paused, looking down at me with a strange desire. "I'm willing to free you from this promise princess, if you'd offer me something of equal value."

I could see where this was going. I'd known what he wanted the whole time, but I'd never give it up. I will not return to being a powerless princess. I don't want more power, but I refuse to give up the power I already have. I didn't notice Caz regarding me for a long moment before he spoke.

"I can give you what you want," Caz said. The smirk on Prince Cillian's face quickly turned into a grin. He was intrigued by his offer. Caz had told me he never wanted power, but I never thought he would give it away.

Even if he wanted to, I won't allow it. Even if he hated me for it. "You will not," I said, holding his gaze.

Caz lowered his head to mine. "I don't mind living without Summer power, princess," he put every effort in his voice to convince me.

"I mind."

"If you're worried that I can't be helpful to you—"

"I forbid it, Caz." He frowned but didn't argue. Instead, he bit his lips to silence himself and looked away.

Lucien offered nothing, and I never expected him to anyway. I faced Prince Cillian, mimicking his wicked smile. "So, will you give me what I'm promised, or your powers? I'll even let you decide which one you'd be willing to spare." Cillian's grin widened.

"Neither," I told him. Watching his face twisting brought me so much pleasure. "But I will offer you something else. Something of less value, I'm afraid."

He scowled. "And what might that be?"

"Your head."

He gave a surprised laugh, looking around at his Winter-guards who went very still. "Is this a joke?" he asked.

I mustered all my strength to keep a straight face as I watched him become dangerously serious. "You made a promise with Icymark's enemy, no? You've betrayed Icymark," I whispered, "you've betrayed your queen. What if she learns of this promise you've made with my mother? I don't imagine an exile would be fitting for the heir of Icymark, wouldn't you agree?"

Cillian bared his teeth at me. "What makes you think

you can threaten me? What makes you think you're safe with me now?"

"That very promise you've made." I drew closer. "You wanted more power and my mother wanted my safety, isn't that right?" My mother might be cruel and manipulative, but she had done everything in her power to change my fate. If she'd promised me to him, it was only because she thought he could keep me safe. Perhaps my mother wanted me to have Winter power to ensure I'd defeat Vironnos. I interpreted his silence as my triumph. "You will let us go, and you will keep your head. That is my offer, Prince Cillian."

His expression deepened into a glower and his violet eyes flashed savagely. Prince Cillian was a child with a strong desire to have everything, he's not a fool to let go of what he has. Nor to stop longing for more. He'd have to let go for a while, but he'd do much worse to get what he wanted. Me. I could see in his eyes that he no longer desired power alone, but also vengeance for what he'd lose. Vengeance for what I'd cost him.

"Are you sure you want to play this game? Very well," he said in a cold voice. "But the next move is mine, princess."

I gave him a mocking nod, mimicking him. "Careful not to play with fire, Prince Cillian. You're not of Summer after all." I warned before turning to the exit with my friends. Leaving behind some memories and new enemies.

I made sure I was far enough from Cillian's sight before I let out an explosive sigh.

"It's true what they say about gingers," Max murmured, "they have a wild side." Lucien and Spore seemed to agree. I didn't have the means to argue. Instead, I focused on the fresh snow covering our footsteps and imagined how the story would unfold.

At the frozen gate, General Jora awaited me with Rue and an enormous two-tailed red fox I'd never seen before. Rue jumped from the general's shoulder to Max. Jora was surprised when I ran and threw my arms around him, and he hugged me tightly, patting my back. General Jora tilted his head back when I pulled away, watching me as though he was seeing me for the first time.

He was proud I didn't give in to the desires he'd mentioned before. "Thank you, General Jora," I said with a smile, "for everything."

Caz bowed as I said his name.

Jora shook his head as if he hadn't done anything worthy of gratitude. "I wish I could join you, princess." He smiled faintly at me, then back at the court. "But I'm afraid I'm stuck with messy politics for now. I trust that you'd send my regards to your mother?" he asked, raising a brow.

I sighed, nodding. General Jora frowned at my expression, "what's the matter?"

"I feel like I hardly know her," I confessed.

He shrugged. "Lady Helia was always...unique," he said, hesitant to continue. "I loved your mother for the princess she was, not the queen she became. She changed, but so does everyone. It doesn't make her worth less. Not to me, at least. Come," he said, taking my hand and leading me to stand beside the two-tailed fox. "This is Red. He owes me a favor."

Red rolled his eyes in a very human way. "I would've never allowed you to save me from that trap if I'd known it come to this."

"Survive before you thrive, Red." I flinched when General Jora placed my hand on Red's fur. "You will take her wherever her heart desires. Do that and consider your debt repaid."

Red let out a sigh. "And where does your heart desire, girl?" he asked.

"Take us to the Mountain of Ruins."

Red inhaled through his gritted teeth. "You're out of luck, girl. I don't know where that is."

"That's alright. You won't be leading anyway," I told him.

"Very well then," Red said, wrapping his tail around his legs. "I vow to take you to the Mountain of Ruins...and not a step further."

General Jora rolled his shoulders. "How does that sound to you, princess?"

"Fair." More than fair. "You've been kind, General Jora, and I'm eternally grateful for all that you've given me."

In one swift motion, he removed his cloak from his shoulders and wrapped it around mine. "Don't let the journey change you, princess. Don't let anything change you."

I nodded, not knowing what to say.

He turned back to Caz and Lucien with a serious expression. "You will be sure to look after her, as she did for you. You're in her debt." He seemed to include Spore by that statement, which served as a command.

"Yes, general," Caz and Lucien said at the same time, and Spore nodded. Lucien finally sounded sober.

Caz helped me onto Red's back and handed me Spore

before saddling up. Max and Rue dug their tiny paws into his long fur as we rode past the ice wall, following Lucien.

At dawn, Icymark was painted gold as the sun ascended into the sky, resuming the moon's position. Under the shadow of Lucien's wings, I couldn't stop shivering from the unforgiving cold. We rode from dusk till dawn without a break. Spore whimpered against my growling stomach, reminding me we hadn't eaten since last evening.

As Lucien dropped to his feet, stretching his wings and yawning, Red came to a halt, brushing the snow out from beneath his paws. It was clear, we all needed a break.

Lucien sat with his legs crossed, arguing, and throwing snowballs at Max. Red rested on a stump, barely covered in snow. With his two tails wagging on his right, he snickered as Max came flying towards him after being hit by a snowball larger than him. Rue picked rocks with Spore a few paces away, deliberately ignoring Max as he called for help.

I went with Caz after he insisted it was time I learned to use my Summer power differently. Fishing, he suggested as we made our way to a small pond which I found odd that it wasn't frozen.

Through the purple-tinted water, I caught a glimpse of colored fish. They appeared almost normal except for their glittering scales and fairy wings at their sides. The smaller ones were completely see-through.

I doubted I could hunt fish with a sword, and I doubted any fire could survive in water, but I did as Caz insisted. Mostly because I wanted to prove him wrong. As a flame ignited in the center of my heart, I imagined a bow and it came to life in one hand. In the other, I drew an arrow, aimed it at a fairy fish, and let go. And just as I had anticipated, the arrow vanished when it came in contact with the water. The fairy fish didn't bother swimming away, as if I wasn't a threat, just a fool.

I shrugged. "Well?"

Caz rubbed his forehead, fingers weaving in his wavy hair. "You weren't focused enough, princess," he said, standing up. "Even if you were, your aim was off."

"The arrow vanished before it hit the target, how could you know my aim was off or that I wasn't focused enough?" I protested.

"Because it vanished," he answered, ignoring my tone. "When using your powers, you have to have a purpose, a reason. Fire can thrive in water if you strongly believe in your reason."

I glanced at the fairy fish, then back at him. "Even if the reason is to eat?"

"Even if the reason is to eat." He nodded.

I breathed deeply and drew my arrow again. Caz was standing behind me, his chest pressing against my back. He leaned in, and with his hands over mine, he adjusted my grip and aim. His chin brushed the top of my head, and I felt as if I were going to sink from his proximity. "Aim the tip of your arrow to the target. Remember your reason and…" he murmured, suddenly aware I'd been staring at him instead. He pulled away, hands behind his back. "And shoot."

My blood raced, and I hated it. I tried everything to ignore it, but I couldn't. Instead, I did exactly as he said and shot, grateful for the small portion of my mind that wasn't occupied by the thought of him.

I stood there watching as the fish floated to the surface of the pond. I couldn't hide my joy at my minor victory, but there was no time to rejoice. So, I straightened up and aimed again.

Together, we caught six large fish in the pond and decided it was enough for the hungry friends awaiting us. My throat itched as we left the pond. There were so many questions I wanted to ask Caz, but I didn't know if I should. I wasn't sure if he'd answer me, anyway. After a few breaths, I decided trying to ask him wouldn't hurt.

"Caz?"

"Yes, princess?"

I cleared my throat. "Do you still want to save my mother?" His brows furrowed, and I went on, "I mean…now that we both know she betrayed Solmark when she made a promise to the heir of Icymark."

"I will not break my promise to your mother, princess," Caz answered. I really should have known better. Caz had promised to protect me, and if I was going to storm into the Mountain of Ruins and get her back, he had no choice but to accompany me. He had no choice even if she was a traitor. *Even if she cursed him,* I couldn't say that. "What is it?" Caz asked, he must've noticed my displeasure.

I studied him for a few heartbeats. "Caz, I—" A snowball to my face cut me off. I rubbed the snow off my lashes and ran after Lucien as he laughed and danced his way around the trees, dodging my every retaliation.

Strike three.

I chased after him, knocked him down, and shoved his

face in the snow until he shouted, "I surrender!" By that time, Caz had already cooked the fairy fish over fire.

We sat around the fire, eating our hunger and exhaustion away. Red crunched down the bones of his fish and licked his paws clean. Spore giggled as he tried to mimic Red. I sat with my back against Red's warm fur and covered Spore and myself with Jora's cloak.

Lucien tossed his dagger between his fingers as he watched the fire, bored with the lack of entertainment. "Would anyone like to tell a story?" he asked, eyes darting around. Everyone was quiet.

"I suppose I could," Red said, his body vibrating against my back. "A tale ancient and true." Everyone shifted to a more comfortable position as Red curled his tail and began to tell the tale.

"Once upon a mortal-less time, there was a mother with five children. The eldest son was cruel, the next two were immature, the daughter was sage, and the youngest son was everything they would never become. Their mother bestowed upon them each a kingdom to rule over and a power to wield. She warned them not to desire for more, but they knew whoever struck first would have it all. For when one line ends, a new and powerful one begins. One moonless night, a tide of curses washed over their lands. The first kingdom fell to cruelty, the next two fell to neglect, one vanished with the wind, but the last one remained standing, pulsing with power, unlike the rest. It wasn't only their kingdoms they lost, but their only sister was also gone. The three remaining siblings bowed before their youngest brother, who welcomed them in with an open heart.

The eldest wasn't satisfied. *Why did he survive against the tide?* he wondered every night. He believed his brother's kingdom was his by right. For whom could be a better ruler than the heartless son of the night?

He went up to the throne when the moon was asleep, he asked the youngest if he could rule for the remainder of the time. The youngest declined and threw him out. 'I will not give you my rule!' He shouted that night.

Banished from the kingdom, the eldest sought advice from a witch he found beneath the thorns not long before the tide came. 'The youngest spun the curses,' the eldest said, 'he wanted there to be one king instead.'

The witch sneered and took his hand. 'Why not become the one and only king?' she said.

'It's too late,' he shook his head. 'He kicked me out of his kingdom,' he said.

'Nonsense,' the witch sneered, 'the kingdom is yours, my dear.'

'I can be the king, you mean?'

She laughed. 'If a sacrifice is made, the past returns, my dear.'

He wanted the past. One where he was glorious and feared. So, the eldest went back on the road to the kingdom he yearned to rule. At the gates, the youngest stood, peering out through the carved wood. 'Why are you back?' he demanded to know. 'I thought I banished you before.'

'I'm here to challenge you for your throne. And let the winner have the kingdoms whole.' The eldest cut his palm with a sharp thorn, and with his blood, the challenge was carved in stone.

The brothers fought with their powers alike, as the others watched from a distance. Blood was spilled that night and the eldest swore to come back and hunt him down. The promise made the night turn red and the plants fell dead. The youngest dismissed the thought of him ever coming back.

When the sacrifice was made, their sister returned from the dead, just as the witch had said. Unlike the past, she had prevailed. And the four siblings lived together in peace until night turned red and history repeated."

Everyone's thoughts were completely consumed by the tale. *A tale ancient and true.* A tale similar to one I've heard before. *The five siblings were the guardians of Everlynia,* I imagined. That must mean…

"The eldest was the Shadow?" I asked, my voice shaking with realization.

He nodded. "It all comes down to you, girl. One way or another…a new future awaits."

CHAPTER 16
MOONLESS NIGHT

I FELL INTO A DREAMLESS SLEEP. No memories of the past, no warnings of the future, no Fateteller. But I awoke too soon. It was still night. The fire was sizzling close to me, where everyone was sleeping. Everyone except Lucien. He was gone, though it seemed he had left not long ago. His footsteps were still visible on the bed of snow. I got up, careful not to wake anyone up, and followed the trail.

Lucien sat at the edge of a bluff, his wings twitched as he heard me coming. I sat next to him, watching the reflection of the moon on the frozen river below.

"What's the matter, Carrots? You couldn't sleep?"

I shook my head. "You?"

"No," he sighed and looked back at the moon. "How do you think it will end?"

I looked up at the moon shining serenely in the sky, unaware of what the future held for me. I hugged my knees. "I don't know," I whispered, "but I don't imagine any of it will be easy."

"Are you worried?" he asked.

"I am," I admitted, wrapping my arms tighter. "But not just for myself. For all of you."

At that, Lucien turned his full attention to me. Surprised that I cared for any of them. Maybe more surprised that I seemed to include him as well. "You can't be serious," he said after a long pause.

Perhaps it is unheard of to care for someone in this land, I don't know. Perhaps being the way he is, Lucien never thought that anyone would care for him. "I'm serious," I told him. "I don't wish hardship on any of you—"

"Why?"

I paused to look at him. "Because no one ever wants that for their friends."

He tilted his head slightly. "We're friends."

Aren't we? I wanted to ask, but his face revealed the answer I wanted to know. We weren't friends. Not even strangers. In his eyes, perhaps he thought we were rivals.

"You ought to be more careful," he said.

"Of you?"

"Everyone," he answered. His eyes shifted to the full moon. "The moon shines brightest just before it's gone. And when it returns it won't be the same," he whispered. "We… we won't be the same. Everyone will transform into the monster that they are. No one will care for anyone. For that reason, you cannot care for everyone. You, above all, shouldn't concern yourself with anyone but yourself. You've got a lot on your plate."

I didn't need to be reminded of what awaited me, even though a part of me had purposefully ignored the part where I'd have to encounter the last Shadow. And I certainly don't want to think about it right now. "Aren't you a little too cynical, Lucien?"

"One of us has to be, Carrots." He smirked, and I was relieved to see him being himself again. "Let's play a game," he suggested.

"A game?" I repeated.

He grinned, the tip of his tongue brushing against his fang. "Questions. I'll ask you two questions; you can skip one but must answer the other. Then you can ask me when it's your turn."

Now that he mentioned it, there were so many questions I wanted to ask Lucien when I met him in the Pixiehouse and again in the Frozen Pond of Secrets. But I knew he wouldn't answer any of them. "Fine. I'll play your game."

He sat up. "You said before that you made a deal with a Fateteller. Tell me, what's the most disturbing thing you learned from your Fateteller?"

I guess I shouldn't be surprised that he wanted to know more about the Fateteller, but I couldn't answer that. The most disturbing was the prophecy my mother changed— and what she did before that. "What's the other question?"

He scoffed, as though he *expected* me to skip that question. "Very well, why haven't you told Caz about our little encounter in the mortal world?"

I did not expect him to ask that question, but it was one I could answer. "Caz promised to keep me safe. If he knew you tried to kill—" I remembered Lucien insisted that he'd *saved* me that day. I sighed. "If he learned of our little encounter I doubt he would let you be our guide to saving my mother, even if you and I had already made a deal. He would have most likely killed you and returned me to the

Solmark Court." I paused, realizing I'd only been selfish to Caz.

"Ah," was all he said. "I thought there was a more… romantic reason. You sure know how to ruin moments like these, don't you?"

"Romantic?" I sneered.

"Yes, yes. We all know you have feelings for me," he reasoned, matching the mock in my voice.

"I don't have feelings for you. I quite dislike you," I said in defiance.

"Dislike is a feeling too, is it not?" He winked at me, knowing well enough that he was driving me insane. "Your turn, Carrots."

I glanced back at the frozen river to recall the Banshee's exact words. *"You will be despised no matter what you do, Lucien.* Why did the Banshee say that? Why would you be despised?"

I thought he ignored me but when I turned to him, he was as still as a statue. Although the moon was shining white, Lucien already looked like the monster he warned everyone would become when the moon turned red. He wasn't going to answer that question, and he wasn't going to ask me for another. So, I quickly averted my eyes from his deadly gaze and asked what I truly wanted to know.

"When we first met, you told me someone wanted me dead because of who I am," I recalled. "Who wanted me dead?"

Lucien was more willing to answer my second question. Maybe because I played by his rules, and he'd have to answer one. And he certainly did not want to answer the first question. "Summer," he answered briefly.

I frowned. "All of Summer wanted me dead?" I inquired. I thought he wouldn't answer truthfully.

He sighed, tilting his head back. "Lord Damien, and most of the high nobles of Summer," he explained. "Now I've answered your stupid question, quit asking me more."

"You suggested this game," I reminded him.

We continued watching the moon in utter silence, feeling something very special about that night. Something I have yet to discover. I imagined what it would be like when the moon was scarlet red. What it would be like to face Vironnos. To fight Vironnos. For some reason, I couldn't imagine what would happen after—as if there was no *after*.

When dawn broke, we returned. We found the rest gathered around Caz and peering at something he was holding. They parted when they saw us coming, turning their gaze to me. I felt my pulse in my throat as I watched them. "What is it?" I asked.

Caz passed the note he was holding to me. It was ripped at the very top as if a knife had pinned it to something. I looked over at the skeletal tree next to us, where an arrow had been drilled deep into its trunk.

I read the message with Lucien peering over my shoulder. There were nineteen words: *BLOOD NIGHT IS NEAR. BREAK THE CURSE OR SURRENDER TO DEATH. BEWARE OF THE DARK RIDERS COMING YOUR WAY.*

"The Darklings," I whispered, "they sent a similar message before, but I didn't think it was possible."

"What?" Caz was furious. It was just then that I realized I hadn't told him about the messenger in the Icymark Court. So much has happened, and I forgot about it. Lucien was shocked into silence.

Red snorted. "I didn't think there was a way to break that curse. Perhaps it's a trap."

I was thankful for Red's comment to break my eye contact with Caz. I couldn't take his accusing stares any longer. "*The blood curse may only break if the rulers join to undo their mistake.* That was what the messenger had said," I told them. "I don't think it's a trap. The Darklings are Shadow worshipers—"

"All the more reason not to trust them. As for the dark riders, they are worse," Max chimed in. "It's no surprise they're pursuing you, fool. They, unlike the Darklings, wish to take their own vengeance."

"Then why send a message to the princess?" Rue interjected, "Why would they want her to break the curse?"

Red waved his tails, slitting his eyes at the note in my hand. "Vironnos is their last living Shadow. Maybe he doesn't want to take the risk of losing his line, because that would fulfill the curse of the past. When one line ends, a powerful one begins."

Rue gasped. "He wants Summer and Shadow united. He wants…"

Me. She didn't have to say it, but we all thought it. I didn't understand the Banshee's statement at first, but I gradually came to. The closer I got to the Mountain of Ruins and Vironnos, the sooner the moon would bleed.

Caz gave a firm shake of his head. "You cannot," he said, "a union with the Shadow means war. You may be able to break the curse, but for how long? All courts will act against you. Your authority over Solmark will be jeopardized. This is not something you want to do, princess. Believe me."

"I don't want to kill Vironnos either!" I snapped, "I don't want the Faye Throne. I don't want to break a curse or end a line." My breaths were ragged. "I just want my mother back. And I want things to go back to normal."

Caz simply stared down at me, a hint of betrayal in his eyes. "It's always what you want," he murmured. I knew he thought that, but it still stung to hear it from him. Worse, I'm not sure if that's what I truly wanted. To be away from Everlynia. To forget about it as though it never existed. *No, I don't want that at all.*

Spore clutched what he could reach of my tailcoat, his eyes gaping up at me. "We have to go," Lucien finally spoke. "Traps or no traps, the Darklings are right about the Blood night. It is much closer than you'd think. But it's not only that, the note is meant as a warning to avoid the dark riders following us."

We rode again beneath the new sun, tailing Lucien's shadow again through forests and rocky frozen rivers. I felt guilty every time Caz drew me closer to his chest when I shivered from the cold. It happened so often, that sometimes he'd know when I'd shiver before I did. He was still furious with me for not telling him sooner, but he did a better job of hiding his temper than I ever could.

Over the cliffs, I noticed some trees falling in the distance. More trees followed in sync along with a gigantic dam that fell piece by piece. Drying snow stirred at the site of destruction, and then it was carried over to us with the harsh wind. My next breath was full of powdery snow and sawdust. I gasped, trying to make out words as the ice below us began to split in two. Red ran faster than the crack traveled, but only by a few paces.

I let my fingers sink deep into Red's fur as he plunged away from falling ice bricks and rocks and trees. For a second, the ground stopped shaking and the crack fell steps behind us. I thought it was over until I looked up and noticed an avalanche starting from the mountain we'd reached. There was no way back, only forward. And forward we went. My breaths were visible like puffs of cigarette smoke.

It took a long moment for the clouds above our heads to reach us with layers and layers of ice. One flew past my head and shattered on the ground, a flying ice shard threatened to stab me in my chest, but Caz was quick to draw his sword to melt it away.

We rode straight through a short tunnel, following the light at the end. When we made it out, it was no longer daytime. The sky was dark as ink seeping into the horizon, and everything went still once more. Lucien plummeted from the sky like a wounded bird and rolled onto the slippery ground. Red dug his claws into the ice to stop, leaving claw marks in his wake, and we rushed towards Lucien.

"Lucien?" I whispered, turning his head towards me. His eyes were closed and he was motionless like the dead. The sight of him lifeless terrified me more than anything else. I slapped my hand over my mouth when I noticed the tips of his fingers blackening, as though he had dipped his fingers in an inkwell.

Caz hurried over and pressed two fingers against his

neck. "He'll be fine," he reassured. His eyes shifted to Lucien's fingers and he frowned.

"What is it?" I asked.

"I don't know. He might've injured himself," he said, putting Lucien's arms over his shoulder and pulling him to his feet. Lucien's wings dragged behind him as Caz rested him beneath a half-living tree.

I watched, worried. There was nothing I could do except wait, and I was never good at waiting. "You're worrying over the wrong thing, girl," Red's voice startled me. "Take a look around."

I did. And my worries were quickly replaced with fear. Aside from the destruction behind us, I never expected to see anything equally daunting. But I was unfortunately wrong. Except for a few stars that flickered mystically, the sky was dark. There was no moon to be found anywhere I looked. My heart knocked against my ribcage, and I knew what it meant. The next time the moon appeared, the night would turn red and the moon would bleed.

"How much time do I have?" I asked, my voice trembling.

Rue looked every bit as amazed as Max. "Three moonless nights before the red night descends," she said and glanced at Red for confirmation. He nodded in return.

"And until then, there will be no daylight," Red added, "if the curse is not broken or a line does not come to an end, we'll never see daylight again. Only the red of the night."

Two more nights. *Two more nights until blood is shed,* I thought.

I curled into a ball as I sat over a hill. Down below, I saw where the ends of Icymark met a dark span of land that blended in with the sky. I was so close, yet so far. The Mountain of Ruins was somewhere in the shadows, watching me from a distance. My mother, the Darklings, and Vironnos were all waiting for me to make a decision. To be free or to be consumed by darkness. To break a curse or to allow it to ruin me.

I couldn't recall the last time I was this indecisive, doubtful, and lost. Perhaps I was naive to think I could ever get what I wanted without getting hurt, or hurting someone else in the process. In mourning for the missing moon, the stars trembled in the sky, the ground shook beneath me, and the ice thawed.

Footsteps sounded near me, and I was only relieved to be distracted. Even if it was only for a few moments. I was surprised to see Caz. I stood, looking over the hill with him beside me. I only hoped he wasn't still angry with me. "How is he?"

"Still unconscious," he said, watching the shadow beyond Icymark. His expression changed quickly when he realized we were much closer to the Mountain of Ruins than he thought. "Many rulers ascended the Faye Throne with a Shadow's heart. Your father, too. I doubt any of them gave it a second thought. What they paid for was worth the price of blood. But you," he stopped and turned to me. There was something odd about him. The way he glanced at me with gleaming eyes like it was the first time he saw me. "You, princess, will not kill for a crown. You will not kill for bloodthirst. And you will not even kill for your mother."

I couldn't figure out if he meant to compliment or insult

me with his speech. Regardless, I listened to him speak about me in a way he never had.

"You have the one quality none of us have," he continued, closely watching my expression. "You may not want the throne, but the throne needs you. I will stand by your side regardless of the actions you'll take. If you decide to fight Vironnos, I'll be there. If you decide to take the Faye throne, I'll be there. If you decide to break the curse and unite with the Shadow…" he said, flinching at the idea of Summer and Shadow together, "I will stand with you. If what it takes for you to win the sea of flames is for me to drown in it, I will do it.

And for that, I need to be honest with you and loyal to you. I must confess to you—you weren't the only one to hide something. Princess—" He reached for my hand as though he wanted to hold mine, but stopped, even though I never flinched away from him. Even though if he looked hard enough in my eyes, he'd find how much my fingers longed for his touch. "You don't know how you're burning me," he said in a voice made only for me to hear.

I wasn't sure if I was dreaming under the stars. I wasn't sure whether I was under an illusion of a cruel curse, or whether it was all real. My lips parted in silence.

"Alexandra," he continued in a whisper. My name on his lips wasn't the same. He reached again for my hand and this time he brushed his long fingers against mine. His touch wasn't a dream or an illusion. His touch was real, as real as him. With his head bent low, he spoke again. "Alexandra, daughter of King Alrick and Lady Helia, I may be immune to your fire, but I am not immune to you. I know that because I burn for you."

When I didn't say anything back, he let go of my hand, reading my expression differently. "You don't have to say anything," he said, face clouded with shame.

"I don't understand," I murmured. My words made him clench his fists and take a step back. Still, he couldn't take his eyes away from me, nor I from him. "You said love is war. You said for someone to fall in love, they must give up half of themselves." He nodded once, recalling every word he'd said that night at Icymark Court.

"And yet here I am," he said, his fists unclenching, and he relaxed a bit. Or gave up. I couldn't tell. "Ready to lose all of me…for the thought of you." He closed his eyes, no longer having the courage to keep my gaze.

I thought he was playing me, I thought he was lying, but I knew better. *Fairies cannot lie.* With that in mind, I stepped forward, ignoring my racing heart, I stood on my toes and placed a soft kiss on his lips. He opened his eyes again, amazed and a little confused. And I was in a state of yearning and desire.

"You're wrong, Caz, son of Lord Damien and Lady Emilia," I murmured. With my hand around his neck, I felt the softness of his curls for the first time. I brought his head to mine, and pressed my forehead against his, letting the warmth in our skin grow hotter. "We don't have to lose anything."

I pulled back slowly, but he drew me closer so our mouths could meet again, and then he kissed me hard. The tip of his nose was cool against my cheek, unlike his tongue over mine. My heart ignited for a completely different reason, and I was certain his did too. The Shadow could've come for us and we wouldn't have noticed at all.

On that moonless night, everything around us made little sense, but somehow, he was the only thing that did.

CHAPTER 17

FINAL VISION

I STOOD IN A DARK, empty throne room with beams of red light passing through the cracks in the stone walls. My gaze followed where they all began, to a stone throne resting against the far wall, and on it, something gleamed in the light. Tempted, I crept up to the throne, hearing my name spoken in a taunting voice with every step.

I couldn't remember how I got here or what happened. All I knew for certain was that I wanted what was on the throne. I desired it so badly that I was willing to make any trade to obtain it. I stood at the foot of the throne, glaring down at a golden crown with twelve red crystals. It called my name repeatedly until I reached for it and held it in my hands.

It was heavier than I thought. Almost too heavy for me to hold. I was about to place it on my head when I heard him call my name.

"Alexandra," Caz called. I turned to find him in horrible condition. His skin was paler than usual, and his clothes were torn, exposing his bruised chest. "You killed them. You killed them both."

I seemed to know exactly what he was talking about. "They deserved to die," I told him, still holding the crown in my hand, which became heavier the longer I held on to it. "They were weak. They betrayed me," I said, feeling nothing. Not a single drop of remorse. Not a single drop of regret.

His purple lips parted. His red eyes did not seem familiar. "I thought you were different. I believed you could become a dignified ruler."

"I am different. I will be feared, Caz. Isn't that much better? I will rule Everlynia in its entirety, and I want to do it with you. Bend your knee and rule beside me."

"Please," he pleaded, his eyes filled with tears. "Don't wear that crown, princess."

Furious with him calling me a princess, I tightened my grip around the crown and raised it to my head. "I am a queen!" I snarled, causing the stones to crumble away. As more stones fell, blood seeped through every crack, quickly filling up the room.

Caz smiled painfully as blood seeped through his shirt, where he was bruised. Shocked, I ran over to hold him before he collapsed, screaming his name. But his body turned to embers and flew past me, each one burned me worse than fire. Later, I drowned in blood and closed my eyes slowly, feeling emptier than ever.

When I opened them, I was walking down an aisle with the Darklings on either side. My legs knew where they were going, but I had no idea why. And when I saw her face, it all came back to me like a punch to my gut. I had chosen to do this. I had chosen to unite with the Shadow, but not just for me. No, not for me at all. My mother nodded with a fake smile, reminding me why I *must* do this. To save *him*, my one and true love whom I've betrayed to keep him alive.

At the other end, the last Shadow awaited me. His tail curled around the stone throne, a gesture of welcoming I suppose. It frightened me how well I knew him. Not as Vironnos, but as my *friend*. Rather, once my friend. When I sat on the throne, I spoke the vow through which I'd be bonded to the Shadow for as long as I breathed. When I was done, the Shadow spoke his vow next. The curse lifted, turning the blood moon to white, and my heart to stone. And so, I became the queen of darkness.

Years passed, and the memory of him never faded in my mind. Caz, the thought of him was what kept me alive. The memory of our last kiss after he was healed from the blow to his heart was the last time I felt anything at all. I'd made a deal with Vironnos to keep him alive. I'd given up my freedom for his.

The War of Seasons lasted for decades until the last Shadow was finally defeated. Countless lives later, the darkness was lost to the light. I was sitting on the throne, stone atop stone, ready for the victors to arrive and put an end to my miserable life. The Court of Shadow was empty. Everyone I had known died fighting my war, still, I couldn't find it in my heart to grieve. I was stripped of everything I used to be, of who I used to be.

Everyone I knew had fallen, and finally, it was my turn. Footsteps echoed outside the throne room, but only one had entered as the gates flung open, then shut by his command. After years of crying my heart out, I couldn't see him at first. And for the first time in a long time, I felt something. Guilt. Guilt for not recognizing the love that burned inside me still.

I couldn't think of anything to say, so I ran into his arms instead, hoping it wasn't another of my delusions. I'd imagined him with me so often that I feared this one time wasn't real. To my delight, it was real. Caz threw his arms around me, bringing me closer to his chest and burying his face in my hair.

He smelled of dried blood and ash, which reminded me of the war and which side he was on. I knew why he came, but I couldn't let go of him, let alone flee. "Alexandra," he whispered in my ear, his voice coated with mutual desire. I wanted him now more than ever. "You know what I came for."

I ran my fingers over the scar on his chest, feeling it through the soft fabric beneath his armor. Caz had vowed to stay by my side, but I forced him to leave me behind. No, I was forced to leave him behind. Years ago, I made the most disadvantageous trade to bring him back from the dead, for life that the Shadow bestowed upon him. A trade through which I saved one life, and doomed thousands of others. Caz came to collect the debt of those innocent lives lost. "I know," I murmured, and he pressed his mouth against mine. I did not deserve a happy ending, not after all I've done. But I needed one last moment with him.

Caz kissed me like it was our first time, our hearts ignited in unison, matching the intensity of the kiss. With it came all of the lost emotions. The pain and relief. The love and hate. The light and—the darkness that flooded my heart as Caz plunged his dagger deep in my chest.

I lay in his arms, feeling my heart throbbing beneath his warm palm. My cheeks were soaked with his hot tears. "I'm sorry," he murmured again and again.

I gathered what was left of my strength to place my palm over his sharp cheekbone, wiping his tears away. "I'm glad it was you, Caz." I managed to whisper before my body turned to embers and was carried away by the gust.

Everything else faded along with his cries, and I was back at the very beginning, standing in an empty throne room in the red night. I realized it wasn't a nightmare, but rather the future that the Fateteller had promised to show me. That's when my shadow transformed into a clone of myself and stood opposite to me.

Her blood-stained hand was dripping to the ground, and she held the crown in the other. "Those were the last visions, living one. Should you choose to defeat the Shadow or break the curse, you will become a fearsome queen with a heart of stone. That is your fate, and one of those visions will be your future. Which one do you choose?"

I shook my head in denial. "None," I said, my voice hoarse.

She sneered. "That's one decision you cannot escape, living one. Defeat the last Shadow to end a line, or break the curse to start a war. Either way, you will become a queen. That is your fate," she repeated.

"And what if I find another way?"

"Impossible. Your fates are what I have shown you."

"What if you're wrong? What if I create a new one?"

"Do you want to challenge me, living one?"

"Yes."

"Very well. If you do find a new path, one that does not require killing or mating with the Shadow, consider your debt to me forgiven. If you don't, however, you'll be in greater debt than you already are. Do we have an agreement?"

I nodded. "We have an agreement."

"It is done. Afraid of losing the boy?" she asked, tilting her head in sympathy. "He is cursed, and you are doomed. You've witnessed it, your paths will never cross the way you wish them to."

I saw the blood moon through the opening on one side of the wall and sighed. "I will become queen, but I will not kill the last Shadow. I will not pay the price of blood for my throne." I watched the Fateteller's face lighten up, thinking I'd finally succumbed to my so-called fate. "And I will not unite with the Shadow either," I said, feeling extreme satisfaction as her face twisted.

She pursed her lips, clearly annoyed with me. "Blood will flow on your hands. You have two nights before you make your final decision, and you will find yourself in desperate need of one before the moon bleeds. You're no fate breaker, living one."

"You know not what I am, Fateteller," I said, turning back to the blood moon and red sky. Weeks ago, I learned I was a princess and an heir in a wonderland. Weeks ago, I thought I was powerless until I learned to use my Summer power. Days ago, I learned I had Spring power as well. Hours ago, I learned I was capable of love. It might be too late to admit it, but it doesn't make it any less true. I belong in Everlynia, and I belong with Caz. "I don't know how, but

I'll find a different path. I know what I want, Fateteller. I will make the impossible possible to get what I want. I vow it."

I promised myself that if there was a way to change my fate, to spend the rest of my life with him, I would find it. I would find it, or I would die trying.

CHAPTER 18

THE DARK RIDERS

I AWOKE with Caz's arms around my stomach and my back so close to his body that I could feel his warmth and calm breaths against my neck. I slowly turned in his arms, trying not to wake him but failing completely. He blinked at me, smiling in a way that made my heart flutter. "Are you real, Alexandra?"

No matter how many times he'd say it, I could never get used to my name on his lips. "Do you think this is a dream?" I asked him instead.

He closed his eyes, lashes resting on his cheeks. "I don't know," he said quietly as if he didn't want to be awakened. "I've been dreaming of you so often lately that reality blurs into uncertainty."

That made my whole face burn, and I was only glad he had his eyes closed. I wasn't going to let him see me like that. If he did, he'd use that exact moment to tease me for the rest of our lives.

I cursed myself for bringing the memories of my last nightmare to my mind. The frightening vision had felt so real. *He is cursed, and you are doomed…your paths will never cross the way you wish them to.* No, I had promised to make this last forever, and I intended to do exactly that. I brought my mouth to his and brushed a soft kiss on his lips. His eyes opened instantly, flashing with surprise. "We are real, Caz," I finally answered.

Caz sat up, dragging me along with him. It was still dark, and I doubted we'd see any daylight until the blood moon had passed. "I am yours then, in reality, and in dreaming, princess." He made it sound like an unbreakable vow.

I gazed up at him as he wrapped his arms around my waist. Knowing Caz, the cruel, cold Summer elf had been dreaming of me made everything else matter less. "When this is over, I want to hear all about those dreams."

He smiled and gently bumped his forehead against mine. "When this is over, we'll make those dreams come true if you wish," he whispered, curling his fingers around mine, he led me back to where everyone was.

"There you are," Red said, lashing his tails when we arrived. "And in one piece too." It was obvious he'd missed us. Under the living half of the tree, he and Spore slept close to Lucien. Max and Rue jumped from branch to branch until they reached us.

"How is he?" I asked.

Red stretched, arching his back. "Take a look for your-self, girl."

Lucien wasn't remotely in a good condition. If anything, he'd gotten worse overnight. The blackness on the tips of his fingers had reached his wrists. His wings had far fewer feathers than before, and those that remained were as hard as slate. "Caz?"

Caz sniffed. "I've never seen anything like this before," he said, "whatever it is we can't leave him here for too long —" he paused, squinting his eyes ahead at the other side of the snowfield. Everyone else matched his movement, suddenly alarmed. Red growled lowly, baring his long, sharp teeth.

Whatever lurked on the other side was impossible to spot in the dark, let alone a foggy night. There was an explosion of snow, and arrows rained down on us like shards. We got out of range in time, barely catching our breaths. I cast a nervous glance ahead as if I could see who was threatening our lives if I concentrated hard enough. There were so many that wanted me gone, the Summer nobles, the Solmark Queen, the heir of Icymark, and…

As the fog lifted, riders emerged from the other side. They appeared to be riding not on horses, but the shadow of them. A mere mist that dissipated as some of them dismounted and charged at us with swords in hand. Their heads were wrapped in black cloth, revealing only their angry red eyes.

I would have recognized those eyes anywhere—the Darklings. No, the dark riders. They worship the Shadow, but unlike the Darklings, they seek vengeance. There were so many of them, so many noises and so many shouts that I couldn't hear Caz when he spoke the first time.

"Princess, get back!" he snarled. Gripping my elbow, he yanked me close to him to evade a dagger flying in my direction.

The dark riders lunged forward, jumping over fallen trunks and mounds of ice as easily as breathing, but they were still far away. Cursing under his breath, Caz glanced at Lucien and then back at me. I hated the way he looked at me, but most of all I hated that I knew he would say next. "I can't leave him behind, but you have to get out of here, princess. I'll hold them back."

"No—" I started shaking my head but he ignored me, and forcibly helped me onto Red's back. "No! I'm not leaving you, Caz!"

"Yes, you are," he gritted his teeth, handing me the weeping Spore in my lap. Max and Rue clung to Red as well. "They're after you, Alexandra. Not me. Not Lucien, but you. You've come so far, but you can't stop now." His lips parted, there was more he wanted to say but couldn't. The dark riders were very close now. Eyes glazing with anger, he turned his gaze to Red and raised a flaming sword. "Take her away from here. Get out of here, Go!"

With that, Red dashed away from the approaching riders, ducking away from the arrows raining down on our heads. I looked back at Caz, watching him fight through the barrage of swords and daggers aimed at his chest.

A group of riders charged after us, straight through the cloud of ash and embers, the remains of their own. The last thing I saw was Caz pinned to the ground with an army over his and Lucien's head.

Fresh tears burned my eyes. All I could think of was what his eyes pleaded to tell me then, and what I wished I could tell him in return. As Red kept changing directions to escape the riders, the sound of the flying arrows filled my ears along with the sound of whispers.

Alexandra, Alexandra, Alexandra, Alexandra, Alexandra. The voices came from everywhere and nowhere at all, hissing my name and making my skin tingle uncontrollably. I heard the pulse of the land as though it was my own. As though I had two hearts beating inside me, each fighting to take control over me.

It wasn't long until one bloomed, followed by a strange sensation. I felt as though I was no longer myself. I was everywhere and everything around me. I felt the mourning stars, the raging mountains, and the shaking ground. An untamed spirit, I reached out to the voices.

"Watch out!" Someone screamed and all I heard was their cries as they were yanked off their horses by something. Before my mind wandered, I saw the lifeless trees groan into action, moving their branches against the wind to throw some of our pursuers and block the way for others. Only a few managed to weave their way through the tangled branches.

"Hang on tight, girl," Red warned before leaping across a massive gorge. A couple of arrows flew at us before we landed safely on the other side. Three riders stood on the cliff edge for a long moment, eyes fixed on me. The middle one nodded once, as if he had captured me despite the distance between us. He raised his sword and motioned for the others to retreat, leaving me more worried than before.

My body felt hot despite my icy fingers. I collapsed, feeling as though I was breathing in thick water. It was strange. Fear was all I could recall. I remembered my fear of being trapped in the boggarts' cage, my fear when I stood before the rulers of Solmark, my fear when I refused the proposal of Queen Rose…on and on until a shudder brought me back to my senses, and I wish it didn't. My leg throbbed with pain. Horrible, staggering pain that numbed everything else.

I wanted to speak, but I could barely manage to catch my breath. My eyes darted to my calf and I almost fainted at the sight of blood seeping down from the tip of the rider's arrow. They must've struck me before I made it to the opposite side of the gorge.

I gritted my teeth and pulled the arrow free, slowly feeling myself drifting away. My sight was the first to betray me, followed by a swollen tongue and buzzing ears.

"She's been poisoned," someone said nearby. I recognized that the voice belonged to Max.

"Will she be alright?" Rue asked.

Warm breaths melted the frost on my skin. "Violet poison," Red inspected, sniffing me. "Time is the antidote. Time she does not have."

Red was right, but it was too late. I had already passed out.

Bathed in snow, I was left alone under another moonless night. *One more night,* that voice reminded me.

One more night before the blood moon ascends.

One more night before the Sea of Flames battle.

One more night before I'd find myself drowning in my consciousness.

I blinked, no longer in Icymark. I was back at the Solmark Court. The pain in my leg had vanished, and I was on my knees, surrounded by the heartless dragon. Rather than motionless statues, the dragons were wandering phan-toms, oblivious to my being there.

"You came," one of the dragons said, the sound of his voice made my stomach roil. He could see me. Could he be one of the Shadow rulers? Was he defeated by a Solmark heir? While others had *some* life in their aura, his was completely dead. More like a memory of a phantom than anything else.

His transparent form made it difficult for me to keep my gaze on him as he shifted closer, his tail dragging behind him. *He cannot hurt me, He's not real. It's just a dream, Lexi.*

He smiled, reading my thoughts as his own. "I've been waiting for you, daughter of Spring and Summer."

The way he hissed drained the color from my face. *The Shadow has been waiting for me!* "What for?" I asked, covering what fear I could with my voice. I knew what he wanted to say, but I wanted him to say it anyway.

"You are our last chance to break the blood curse," he answered, nothing I haven't already heard. "Only by you can the truth prevail."

If the clock ticked back a minute for every time I had to repeat myself, every time I was told who I was, every time I was told what I must do, I'd be back in the mortal world where the thoughts of faeries and strange lands didn't exist.

"I will not join the last Shadow if that's what you mean. I will not kill him either." I've seen the great misfortune if I took those chances, and I vowed to do whatever it took to find another solution. Another fate.

I had never seen a dragon scowl before, yet again I'd never seen a real dragon before. He wasn't angry by what I'd said, he was confused. "And you're certain of this?" He curled his tail. "You don't want to be the hero. You don't want to be the villain. What *do* you want, daughter of Spring and Summer?"

Terrified as I was, he kneeled down for an answer. One that I had but don't know how to achieve yet. "I don't want to be manipulated by some fate. I don't want to change. I don't want to lose anyone. And if I must become a queen, I don't want to lose myself for it."

He wasn't pleased with my answer. "I've asked for what you do want. Not what you don't want."

I nailed him with a sharp glare. "I want to be free," I said with as much confidence as I could muster, "free of prophecies and curses. I want to make my own fate. Most of all, I want to be with those I care for, and…I want to be with the one I love." I felt embarrassed admitting what I felt for Caz out loud. I am ashamed of leaving him behind with the dark riders. *This is a dream,* I realized. *I shouldn't waste more time. I should get back—*

"To achieve that fate, you must break the blood curse," the dragon said, his figure drifting away. I wanted to remind him of my opposition to uniting with the last Shadow, but he cut me off before I could even begin. "There's one way to cast a curse, but not only one to break it."

My breath hung immobile in my lungs. I knew it! I did have another choice. "How?" I hurried, "What can I do to break the curse?"

"Find the truth I failed to accept, daughter of Spring and Summer. And don't let the red night sway you into anger the way it did me. If you avert from the truth, you'll lose everything you want. You'll lose yourself too."

"How do you know this?" I asked, watching him change slowly into stone. "Who are you?"

"The Shadow Guardian." His voice came after he'd been turned back into a heartless statue.

"Ginger?" a voice echoed from nowhere. "Ginger!"

A weight pressed on my chest, and my eyes opened to stare straight into Max's face. "Well, what do you know! The ginger managed to overcome even the poison's effects, and in little time too," he said with a lazy blink.

I got up quickly, sending Max rolling off my chest, grunting with effort to balance himself on slippery ice. "How much time has passed?" I asked, adjusting my eyes to the darkness of the grotto I found myself in. I had no memories of how I got there, but everyone was there with me, waiting for my awakening.

"Not nearly as much as it should have," Red answered, his two tails twirling smoothly, in and out of Spore's reach as he pinned his focus on them like a cat does to a laser pointer. "You surprise me, girl. Violet poison isn't so easy to overcome."

I realized then that the stinging pain in my leg had lessened to something I could convince myself to ignore. Staggering forward, I pushed my weight against the cold stone to stand on my feet. A rush of pain stung me like an electric shock with each step until I quickly became used to its familiar shock.

Red inspected me with a wry look on his face. "Going somewhere?"

I kept moving with effort. "I have to go back for Caz and Lucien. It was a mistake leaving them behind."

"*What?*" Rue shrieked, pushing Max off balance again

as she waved her arms around. "You can't go back to the riders, princess. You barely escaped them," she said, pointing to my wound as though it wasn't obvious enough.

"I'm going, Rue," I said.

"What has the Violet poison done to you, ginger? Just when I thought you could be sane," Max grunted, planting his tiny claws in the ice to stand still. "You ought to make things worse? What if they're already dead?" Rue shot him a quick glare to make him stop mumbling nonsense after she caught my expression turning into something of fear. The last thing I wanted was for my mind to be consumed with horrible thoughts. Max sighed. "All I'm saying is that she doesn't even have a plan—"

"I do have a plan," I snapped, coming off the wall. "I'm getting them back."

Red yawned, relaxing his tails for Spore to climb. "That is not a plan, girl. A plan is a strategy."

"One that you do not have, ginger," Max added, pointing a claw at me.

I watched them take each other's side for a moment too long, then remembered that I don't owe them anything. "You don't have to come with me. I can bring them back on my own," I said, too breathless to argue.

Red snorted. "Don't be ridiculous, girl," he said, as Max nodded furiously and Rue stood silent, indecisive. "Of course, we are coming." Max's nods quickly turned into shaking his head in disapproval, but he didn't object further when Rue snatched his arm to get moving.

∽

For several minutes, we scoured the dark riders' camp for signs of Caz and Lucien. Red's plan was simple: first, we had to discover where they were keeping them. Second, I'd use Summer power to set a fire somewhere far away, causing the riders to scatter. Finally, we'd sneak around the camp while the riders were away to retrieve them. As Red, Spore, and I waited behind a large boulder a few paces from the camp, Max and Rue had left to complete the first part of the mission.

The dark riders gathered around like a pack of hungry wolves. Dozens of them. Females and little ones too. They looked different in many ways, but they all had long, curled horns and shark-like teeth. Someone was preaching about the approaching blood moon and the ultimate sacrifice. They were attentive, and some mumbled along with the preacher as if reciting a poem.

"A curse is a coward's weapon!" Their preacher shouted, drawing nods from everyone his eyes landed on. "One they bestowed upon us. One they used to place new cowards on their throne as they pleased."

"Summer has taken many of our own. We have allowed their fire to reach our darkness for far too long." A rider, the same one that struck me with his poisoned arrow, had said. He wasn't wearing his mask, revealing his shark-like teeth. "But they will not take the last Shadow from us!"

The ground trembled with their yells. "Vironnos! Vironnos! Vironnos!" they shouted again and again, clanking their weapons as they raised them high above their heads. The little ones cheered with the same energy, though I could tell some didn't fully comprehend why.

"You still want this, girl?" Red asked, waving his tail. I

knew he didn't ask about the mission, but what was coming after. "Ambition cannot be burned. Not even with your fire."

I looked back at them with a smile I plastered on my face. "Perhaps you're right," I said as I continued to watch them. I wanted to remember their faces, to remember their persistence. Quickly they became another reason to find the truth. Not just for me, but for everyone. "But they're not the only ones with ambition."

Muffled steps hurried towards us, and I turned to find Max and Rue returned. "What have you found?" Red asked before I could get the question out.

Of course, we had to wait for them to stop panting first. Though I felt those were the longest seconds of my life. "There's a cave south," Rue said, gasping for air.

"Two guards are stationed outside the entrance," Max added, "though we couldn't look inside, I'm sure what you're looking for is there."

"Not what, but whom." I raised an eyebrow at him and he snorted.

Red twitched an ear. "How uninteresting. Have you forgotten what you must do, girl?"

My heart ignited naturally and easily as I breathed in the harsh air. I pulled my arrow as Caz taught me, aiming at a fallen trunk in the opposite direction, and released. Screams were lit like wildfires throughout the camp as a cloud of smoke rose above treetops. As we'd hoped, a fair amount of dark riders charged after the signal of smoke, but not enough. I shot another arrow several paces west, drawing more riders away. Another and another until very few remained.

We had little time to move before they'd discover the

false alarm. Circling the camp, we dodged out of view until we came very close to the cave Max and Rue had discovered. The guards had doubled in number outside the cave's entrance, but it wasn't a problem for Red to lure them away with the sound of claws scraping into the woods.

As they ran away, the guards yelled for others to take their place while they pursued the monster. It would take the riders several minutes to reach the entrance. Enough time for me to sneak inside and get Caz and Lucien out. I moved quickly, cursing the pulse-like pain in my leg.

The cave was quiet and dark as a cemetery. My footsteps, no matter how lightly I stepped, echoed like thunder inside. The air began to smell of metal and blood, a scent that burned my lungs like acid. The noises of chaos and shouts from the outside were replaced with slow, ragged breaths somewhere deeper into the darkness.

My muscles stiffened as I followed the sound, hoping I wouldn't find any of them hurt. "Caz? Lucien?" I whispered, letting the walls carry my voice around. There was a clanking of metal, and then it broke with a low growl. I imagined it was someone breaking free, but I couldn't see who, and when I got close enough, I found the chains broken with no traces of a prisoner.

I didn't have to look further to find Caz, unconscious. His head was bent so low I couldn't see his face, and his wrists were chained in iron to the ground. The closer I stepped to him, the louder that voice spoke in my head, telling me to run away. His flesh turned purple where iron touched him, melting into his skin. I had read about what iron does to fairies, but it was horrifying to actually see it.

Gritting my teeth, I slashed my sword, fire against metal

until he broke free. Caz fell slowly into my arms, his body cold as the dead. The silent moments stretched. I never should have left him alone. I sagged against his chest, letting my tears soak his black shirt as I listened to his slow heartbeats return, then thudding rapidly.

His hand came up to stroke the back of my head, making me shiver. "You shouldn't be here," he whispered under his breath, eyes glazed. Blood dried at the corner of his mouth. His face was so pale, I could see his veins through his sheer skin.

"There's nowhere I'd rather be." The look on his face was almost reassuring. I pulled him up with me, and together we headed out of the cave. Caz had looked back once, frowning as if he'd missed something. Before I could ask what it was, the new guards arrived at the entrance.

Four riders with teeth as sharp as their weapons and horns curled around their heads walked slowly towards us, eyes gaping at me, wondering why the mouse came back to the hunter's trap. But I was no mouse, and this was no trap.

Their mouths curled into hideous smiles as a sword appeared by my side quicker than they could blink. Evidence that I was who they were looking for. Judging by their faces, they wanted a fight. Good. A fight is exactly what they would get from me.

One whistled softly. A tune that summoned more riders than I'd expected. They appeared from nowhere, from behind rocks, from trees, and even from thin air. Someone tugged at my sleeve, and I turned to Caz, looking up at me in terror. *Run!* his eyes seemed to scream. I shook my head. Never again.

I raised my sword as the riders scurried toward me with

a howl, only to be stopped by a thunderous screech. Loud enough for the riders to drop their weapons and cover their ears. Red eyes were no longer threatening, and no longer gaping at me.

Caz stood close to me, guarding me from whatever sat atop the cave. When I raised my head to stare at it, my body felt as though it belonged to someone else. I could no longer *feel* myself. There he was, less than twenty feet away—

Under the moonless night with his wings spread wide, threatening to knock down the stars with his screeching, was the last Shadow. Vironnos.

CHAPTER 19

BETRAYED, DESPISED, AND LOST

THE WORLD BLURRED. I stood rooted to the spot as Vironnos fixed his calm, predatory eyes on me. Smoke curled lazily around him like a cloud, and the jagged spines down his back cut through the air like a hundred blades as he shifted. Vironnos was there, gazing at me like an old friend who couldn't decide whether to attack or let me go. Those eyes— if I didn't know better, I'd have sworn we'd met before. But I did know better. The last Shadow wouldn't have spared my life if we'd met before, or was it that he couldn't make a move? Was it the absence of the blood moon that kept him from attacking when he had the chance?

This is insane, you're making it all up! It was all in my head. There was no proof, only my own suspicion.

There was a flash of fur, and Red was beside me in seconds, gazing up at Vironnos whose scales changed colors as he swooped into the air. Completely ignoring us, Vironnos went straight towards the dark riders.

"This is our chance," Max panted as he poked his sword

into my arm, finally drawing my attention away from the last Shadow. "We leave now, ginger!"

"No! We haven't found Lucien yet…" I looked down at Caz, his knees were pinned to the ground, and he smelled heavily of iron. He fell silent, his body still shivering. The others, too, remained quiet, waiting for me to accept that we didn't have time. I knew we didn't. I clenched my fist so hard that my nails scraped my skin, letting the fresh cuts burn against the cold wind. I hated the idea of leaving Lucien behind, but I couldn't risk their lives for it. *I'm sorry, Lucien.*

"Fine," I finally said, offering my hand to Caz. He took it, and I pulled him up. "We're leaving for the Mountain of Ruins, I can't defeat him with all the riders here."

Even after the dark riders' camp seemed as small as an ant from the distance we rode, the deafening roars still filled my ears. Nobody pursued us. Not even Vironnos, though he probably knew where we were headed anyway.

Caz had his head on my shoulder the whole ride, as though he was drawing strength from my proximity. I placed a hand on his head and felt him flinch at my touch. "We'll be there soon, Caz." He hadn't said a word since we left the cave, and I felt him drifting away from me. Maybe I couldn't help him, but I knew my mother could. I'd always found new ways to be in trouble, and she'd always known what to do. I suppose that was what mothers were supposed to do.

Red suddenly stopped, and that was when I noticed Caz had fallen onto the bed of snow, breathing slowly.

I pulled Caz closer to a tree which he sank back against. I glanced up to meet his hollow eyes, stripped of light before they closed completely. His chest was heaving. He occasionally winced from the pain that surged through his body, which might as well have surged through mine, because I felt it all.

I felt the rhythm of his heart as though they were mine. I took his hand, and in unison, our heartbeats quickened like they were linked by an imaginary bond. No, not imaginary. It was all too real. This iron poison was stealing him from me. Little by little.

Minutes passed and I continued to stare at his chest as it fell and rose steadily. My mind was a mess of thoughts, and I was a lost explorer trying to find my way out when I realized Caz had been awake for most of the time, secretly watching me staring at where his heart was.

"You're not thinking about breaking it, are you?" His voice startled me, but I was happy that he sounded more like himself. Perhaps all he needed was a little rest.

My face heated as his words sank in. I shook my head furiously, and he *laughed*. I never thought Caz was capable of laughing. It was a pleasant sound that I could never tire of. I decided I was greedy for wanting all of his laughs for me alone, even after he winced from the pain it had caused him.

"Good, because no one has ever come this close to my heart."

Does that mean…I had to look away to ask, "I'm close to your heart?"

"No," he said to make me look back at him in an instant. "*You are* my heart, princess. You are my everything, I'm sorry it took me this long to realize it."

I leaped to my feet and kicked snow at him for making me flush with embarrassment. All he did was laugh some more before he gingerly pulled me down to his chest. "Stop it," I told him, even though I never truly wanted him to. Sometimes I wish he wouldn't listen to me, but this time he did. Still, his smile was painted with permanent paint as he continued to glare at me.

He reached behind my neck and, as his icy fingers touched my skin, I let out a tiny gasp. "It's yours," he said in a serious tone, as he brought my palm over his pounding heart with his other hand. "It's all yours, my love."

"Are you sure you want that?" I whispered, my thoughts were on my tongue before I realized. "I'm rather clumsy."

He sobered. "I'll take the risk. With you, I'll take any and all the risks. If you wish to tear it apart, my love, then I'd only be grateful to have made your wishes come true."

I'd never wish that. He knew it, too. I traced his heart with my thumb, and he seemed to melt under my touch. *I may be immune to your fire, but I am not immune to you. I know that because I burn for you.* Those words scraped the back of my mind. Was he burning for me now?

"And…what if I wish to accept it?" I asked.

He pulled me so close to him that our breaths became one. "Then I'd have to get used to this endless dream of us," he said, his voice soft and firm.

Before I could say anything else, he brushed his lips softly against mine, and then kissed my forehead. My breath hitched as he wrapped his hands around my shoulders and I rested my head on his chest. We watched the stars twinkle brighter than ever before. I knew Red and the others were nearby, but all I wanted was to spend a few more peaceful moments with Caz.

"I used to like them, you know," he murmured, letting

his fingers tangle mine, "the moonless nights. No one recognizes how beautiful the stars are except when the moon is gone. And even by then, everyone is too scared to notice."

It wasn't hard to imagine why. "Are *you* scared, Caz?"

"I'm terrified," he confessed, his chin resting atop my head. I felt those words, felt them like a boulder resting atop my chest. I straightened. Our eyes met, and I understood why he was terrified.

He looked at me like I was a complex riddle that made the difference between life and death for him. "You didn't kill them," he murmured, only to confirm my suspicion. I had been wondering when he would mention that. I shifted uncomfortably in the snow.

It scared me to see him like this. He looked so concerned. Unrecognizable, even. Back then I did have the chance to strike first, but I didn't want to. The dark riders had their reasons to hate me, they shot me, poisoned me, and still…I couldn't do it. I didn't want to let anger lead me closer to the Fateteller's vision. A future certain of death.

I looked away. "I didn't."

He frowned. "Why?" I couldn't believe it. Did he want me to? Did Caz want me to kill the riders…no, he only wanted to know if I could. He was worried that I'd fail him, worried that I wouldn't be able to defeat Vironnos, worried that I'd give up everything if it meant I had to kill someone. That much was clear in his eyes.

I said nothing. I scowled and rose quickly, feeling panic rush through me like adrenaline, sending my senses into space.

Caz rose too, grunting with effort. He pressed his hands to my face, forcing me to look him in the eyes. His hair fell across his forehead "Alexandra," he said my name like he was desperately trying to help me understand what was at stake. "Tell me, why didn't you use your powers to protect yourself? Do you not care if you're hurt? Do you not care for your life?" His concern was now obvious, and so was his anger. "You can't win like this," he said, like an accusation. "I told you I'll stand by your side regardless of the choice you'll make, but you can't win if you don't fight to live. You can't win if you don't kill. That's the only way. Promise me you will."

"No!" I pressed my hands to him, and he winced at the pain. "Caz, I don't have to kill anyone." That's right, Caz didn't know everything I did. Even though I only knew little. "You think there's only one way to break the blood curse, but that isn't true." His brows were drawn together in an instant. "I'll find the truth. And there will be no bloodshed when I do, Caz. There won't need to be, I promise."

He slowly withdrew his hands. A gesture that he'd given up. "Don't make promises you can't keep. It's called the blood curse for a reason, princess. You're not obligated to change that," he said in a tired voice that made me recoil. *He's wrong,* I thought to myself, *he must be.* I shook my head slowly, fighting back tears. Why couldn't he understand? Why couldn't anyone? "I know it isn't like you to hurt anyone, but you cannot always stand back. Not everyone will be as forgiving as you, certainly they weren't. Did you not think I'd notice that injury of yours?"

The mention of it made my leg throb.

He sighed. "My last lesson is this: if you cannot be as cruel as your enemy, you will succumb to defeat. Victory has a cost—you can either pay it or be it."

"Why are you telling me this, Caz?" My voice choked with tears that stung like fire. I felt as though I didn't know him anymore.

His eyes held no explanation. A moment passed, two. "What good are your powers if you cannot defend yourself, Alexandra? When the time comes, you can't hesitate like you did with the Darklings." He read my expression and went on, relentlessly. "They tried to kill you more than once. They would have tried again without a doubt if your mother hadn't brought you here."

He was wrong enough to make me wince. "It wasn't the Darklings, Caz."

His frown deepened. "I don't understand," he said, more to himself than to me. "Only the Darklings have the ability to portal to the mortal world. Other than them…" His eyes widened dangerously, and I shrank back as he clutched my shoulders so tightly that I was certain he'd been in more pain than me. "Who was it? Alexandra, tell me who it was," he said, urgently.

I felt lost. I knew keeping that secret from Caz was a mistake, but I didn't know how big it was until I looked into his eyes. There was more than just rage and frustration. Far beneath those emotions was betrayal. The wind howled, blowing the snow everywhere. For a split second, something was there then vanished. "Tell me," he repeated in the same tone, though his voice almost broke. "Who was it?"

I swallowed and parted my lips to say the name when *he* spoke instead.

"Did someone summon me?" Lucien asked, perching on a large branch above our heads. He landed with his wings spread wide, and his feet deep in the snow. He looked more like a shadow of himself. He was panting, and his chest heaved rapidly. The blackening that was once on his fingertips had spread all the way up his neck and onto his face like tree roots.

Caz stepped right in front of me, a shield of heat that melted the frozen bullets racing through my spine. Betrayal floated into view and flooded over me as he gave me a quick glance before turning to Lucien with disdain. "You tricked her, didn't you? Trickery is lowly, even for someone like you."

"*Especially* for someone like me. Which is why I gave so many signs, but you were so blind weren't you, Summer bastard?" He laughed without humor. "The way you gave in to your emotions every time, the way you trusted her without a second thought. Some might call it love."

"What's going on?" I asked Caz.

"It's my fault. I should've known when you asked me to take you to the pixiehouse. I should've known then," he murmured answers but didn't as much as blink in my direction.

Should have known what? What does any of that mean? I wanted to ask, but I was lost in the wilderness of my own creation.

Lucien took a step towards me, crunching the snow beneath his boots before Caz's gaze pinned him to the spot, and he thought better of it. "Trust makes you vulnerable. It makes you weak," he went on, just to spite Caz. And his work did not go in vain. "You trusted her, but she trusted *me*." I didn't realize how stupid I was for not telling Caz sooner until I saw his features faintly begin to twist. "You're both so weak, it makes me *sick*."

286

Caz's jaw twitched, and his knuckles turned white. "The favor," he whispered, "what will you ask of her?"

I forgot about that part. I thought I was doing the right thing when I made that deal with Lucien. A favor for a favor. Now that I saw the wicked look on Lucien's face, I deeply regretted that deal.

Lucien grinned at me. Strands of his ink hair fell onto his eyes, but it wasn't enough to block the pointed look he sent my way. "Who knows," he said quietly. "Maybe I'll make her my mate."

That was all it took for Caz to lunge at him punching left and right with the little strength he still had. He knew he couldn't win, but he had to try.

"No! Stop it!" I shouted, but no one listened.

Lucien wasn't surprised, he wasn't compassionate either. He landed a hit with his knee that sent Caz staggering a few steps back. "You should've agreed to that duel when you were stronger, Summer bastard."

Caz spat the blood from his mouth and charged again, determined to tackle Lucien down. He landed a couple of punches before a kick to the stomach knocked him on his back. "You're pitiful, Caz. All your efforts to protect your princess meant nothing at all when you brought her to me." He rose to his feet, his wings shaking off the snow, as he wiped the blood at the corner of his mouth with his sleeve. "I suppose I should thank you for being such a fool. You did everything I wanted, and I didn't even have to ask."

With a roar, Red jumped from behind Lucien, teeth flashing. He must've heard me screaming and came back. Red was above his head, claws poised to sever his head with a single strike, when he froze. Max, Rue, and Spore were on his back, each ready to fight. But they, too, were froze. Except for Caz and me, Lucien made everyone as still as stone.

Caz grunted, pulling himself back up, he turned slightly to regard me with worrisome eyes. "Caz, please," I cried, "what's happening?" I begged, and a tear slipped from my eye. I felt as if the world was collapsing and I was left out of it all, even though a part of me was screaming it was my fault. "Tell me what I've done." *Someone, anyone, please tell me what's going on.*

Lucien barked out a laugh that forced Caz to lower his gaze. "You naive, little princess. There's a certain beauty in ignorance. Don't you realize what you've done? All the secrets you kept for yourself; all the deals you've made will break you. Little by little they'll ruin you. You are your own enemy, my rival."

I was fighting to get the words out, fighting to believe them. "I'm not your rival, Lucien. You're not mine."

"Yes, he is," Caz gritted, annoyed with me. "But you're not his only rival." He pulled his dagger, relentlessly thrusting it in Lucien's face until it managed to leave a mark a few inches from his eye. Caz was a lot weaker than before, but he displayed greater hatred for his opponent than he did to Titan. In that, there was no comparison.

They spun around to face each other again. "I'm everyone's rival. No one's friend. But you know what?" Lucien sniffed. "I'm not the one to blame. Your kind persuaded everyone that we were the ones to blame for the blood curse. That only by our sacrifice will great rulers rise."

"You'll have me believe your kind is innocent?" Caz swung his dagger, but Lucien twisted his hand and squeezed down on the iron wound before it could reach his chest, burying the dagger beneath the snow as it fell. Caz hurled him down with no remorse, but they rolled quickly, and Lucien landed on top.

"*Innocents?*" Lucien snarled, punching Caz repeatedly. "You think there are innocents? No, we're both guilty, Summer bastard. Somehow, we were the only ones paying the price, but the time has come for each and every one of you to suffer the way we did. If our fire won't kill you, our darkness will. As for your king, I'll shred him to pieces and when I'm done, I'll bring him back alive for more. You won't be able to see it, Caz, so better imagine it."

"Enough!" I roared, tasting my own tears in my mouth. Lucien looked up at me, his fists were stained with Caz's blood. "Please, just stop hurting each other. Come to your senses, Lucien; you don't have to do this. Whatever this is, it's my fault. So please, let him go."

"You don't know me," he muttered under his breath.

"I do, and you're not like this—"

"You don't know me!" He shouted, startling me into silence. When he read my face, he scoffed, relaxing his grip on Caz's throat. "Don't look so astonished, my rival. Your mother hid you well for seventeen years until you became poisoned with emotions. Dangerous emotions that blinded you and made you believe there's good in everyone, even someone like me." He stood and dragged Caz until he knelt before me, out of breath. "You're so lost, my rival."

A shield of smoke stood between us like a sheer black blanket as Lucien reached behind his back and pulled his crystal dagger. "So let me help *you* come to your senses, yes?"

"Lucien, no!" I ran to him, but the shield of smoke flung me back with a zapping sound that rocked my body. There was a bolt of pain in my head, and the snowdrift did nothing to ease my discomfort. I blinked, raising my head to glance at the blurry sight of Caz and Lucien as something warm dripped from my head and onto my face. Another blink and I saw him pointing the dagger to Caz's back. "Let him go!" I cried, or screamed, I couldn't tell. Fuming, I rose, feeling my head thudding. "Lucien!"

Rage made my blood boil. "Do you still not understand what I am?"

"I don't care what you are," I answered, the words escaped through my teeth. "Let. Him. Go."

Caz appeared lifeless before him, but he lifted his head to look at me as if it was the last time he'd be able to. Blood poured from his mouth and nose. I realized too late that it was all my fault. If I hadn't kept any secrets from him, this wouldn't have happened. If I hadn't trusted Lucien, this wouldn't have happened.

It was all my fault, and Caz was paying for it. *If you're not careful, son of Lord Damien, your heart will betray you.* The Banshee's words hit me like a bolt of lightning. I was his heart, and I surely did just that.

I loathed the agonizing way he looked at me, but I didn't want to turn away. He didn't want to, either.

"Do you still wish to know what I whispered to the Frozen Pond of Secrets?" Lucien's smile turned predatory. "Why I'd always be despised?"

I hesitated. I was afraid of what he'd say, but even more so of remaining in the dark. I wanted to know why he changed, why he's suddenly calling me his rival. Had I misread him so terribly?

He didn't wait for me to answer. With the dagger's sharp edge aimed, he said, "I." He drove the crystal dagger into Caz's back and the pain shot up through mine. "Am." Deeper and deeper until the soaked tip reached his chest, dangerously close to his heart. Through it all Caz did not wince. It was as if he'd felt a greater pain that a dagger wound to the chest meant nothing at all. "Vironnos."

I wasn't sure what happened next. I found myself kneeling beside Caz, his head cold in my arms and my tears falling into his hair. I sobbed, screamed, and felt the ground shift and tilt. Seconds dragged. One moment I was conscious and the next I was sinking in memories, visions of Caz in the past and what could have been. For several moments I'd forgotten what happened until I looked down at him, and I remembered the nightmares where Caz had the same wound, and in both, I was empty.

Caz was right all along. I'd been a fool to believe there was another way to end this, to create my own path. Torn between rage and despair, I gave in to that emptiness. There was nothing more I craved than for things to go back to the way they used to be. I wanted Caz alive. Alive and away from me. Away from his greatest regret, which now had to be having feelings for me.

Caz was gone, and the last memory he had was of me betraying him, foolishly and selfishly betraying him. Choking on tears, I realized everything I believed in was wrong. There may never be a different path. My fate was sealed, I saw what would happen once I reached the Mountain of Ruins. But what if I gave up now?

I glanced up at Lucien—Vironnos, who seemed almost sorry until he plastered a wicked smile on his face. *You're so naive, he'll never be sorry.* I had to try, there might still be a chance. "Save him," I whispered, my throat ached as I spoke, and my voice became strange to even me. "Heal his wounds. Let my friends go. Let me take my mother with me and you'll never see me again. I'll go home and never return to Everlynia, I promise." My voice broke on the last word, but I went on. "There will be no Solmark heir to challenge you, Vironnos. I will never be a threat to you."

Vironnos' gaze lingered on Caz and then back to me. "Tempting offer, my rival. But I'm afraid you cannot leave. A curse does not simply fade with an heir, it may only die with an heir. You see, our choices aren't ours to make, even if we are the ones being sacrificed. Cruel, isn't it?" There was some truth in that, even *I* began to believe it. "Save your anger, you'll need it tomorrow. It might actually save you."

Even though I expected terror to weave its way into my veins, it didn't. Caz had told me the only way to win, and Vironnos had shown me. Still, Caz will not die. I've decided to do whatever it takes to bring him back. Rage flooded and spilled over me as I slowly came to terms with the fact that I would have to kill. Tomorrow, I would have to kill.

"Come now," Vironnos said, his voice cutting through my thoughts, "we both still have a deal to fulfill, and an act to play."

CHAPTER 20

MOUNTAIN OF RUINS

THE SEVEN OF us rode again for the Mountain of Ruins with Lucien—Vironnos—in the lead as usual, but it wasn't the same as before. We were nothing like we used to be and to keep going, it would have to get a lot worse.

Except for a few times when his body trembled to cough up blood, Caz was impossibly still on Red's back. I had one hand pressed on his chest, half-expecting his heart to stop thudding through the soft fabric any second. Half-expecting to lose my mind.

No, I will save him. I vowed to find a way for us, and if that's too late for that, then I vow to find a way for *him*, even if I had to lose myself along the way. "Everything will be fine, Caz. I promise." I whispered those words into his ear, unsure whether he heard me or not.

Rue caressed my cheek with her paw, and it took everything in me to hold back my tears. "Do not give up now, princess. This is your story."

"Is it?" I scoffed, and my voice wavered. "I don't recall writing that beginning."

Her shoulders lifted in a shrug as she pulled her paw away. "No one gets to write the beginning of their story, princess. But you do get to choose the ending. Choose it wisely."

I looked up at the shining stars, wondering if I'd be afraid to look up tomorrow when the blood moon rises. "I don't know, Rue, I'm not exactly looking forward to the ending. None of my choices are exciting."

"Then choose the one you'll least regret," Rue said with a smile as Red lurched to a halt.

I leaped off Red, one foot in Icymark, the other in the deep mud of the Mountain of Ruins. There was nothing to see through the darkness that hung over the horizon like a giant cloak in which Vironnos disappeared. I didn't even hear the four Darklings that emerged from the shadows, making their way toward me. I quickly aimed a blazing arrow in their direction, but only one of them stopped. The Darklings dangerously resembled the dark riders with their twisted horns, which made me far less comfortable being around them again.

"We welcome you, Princess Alexandra," he said with a bow. I recognized the Darkling's voice instantly, he was the messenger from the Icymark Court. The other three only stopped to quickly bow, then they were drawn to Caz's blood like a starving vampire. My eyes followed them. They mumbled something among themselves before carrying him along, making their way back into the mist.

"Where are they taking him?" My voice stumbled with panic.

"Don't worry, Your Highness, the Grand Healer will

attend to his wounds if it's not too late. This way," he made a gesture, wanting me to follow him somewhere.

I hesitated, turning back to my friends one last time. Red's tails wagged slightly as he lowered his head to my reach, allowing me to pet him without glowering at me. Spore crept into my arms and mused the only word he knew.

Red straightened. "My debt is paid, girl," he said, reminding me of General Jora's favor.

I nodded. "Thank you," I whispered as my eyes met Rue and Max's gaping at me, "thank you all. For everything."

Rue gave a little curtsy that mocked the one I gave to Valor. "May you be the victor, princess," she said.

"May you be the victor." Red and Max spoke in unison, which made the Darkling waiting for me clear his throat very loudly. Everyone knew there may only be one victor. I was just too late to accept it.

My eyes teared up, but I quickly turned away. "Ginger!" Max shouted, stopping me in my tracks. I saw Rue fixing him with a look, which probably threatened him to say goodbye. "You are a true princess," he said, and I realized it was the first nice thing he'd said to me. "You're just one with a *terrible* knack for trouble."

I chuckled, which made Max scowl. "And you're a true knight, Max," I told him, "just one with a *tiny* sword." I waved goodbye before following the Darkling into the mist.

Following a Darkling in the night proved a real challenge. He moved soundlessly, his figure blending in perfectly with the darkness. I narrowed my eyes to him for as long as I could, but every time I blinked, I lost sight of him. I thought he'd abandoned me numerous times until I caught a glimpse of his red eyes flickering from a distance.

Eventually, after getting lost countless times and having to search for glowing crimson eyes in the night, the mist cleared, and I found myself hundreds of feet above the ground. I was standing on the edge of the mountain, and one step to the left would have taken me down to my death.

My heart leapt into my throat as we spent long minutes climbing curved stairs that were carved out of the mountainside. They rose high above the clouds and ascended to the summit, where the Shadow Court resided.

The Darkling pushed the door open, and it swung back with a creaking sound that shook the soiled chandeliers, showering dust onto the floor. I took a deep breath and stepped forward. The court was built within the mountain, with walls made of smooth and jagged stones that were smeared over with blood-red paint. Illustrations of the blood moon over the flaming sea stretched from one corner to the next, ending only a few inches from the start line. The smell of herbs and moss was heavy in my nose.

From the shadows of the court emerged the rest of the Darklings, surrounding me like the statues of dragons in the Solmark Court. My stomach tensed. Their expressions conveyed hatred, resentment, fear, interest, pride, disgust, and far more emotions than I could count. Far more than I could bear at once.

The crowd behind me separated, and I heard her voice. "Alexandra?"

I spun around so fast that I almost tripped. My mother's

eyes were alight with joy as she rushed to embrace me, her arms wrapped so tightly around me it made me forget about anything that mattered. I sobbed into her shoulder, soaking the sleeve of her silver gown as she stroked my hair, murmuring comfort words.

She did not pull back until my tears dried at the corners of my eyes. She studied my face for a moment before her hands went up to my head, wiping blood off my hairline. "What happened to you?" she demanded with a pale face.

I blinked back tears, not wanting to remember what happened. My mother sighed, then took my hand in hers and led me to where she'd been spending her days. And, to my surprise, it looked nothing like a prison.

Despite everything being coated in the darkest shades of black, the room was dazzling. Fit for the Shadow rulers, I thought. Next to the bed with black sheets and fur thrown on top, a small opening in the wall served as a window. Plants were creeping into the room from the mountainside and onto the bed frame with will-o'-the-wisps dancing around the stems.

I sat on her bed, drawing a few will-o'-the-wisps around me and Spore, who was jumping on the bed beside me. "I borrowed this elixir from the Grand Healer," my mother said as she knelt before me and gently wiped the blood off my face with a clean, mint-scented cloth. I winced, feeling my skin burn as if I had come into contact with acid. When she removed the cloth, I touched the wound and felt that it had completely healed, though the throbbing burn made it hard to accept. "Ironically it's called Painfader."

I chuckled a little. "Of course it is." She opened her mouth to say something, then closed it again. I knew what she wanted to say, and I had to bite my lip to hold back my irritation from being left in the dark. "Why didn't you tell me about the blood curse, mother?"

She licked her lips and sat beside me on the bed, reaching to brush my hair back, as she always did. "Lexi, I…I didn't think it was the right time," she admitted quietly. "When I told you all about Everlynia, it seemed like it was a lot for you to accept, and it was. If I had told you *everything*, you would have been terrified. I wanted you to trust me, not to be afraid of me."

There was a pause before she spoke again. "You must've seen awful things, my dear," she murmured, squeezing my hand. "I thought I ordered Caz to look after you, how did you manage coming here on your own?"

"I didn't. It was Vironnos who led me to you," I said, and her eyes widened in surprise. Or possibly fear. "And Caz…" my eyes quickly misted with unshed tears. "It's all because of me…I don't even know if he'll make it—"

She stood. "Tell me you didn't make a deal with him," She whispered in a trembling voice. When I didn't answer, she gripped my shoulders, pulling me to her. "Alexandra, tell me you didn't make a deal with Vironnos!"

I've never seen my mother so frightened. What would she be frightened about when it's only me who'd be doomed by all this? "I did," I admitted, much to her displeasure. "I didn't know it was him."

"You can't." She shook her head, long fingers digging into my flesh. "Everything will be ruined if he asks you to break the curse," she said, speaking more to herself. "You can't be the one to break the curse, Alexandra. I will not allow it—"

"Of all people, I thought you would understand." She had the audacity to look confused. I pushed her hands away. "I'm sick of everyone telling me what I should do. This is my story. *I* will choose the ending. Not you, not Vironnos, *me*. I will not unite with the Shadow." Relief settled on her features, but not for long. "Though I will break this curse." I started walking to the door when she grabbed my arm.

Pursing her lips as if she had tasted something sour on her tongue, she plastered a pitying look on her face. "You think *you* could find what countless rulers had been searching for centuries in a single night? You're playing with fire, daughter."

"Turns out I'm quite good at it." I jerked my arm free and made my way across the room. At the door, I looked back at her. "I've had the pleasure of meeting General Jora. He sends you his regards." She nodded, not having the courage to look at me.

Unaccompanied, I roamed the Shadow Court freely, allowing myself in deserted places where I could've sworn I heard voices echoing throughout, only to be proven wrong. I wondered if the Darklings I saw before were a figment of my imagination. I wondered if anyone lived here at all.

There were only a few lit candles scattered across the halls, barely enough for me to keep going. To find anything that could help me discover the truth. The thought of proving everyone right made my mind throb with rage.

I will find the truth, I told myself. *For him, I will find it. Tonight.* I was so engrossed in my grim thoughts that I didn't see the arm-thick stem creeping in through a window. I tripped and fell on my knees and hands, bumping my head on a closed door and cursing myself for arousing the pain from the rider's arrow.

I groaned, watching the stem as it slowly creeped back out. As if its only purpose was to humiliate me. "Great," I muttered, "even plants find me offensive."

The door creaked halfway open, making my heart leap to my throat in a matter of seconds. I expected someone to jump out, but no one did. Behind me, footsteps echoed through the hall, closing in as their whispers became louder and louder. Not knowing where else to go, I hid behind the open door, listening to the Darkling's conversation and my own heart beating in my ears.

"He's mad!" Someone rasped.

"Hush! Quiet, fool," another whispered. "He's our ruler."

"Yeah? For how long? One more night? He is the *last* Shadow."

"It's just a prophecy!" The other darkling raged quietly. "A weak prophecy brought to our ruler by the deceiving heir of Icymark. How convenient for him to make matters worse for both the Shadow and Summer just a day before one of them is sacrificed."

My mouth dropped open. *Cillian was here?*

"What Cillian proposes is absurd. Vironnos is powerful. He's more powerful than you'd think," he went on desperately to reason with him. "His reign will not come to an end, not tomorrow."

"No." The other one said with a composed voice. "If he won't do it, I will."

"What do you mean?"

"I'll kill the Summer heir myself. With her gone, there will be no blood moon. The prophecy will die with her."

The damn door creaked again, and I froze behind it as the Darkling stepped in. He was inches away, scanning the darkness with a knife in his hand and listening to the faintest sound. I held my breath as long as I could, knowing full well that I'd have to kill him first.

Faster than my heart could ignite, he clutched the doorknob and shut it behind him, making the chandeliers above my head tremble. Then, he locked me inside without an ounce of light. "What will you do about the exiled queen?" the other asked, voice fading with their footsteps.

"I guess I'll have to kill her too."

I desperately wanted to get out, to warn my mother before it was too late, but it was pointless. The door did not budge. I groaned, banging my head against it as I sank to my feet.

There were so many places I needed to be and many things I needed to do, but there was no time. And I was locked in the darkness—

As I'd given up hope, I heard my name. Then, a beam of light danced around my fingers, calling to me in whispers that drew me up to my feet and across the piercing darkness like a lure.

My heart thundered in my chest. I didn't know where I was going. And worse, I could not stop myself. I went down flights of stairs and straight through curtains, hearing my name in a dozen different voices. With each step, they got louder in my head, strings that moved me like a puppet to places I'd never find on my own.

I closed my eyes as the voices screamed my name at full blast until my ears buzzed, and I fought the urge to faint. Suddenly, everything stopped. I opened my eyes slowly to find myself standing before a freshly painted door less than half my height. I opened it and crawled inside, leaving a trail of red paint from my fingers where I'd touched the knob.

Inside, the unmistakable scent of medicine overwhelmed my senses. All I saw in the small room were potions kept in clear glass. Each one of them had its own scent and color. None were pleasant. In some, I saw rotten petals of flowers. Others had an eye, a finger, or a dried pixie floating within a liquid mixture. I gagged at the sight.

Past the dozens of shelves with potions, there were stacks of coffins. I did not dare look inside. Not sure where I was going, I went deeper. Even though I couldn't see anyone in the distance, I felt eyes following me everywhere I went, closer than my own shadow.

I stepped into a puddle of blood that wasn't there before. Watching it, the puddle became larger and larger as more blood seeped down the walls. I had to crane my neck up to see the freshly harvested hearts beating in every corner. Eleven, I counted. Each one of them was in a race to beat faster, but somehow it didn't terrify me. Somehow, I wanted to listen to them as though they were telling me something. As though they were telling me the truth—

"Is it a pleasing sight for you, Summer Princess?" Just like before, everything stopped. There was no blood anywhere, and the hearts were nothing but stones engraved into the mountain. *Was I imagining again?*

I reeled back in shock, facing the three-foot-tall redcap

with eyes as white as her claws. Shooing me away, she inspected her collections of potions, one by one. When she was confident that I didn't steal anything, the old redcap narrowed her eyes at me and asked again. "Well, is it?"

I shook my head earnestly.

"Pity," she said, "I guess now I wouldn't enjoy the sight of yours up there as much. What are you doing here anyway? And how did you get in here?" I opened my mouth to answer when she sighed, waving her hands in my face. "Never mind how, just keep out of my way. I have another Summer lunatic to deal with."

Caz? "Are you the Grand Healer?" I asked hastily.

She noticed the paint on my fingers and rolled her eyes. "I'm afraid so," she said, returning her gaze to her potions as she searched the shelves for one in particular. "Where are you…Aha." She shoved a mixture as black as ink, fighting to break the glass, and reached for one with a mosaic of colorful clouds.

"What is it?" I asked, following her as she opened another door. Crawling inside, I watched her climb up a bed where Caz laid topless and barely breathing

"Caz!" I dashed toward the bed, stepping on books in my path, which didn't please the redcap one bit. "What have you done?" I asked, my voice wild with panic. His chest was dark, as if he'd been burned from within, and his blood had soaked the sheets to the point that it was dripping onto the floor.

Seeing him like this all but made me up in arms over the fact that I'd been so foolish as to trust Lucien. And even a bigger fool for not telling Caz from the start.

It wasn't the redcap's fault, it was all mine. "Please, do

something," I begged her. She continued to stare at me for another moment before opening the vial and pouring a droplet into his mouth.

"Timewinder," she whispered. "It is strong enough to heal even a broken heart, but only if *he* was strong enough to pass the trials."

"What trials?"

"He must accept all the choices he made knowing the consequences of them. He must face his fears, failures, and regrets. For the Timewinder to work, he must live his nightmares."

So that was the cruel price he had to pay. "That's awful."

"It wouldn't be so awful if he had something to live for," she reasoned.

I knelt, running my fingers through his hair. "Come back to me," I whispered in his ear, "and if you hate me, come back and tell me how much you hate me."

The old redcap sighed. "He can't hear you."

Guilt gnawed at me. I shed some tears, watching them scatter around his temple and then sink in his hair. I've betrayed him, and I knew I wasn't worthy enough of a reason to live for. I wasn't worthy to fight for. Still... "You gave me your heart, Caz. Don't you dare take it away now." I pressed my forehead to his. "I will make things right, that I promise. Don't give up on me just yet, Caz That is an order." I placed a kiss on his cold cheek and rose from the bed with the redcap.

"Touching," she mocked. "Though it might have been a waste of words, Summer Princess. If you intend to break the curse by finding the truth, you might as well accept defeat now."

I frowned at her. "Whatever do you mean?"

Carefully closing the vial, she returned her attention to me. "Why do you think so many Shadow rulers have been sacrificed?" When I didn't answer, she went on. "Because they wanted to be the heroes. Every one of them sought the truth to save those who they loved most, and to save themselves, of course. If that is why you're seeking the truth, then you will fail like the other Shadow rulers before you. But..." Her smile grew eerie. "What if you're willing to give it all up for the sake of truth? What if, to get everything you wanted you must lose it first? After all, you cannot find what you already have."

Strangely, everything made perfect sense to me. Her words were the key to unlocking my memories, and every moment I'd spent in Everlynia flashed before my eyes. I had long thought the more I sought the truth, the less I knew. I looked back at Caz, realizing how mistaken I was. The truth had always been in front of me, and it could've knocked me down with a feather. It was one I chased when I should've run away from it.

In that moment shock faded, and rage rushed in uninvited. The redcap must've read my mind, because the next thing she said was, "You know what you must do, Summer Princess."

"I know my choices," I said quietly to myself. It may cost me everything that I am, but I'll learn to live with it. I'll have to. The Sea of Flames had already begun; waves rose and crashed within me, buzzing with the horror of the truth. "With fire, I will make it."

CHAPTER 21

BLOOD CURSE

BLOOD GREETED me when I returned to my mother's room, barely conscious of my surroundings. I had forgotten about the Darklings that wanted to murder me before the blood moon. Now, their bodies were piled beside the door frame, motionless. I should've known the former queen of Solmark is no stranger to violence.

"Alexandra!" My mother called with relief. "Where have you been? You've been gone for hours. I thought something happened to you." She rushed to embrace me, her hands left stains of blood on my shoulders. My own clothes were soaked with blood. Caz's blood. Spore jumped down the bed and staggered towards me, clutching my leg. I was relieved to see them unharmed.

When I didn't embrace her back, she pulled away, noticing the blood on me. "Are you hurt?" she shrieked.

I shook my head. I was too tired to speak. Too tired to think. I let her lead me to the bedroom bench. "What happened?" she asked.

"You tell me," I said, smacking her hand away, making her frown deepen. "Why did you curse him, mother?"

I meant to be vague about it. I wanted to give her the chance to speak on her own, but she didn't. And because she couldn't lie, she remained silent.

"Why did you curse Caz?" I asked, more clearly. "Why did you want to curse Lord Damien's son? How was he a threat to you?"

"How do you know about this? He couldn't have possibly told you…" Her voice trailed off, and she realized I must've made a deal with a Fateteller to have seen the past. She also sensed that I didn't see everything, which helped her contain herself. "Don't ask questions you don't want to know the answers to, daughter." She paced the room with a hand to her mouth.

"Oh, but I do." She gazed back at me with a look as if she was pleading with me to stop. "Lord Damien came very close to the truth, didn't he? So, you threatened him."

"The mortal world made you weak. You don't know what you're talking about." Her face flushed with anger. It was the first time I'd seen her like this.

"You're not the Spring ruler, mother." I stood, intimidating her. "You're the Spring guardian. The one that mysteriously disappeared just before the curse was spun. It was you, wasn't it? The greedy, exiled ruler who sought glory for herself."

My mother grinned wickedly. "I wanted nothing but for you to be the victor. I have sacrificed so much for this very day. I will not lose everything that I longed to have for your sentiments!" she raged, pointing at me with a long finger.

"All these years I thought you protected me because I

was your daughter, but no. You only ever saw me as a valuable chess piece. You don't want me to be the victor, mother, you *need* me to be the victor. You need me to kill the last Shadow for you, so you can have unmatched power.

"Because of you, I spent my life in a world where I didn't belong. Did you really think everything would go the way you planned? Hiding me from this one and promising me to that one…" My throat ached. "I don't belong to you, mother."

She turned away from me, crossed her arms, and gazed out the window at the bed of clouds a few feet below. "You were born a Solmark heir. Your life isn't yours to gamble with, and your choices aren't yours to make. As the Spring guardian, I'm no different. I knew one of the guardians would covet greater power, and I needed no prophecy to know that was true. Needless to say, I'd rather kill than be killed. So, I spun the blood curse, and waited.

"I've been waiting centuries for the ultimate prize. The day when a line ends, and I become unstoppable. I had no choice, but to strike first."

"You *had* a choice, mother. And you chose yourself."

"Just as you should," she said, stepping away from the window. The mountain roared, and the court trembled as it was slowly bathed in fiery hues in a heartbeat. My eyes went straight to the sky, and I froze. "And quickly, because your time is up, my daughter."

The blood moon rose slowly, casting a frightening glow that bewitched my soul, tangling my senses. Instantly, I felt a change in me, almost like the worst part of me had awoken, fought to take control, and won. I remembered what Lucien had said about the blood moon and I felt it all now. I became the monster he warned about, thirsting for blood and power.

What am I doing? I don't want this. No, someone please—

Drugged by the blood curse, I forgot why I wanted to break it. No reason came to my mind. I couldn't think. I couldn't breathe. All I could do was crave blood. More than the sea in which I was already drowning.

Everything was wrong, but it felt right. It felt so right… until I heard the rulers' hearts thundering louder than the silence in my ears. They were all there with me, pulling me from the depths of the darkness.

Suddenly, I became conscious of them all, of their desire to find the truth, and of their sacrifice. I realized I was not alone. Like me, the Shadow rulers were only victims in my mother's cruel game of power.

Through the swirling possibilities in my head and the morbid desires the blood moon had forced me into, I found my way out. Perhaps too quickly because my mother reacted as if I had shouted her secret from the rooftops. She couldn't hide her shock if she tried.

She opened her mouth, but I spoke first. "Do not be alarmed. Your curse will not change me," I told her, "I will not lose, mother, not to you. Not again. I have already made my choice."

"Your choice might just bring the destruction and chaos told by the prophecy—"

I took a step toward her. "Save your pathetic attempts to sway me into your game. Power isn't what I seek."

"Is that so? Tell me, daughter, will you allow thousands of innocents to die just to spite me?" She closed the gap between us. Despite being so close to me, I hardly recognized her anymore. "Make no mistake, if you fail to defeat the last Shadow, every drop of bloodshed will be on your hands. And there will be plenty. Vironnos will destroy Solmark beyond a shadow of a doubt. Everyone you've ever met will perish. Caz, too."

"Stop! You've done enough, don't you dare speak his name," I raged.

Her head tilted back slightly as she looked down at me. "Yes, I have cursed him, but will you doom him?" My heart tore against my chest. I thought I had made my decision, but now it all seems so surreal. I can't let Vironnos live, knowing he'll eradicate Summer as easily as he'd plunged his dagger into Caz's back.

The more I considered why he did it, the clearer it became. Vironnos *wanted* me to fight him. He never asked for a union, even after hearing Prince Cillian's prophecy. I wondered why. Has Vironnos already made his decision to surrender to his fate?

"I'll give you one last piece of advice, daughter: power belongs to those who dare to seize it. You have a chance to be the hero. Do not squander it."

My heart felt as though it stopped beating as chimes sounded throughout the court, each one felt like a smack to the face.

"Go on, then," my mother said with a smirk. "The battle has begun, and someone must drown in the Sea of Flames."

A crowd of Darklings gathered in an open arena, filling every seat. The blood moon shone the brightest above their heads, spilling rays over me as the gate lifted and the deafening sound of cheers erupted like a volcano. I could feel everyone's anticipation in the air, and the worst of them all was my mother's. One look at her and all my thoughts were reduced to ashes.

I considered giving up the fight just to spite her, but I would also have to give up countless lives for that cheap revenge. *There has to be another way,* I thought desperately.

"Is it anything like you've imagined it, my rival?" Vironnos' voice was in my ear. I liked him better when he used to call me that stupid nickname.

I slowly faced him and froze. He was a dragon, a monster with scales that could easily cut through my flesh. I didn't give him the satisfaction of looking trembling in his presence. "No, somehow I never imagined this day."

Vironnos lowered his head. "We were born only for this day, my rival. The way I see it, you and I were meant to be sacrificed. To rule or to avenge, we're merely pawns." His voice broke through the applause.

"Is it too late for us to be free?" I asked foolishly, gazing at the thirsty moon in the red night.

I found Vironnos shrinking under the bloodlustful gazes of the Darklings, and I dreaded what would happen to them after their last ruler was sacrificed. Lives will be lost either way. "Do not fear, my rival. Your fate has been told," he said without looking at me. "Tonight, you will deliver the killing blow. However, I must warn you that I will not be sacrificed without a fight. In terms of your debt, I want your word as a queen, not as a princess, that no harm will come to my subjects."

"You have my word. Though you must know, I do not leave things up to fate," I said, and only then did he spare a glance at me before strolling to the battleground.

The applause came to a halt as I followed him into the center with a flaming sword half my size. Each step felt like I was walking on blazing coals. Vironnos slowly spread his wings, gazing down at me with his inhuman eyes as his scales glistened red in the ring. A single chime echoed through the silence, and with a roar, he struck first. The battle had begun.

I barely evaded his sharp claws as they flew past me and creaked the stones, sending a million pieces flying to the crowd. He lashed again with his long, spiny tail. I struck fast, sinking the sword deep into his flesh, but it wasn't enough to stop him from knocking me to the ground.

For a moment, I lay there, my head throbbing from his screeching. Vironnos slapped his tail against the ground, splattering his inky blood everywhere, but I was quick to get out of the way and catch my breath. Next came the fire, spilling out of his mouth like molten lava, quickly filling the ring.

To me, it felt a lot like air, harmless. Fire couldn't hurt me, so I thought perhaps I could use it to my advantage. I knew the slightest sound could give me away, so I snuck through the crashing flames, making my way closer and closer to the dragon all while feeding more fire to the sea. All while I fought to find a way to end this nightmare.

I spotted his figure through the rising waves and had to trade my sword for a better weapon. *Summer power is more than fire,* Caz had once told me. *If it's used with a strong purpose, it could strike even a dragon.* What's a better reason than staying alive? Using the sea, I sent dozens of daggers his way. He screeched louder, voice rumbling in my ears. He lashed his tail savagely, clearing the view.

Vironnos was a lot closer than I'd hoped. One moment he was where I could see him, the next his claws sank into my side, and with his tail, he sent me flying against the wall. I was sure I heard my bones breaking as my back clashed against the hot stones.

Vironnos, who was once my friend, seemed as surprised by his own attack as me. He realized the prophecy could be changed. So, he kicked more stones to crush me. Despite the pain, and despite the bleeding, I rolled out of range in time. Darkness surrounded the edges of my vision, and for once I saw everything clearly. The stones hit the ground hard enough for the storm of dust to hang immobile in the air.

The Darklings roared, calling for him to end me.

"Vironnos," I called his name, and everyone went silent, disappointed to have learned I was still alive. He couldn't find me behind the rubble if he tried. "Enough blood. Enough sacrifices. We are not pawns. We don't have to fight. We were so blind to see it, but the Shadow rulers knew this, surely there's another way."

"There isn't," Vironnos said, but he wasn't a dragon anymore. And I didn't have to see him to know. "We are fated for *this*. We are fated to be rivals. The blood moon is more than a curse, it has shown us who our enemy is. Summer is my enemy; *you* are my enemy."

"You seem to be forgetting something," I rose, as the dust finally faded. Blood seeped down to my feet. "I'm not

Summer." A crack ran down the middle of the arena, and the Darklings screamed. Some scrambled out of their seats, some fled. Pebbles rained down on the ring from the side of the mountain. In his faerie form, Vironnos' eyes widened. "I'm more than that."

Power surged through me stronger than I'd ever felt, Summer and Spring intertwined inside me. I lunged at him with my sword like a striking serpent as the shattered stones flew at him like bullets at my command. Still, none reached him before I did. My sword was at his throat before he could draw his dagger. The crowd gasped in surprise. This was it, the killing blow. I raised my sword high above my head and drove my arms down with a scream of triumph.

Despite knowing better, I hoped it would all end here. The arena fell silent. My ragged breaths were all there was to hear. I felt a thousand gazes on my back. "I'm Solmark," I panted, "and you're not my enemy, Vironnos." I rose slowly, one hand pressed to my side.

My sword dug into the ground, a few inches from his neck. He didn't as much as flinch, and for the longest moment, he was still as a statue. Then, he frowned, almost angry that I didn't kill him. I offered him my hand, dripping with my own blood, and he took it. Vironnos winced. It was only then that I noticed the blood on his wings. He was hurt too. In that matter, I found us equal. "I don't understand." His voice was the proof he was utterly lost.

I turned to the crowd instead of facing Vironnos, noticing my mother was already gone. I raised my voice loud enough for all to hear. "We are the masters of our fate," my voice echoed back to me, "we cannot fix the mistakes of those who ruined us, but we can choose to no longer be ruined. I will not fight for a curse. I will not fight for revenge. And I will not fight for a throne." I felt their curiosity getting stronger in the air. "I will not walk on the path of those who wronged us. Tonight, I will not let a curse blind me, I will not let a curse choose my enemy, and I will not let a curse choose my fate. Tonight, I'm taking the reins. We may not have the power to change history, but we do have enough power to choose a better future.

"I'm Alexandra, daughter of Spring and Summer, princess of Solmark, and heir to the Faye Throne, and I acknowledge you not as my enemy but as my friends. From the youngest Darkling to your ruler, I choose to be your ally." I said, looking back at Vironnos, whose eyebrows were shot up in astonishment, rendering him immobile.

"Hatred has blinded us for long enough, but I will not allow it to consume us. We are rulers, Vironnos, not followers. Change must start here, and it must start with us. Will you deem me worthy to be your friend, or will you deem me your enemy?"

His eyes darted to the Darklings before he took a step towards me, another. "You have called many things before, devil, irrational, player, *raven thing*..." I winced as he said that one, hoping it didn't offend him as much as I'd thought when I said it. "And a friend," he said with his usual smirk. "You had the chance to slay me, but you showed me mercy instead. Before, you have saved me more than once. And although you did have to be drunk to have praised me, you had said that you saw something good in me. I want you to know this: I'm only good when I'm with you."

"What are you saying, Vironnos?" I mumbled stupidly.

He grinned. "I'm saying I want to be your friend,

Carrots, if you'll have me." He opened his arms, and I staggered to him. The sound of my footsteps were quickly lost in the cheering that spread like wildfire.

His wings wrapped around me much like his arms. "Are you sure you want to be good, Vironnos? Your reputation might be ruined." I mocked what he said at the Solmark Court when I saw him for the second time.

Grinning, he pulled himself away slowly, still holding my shoulders. His gaze flashed behind me, and his face twisted. Vironnos spun us so fast, my side protested from the sudden movement. He flinched as a bolt pierced his shoulder, sinking to his knees, he pulled me down with him.

The Mountain of Ruins raged once more, bringing rows of seats falling to the ground. The Darklings who could, began to flee. I wasn't nearly as aghast by that as I found my mother standing in the ring with a crossbow in hand. I knew she would never be satisfied with my choice, but to kill Vironnos herself?

"I should've known, you're too weak to kill anyone," she gritted out.

"Stop!" I pleaded, but she shot the next bolt anyway. Vironnos cursed as the bolt thudded into his arm.

"You're so pathetic I can hardly muster the will to draw my next breath in your presence, daughter. You think you can make new alliances?"

"All of this for more power?"

"It is what is rightfully mine!" she roared. Her silver gown was tainted red. "You cannot fathom how much I've lost, how much I've sacrificed all to see you end a line, but what have you done?"

"This has to stop right now," I said quietly as she tightened her grip on the crossbow. "You will not have your way, mother. Accept that you've already lost."

"The last Shadow must die here tonight."

"No. I will not play your game, and neither will Vironnos. Together, we have chosen to unite as one. Together, we have broken your curse."

The crossbow wavered in her hands as she gave a menace of laughter, making my muscles clench. "Did you really think unity is enough to break this curse? Without blood, you have accomplished nothing."

"What?" My voice faltered. I didn't believe her. She had so much to lose. A corner of her mouth lifted, and I realized whatever she would say couldn't be a lie.

"You're not finished, you see. I have spun this curse and I know that subjects of the Shadow and Summer will all suffer one by one if a ruler isn't dead tonight. The longer the blood moon lasts, the more sacrifices will be made. You cannot escape this, not until you kill him. Not until a ruler is dead."

Now, I believed her. My mother would have never made a curse this cruel to be broken so easily. I looked back at Vironnos, drenched in his own blood. Tears seeped down my face faster than I could blink them away. "If I choose to kill a ruler tonight, will the curse be broken? Will I finally be free?" My chest felt hollow, like a part of me will soon cease to exist.

Vironnos' eyes were immediately drawn to me in awareness. He swallowed. "Alexandra, don't."

"Yes," she answered, sounding too pleased. "The only way for this curse to be broken is to offer a ruler's blood. Do him a favor and put an end to his miserable life. He's dead anyway. Make your choice."

My temper sparked, setting my heart on fire. My teeth clenched, almost breaking from the pressure. "Then I choose you," I said, shooting a flaming arrow. Her crossbow clattered to the ground, and she realized what I did a second too late. The weapon faded, and my hands shook uncontrollably.

Blood seeped from the corners of her mouth, and my mother dropped to the ground with a pierced heart. She stared at me with a shock and disbelief that would haunt me forever. "Alexandra…what have you done?" Her voice was a whisper.

"This had to stop, I meant it." She gasped for air, turning her head to the gleaming blood moon. "With you gone, there will be no more sacrifices, no more blood curse, no more waiting." Her years of scheming have finally come to an end.

Ashes began to swirl around her like a storm of death, slowly decaying her body to embers. She looked back at me with a frightening look that begged me to save her despite knowing it was impossible. A part of me wanted to save her, but that part was slowly dying with her. It was hardly the moment, but I learned then that some choices cannot be undone. "I…underestimated you, d-daughter," she stuttered, her eyes glazed with tears. The blood moon faded to white, lifting the horror of the curse.

"Goodbye, mother," I whispered as her empty silver gown fell soundlessly to the ground. Closing my eyes, I finally collapsed from the pain in my side, knowing that my mother had died, and with her, her curse.

CHAPTER 22

A NEW BEGINNING

"You have carved your own path, haven't you, living one?" the Fateteller asked, her voice echoing. She was nowhere to be seen, but I knew she wasn't pleased.

"I have," I answered. "And I have won your challenge, Fateteller. My debt to you is forgiven."

"I'm afraid so," she hissed, "but this is not goodbye, my dear, for no fate is free of danger." She had come to say exactly what I had expected from her. "Until next time, my queen." Her voice faded into a whisper, and the world around me shattered into a million pieces.

When I awoke on a bed, the pain had lessened, and my view of the rusted chandelier was quickly replaced with Vironnos' beaming face. His coal hair fell to my eyes. "Carrot's awake! I win the bet."

Groaning, I pushed his face away from me, bringing myself in a sitting position. "Were you betting on me to fall into a sleep like death?"

"I would never!" he protested, "but he did," he said,

pointing to Spore, who was sitting atop my blanket. Spore chuckled nervously, crawling down the bed.

Vironnos was topless, except for the bandage wrapped around his chest and shoulder. Judging by that and the gleaming moon, I realized not much time had passed since the curse was broken.

I glanced down at my hands, still shaking with the choice I'd made. I knew I'd made the right choice, still…

I surrendered to the weight of my emotions, letting my tears run free. Vironnos sitting on the edge of the bed, pulling my head into his chest, all but made me sadder. "What happened was…" I cried, "it was…"

"Let's never talk about it," Vironnos said in a gentle, understanding voice.

I pulled away to meet his golden eyes. "But…what about the nightmares?"

He seemed to understand exactly what I was talking about. "It'll go away." His hands framed my face, wiping away another fallen tear. "There's no place for them in a new beginning, my friend."

I smiled, trusting he'd be right about this. He must be. "You know, I never imagined you'd be so sentimental, and friendly. It suits you."

"Oh, must you torment me so?" he said, sounding anything but tormented.

The door flung open, and the Darkling messenger barged in, panting. His eyes met mine, and he bowed to both of us. "Your highness, the Grand Healer wishes to see you. Immediately," he said urgently.

"The Grand Healer?" It struck me like a hurricane. "Caz!" I rushed out of the bed, feeling my heart hammering against my chest. Blood quickly soaked the bandage tightly wrapped around my stomach, but I didn't care.

I ran through the halls, ignoring the bowing crowd of Darklings as I dashed by them, nearly tripping and planting on my face a couple of times. My hair was a wild mess, but I didn't care about that either.

I'd been on pins and needles waiting for the Timewinder to work. The trials had only two possible outcomes: Caz was either strong enough to endure them, or he wasn't. Just then, the thought of my betrayal blinded me yet again. I had asked him to come back to me, but was I deserving of that? I had kept secrets from him when I said I trusted him. Secrets that nearly ended him.

The messenger stopped at the door, waiting for me to walk in first. When I did, the clean, empty bed mocked me. The room was dark. There were no candles, no potions, no Grand Healer. Only the glistening moonlight inside, filtering through the openings in the stone wall. I was struck with a dreadful feeling that refused to go easily. *I did this. I—*

"Princess!" His voice came to rescue me from sinking below the tide of guilt.

I whirled around, eyes stinging with tears. Caz stood near the doorframe. He wore a loose black shirt with a deep drawstring collar that revealed the healing scar on his chest. Walking slowly to each other, we met in the middle of the room. His gaze never strayed from mine as I traced his cheekbones with my hand, hoping I wasn't just imagining him. He looked much better. The burns on his wrist had vanished, too. I slid my fingers to his neck, listening to his breath hitch as I weaved them through his soft hair.

So close I had to tilt my head to meet his gaze, shining

brighter than the drifting moonlight. It was him. "You came back." Tears welled, and I let them stream down. I wasn't afraid to show him my emotions anymore. I had made a vow that I will never try to hide from him if he'd ever return to me, and he did. That must mean… "I'm so sorry, Caz. I imagine it wasn't easy for you to face your past, your choices, and regrets. I know you must have been afraid of it all."

"I was. It haunts me still," he said, making it sound like an accusation. My hand trembled as I yanked it away from his hair. I'd been right to imagine the hate he would bear for me. He resented me. I took a shaky breath. I had told him to come back even if he hated me, but it tore my heart to hear it. I thought I had the courage to keep my glare in place, but I didn't.

I tried taking a step back, but his arms were on my waist in no time, pulling me closer than before. Surprised, I glanced up at him. For the first time, he looked frightened, holding on to me as if I would disappear. "*You*," his voice barely above a whisper, "you don't know what you did to me. Nothing would ever scare me more than the thought of not being with you," he murmured, his ocean eyes boring into mine.

My tears of guilt were quickly replaced with tears of joy. I pressed my fingertips to his chest, feeling his heartbeats quickening under my touch, desperately telling me it was still mine. "Caz, does that mean…you still love me?"

He swallowed, tightening his grip. One hand came up to brush a strand of hair away from my cheek, and suddenly I was aware of my embarrassing state, dressed in a nightgown two sizes too big, and my tangled hair in shambles. "Alexandra, I never stopped loving you."

Caz lowered his lips to mine, kissing me in earnest. This was what forever felt like. It was beyond my wildest dreams. *He* was beyond my wildest dreams.

I held onto his neck even as he pulled away, smiling. "It's funny," he said.

"What is?"

His dimples returned, working its magic inside my head. "You remind me of a girl who forbade me to hold her in my arms ever again."

I laughed. "How odd, and you remind me of a boy who claimed he took no pleasure in holding me longer than he had to."

I stood on my tiptoes to meet his lips, and he held me like that for a moment. "What are your new commands, my queen?"

I smiled. "Never let go." We kissed again as the sun rose slowly, taking its rightful place in the sky. I knew then that this was my new beginning.

FOUND IN EVERLYNIA

Breaking the blood curse was one thing, claiming the Faye Throne of Solmark was another. I bit my lower lip as I paced back and forth in the throne room of the Shadow Court. My heart never failed to creep into my mouth every time I was reminded of my coronation ceremony next week.

Caz, Vironnos, and Spore all sat on the throne's steps, watching me quietly as I took deep breaths whenever I felt suffocated. I had spent the last few days trying to get Caz and Vironnos off each other's throats long enough for them to sit in peace, and in the same room with me. Under merciless pressure, I made Vironnos apologize for his actions, and knowing Caz, he would never admit to forgiving him, but I knew in his heart, he did. Maybe he understood why Vironnos had to do it, to provoke me to fight because he knew I cared about him.

"Relax, Carrots," Vironnos groaned, his dark crown gleaming atop his head as he rested his chin on his palm. "A coronation ceremony is supposed to be fun. Must you find fault in that too?"

"Easy for you to say. The Darklings have accepted you as their ruler despite your choice to unite." My stomach dropped to my feet, and I kept shifting from one foot to another. "For me it's different. The Spring will hate me for the choice I made, and the Summer will hate me for the choice I didn't make."

"Killing me, you mean," he said, laughing without humor. "Yes, I suppose you're not among their favorites."

My shoulders slumped. Caz, fully aware of my defeat, stood. "Tell me this, if you would do it all over again," he said, and we all winced at the thought, "would you have chosen differently?"

"No," I said without hesitation. I would not have changed a thing, that much was certain.

His hands were on my shoulders, comforting me. "Then you have made the right choice. Believe in that." I looked over his shoulder, Vironnos and Spore nodded in agreement.

I sighed. "You are the first ruler to have broken the curse *and* saved thousands from ruin," Caz went on, "You are their queen regardless of what they think or believe."

"That's not the kind of queen I want to be."

"The kind of queen you are is righteous. Everyone in Solmark knew the daughter of Spring and Summer would return a victor. You're not only victorious, but you are their savior. They will only ever doubt you if you doubt yourself."

"Pretty boy is right," Vironnos said, rising. "Besides, what are you afraid of? You won't be alone."

I frowned. "You're coming too?"

He grinned. "You'll need a faster ride if you want to arrive at your own coronation in time, Carrots."

Turns out, riding a dragon is not as scary as I'd imagined. Soaring through the clouds, I closed my eyes against the singing wind, billowing my hair in every direction possible. But when we were beneath the clouds, the wonderland of Everlynia stretched out like I've never seen before.

From high above, the beauty of Icymark seemed like a pearl gleaming in the depths of the ocean. Every inch of the snow, every person I'd met, every little adventure I had sewed into my memory like a mosaic of fabrics.

Far past the howling wind screeching into my ears, came the danger of the Vileforest. Endless thunderclouds shielding the forest from the sunlight. Even from this height, I heard the bargaining and waging of the Enchanted Abyss. I smelled the spices and blood, saw the light of the floating candles, and felt the chaos of the Market. Further in, I saw the dazzling twisted oak tree of the Great Whisperers and the forest's maze.

My emotions stirred as we passed by a field of Teal flowers, petals drifting with Vironnos' wings. I wondered how many more fields it would take to remedy the pain of the past. All of my memories, the good and the bad, huddled together.

One region slowly bled into another until the warm breeze of Solmark kissed my face as we arrived at dawn. While I didn't expect to find so many subjects, and all of the

Solmark nobles waiting for me at the court's entrance, I felt a strange sense of belonging.

The courtyard appeared brighter than I remembered, with pastel fabric braided around banquet tables set to last a fortnight of balls to celebrate the coronation of a new ruler. Flowers bloomed far beyond the eye could see, some were plated gold from the fountain. Music of spring played from inside the court, carrying a special kind of enchantment to my ears.

The nobles' faces grew solemn at the sight of the fearsome Shadow, Vironnos by my side. Compared to him, the statues of the dragons were the least frightening. I hopped off the dragon's back and into Caz's arms along with Spore. I admit that I enjoyed witnessing Lord Damien's confusion turning to fear as Vironnos shifted into a familiar form.

One by one bowed once I was close enough. All except Lord Damien and his son, Liam who held his chin high as if to oppose me. "We are pleased for your safe return, my queen," Lord Damien said, as if the words had been forced out of him.

"Are you, really?" I asked, darting my eyes from him to the Spring Lord, Aries, giving him a curt nod. If I had a single doubt of Lord Damien despising me before, I had none now.

He pursed his lips, barley containing himself. "Of course," he said, sharing a glance with his son. "I cannot lie."

I stared back at him. "Yes, but you never told the truth either," I reminded him.

"The wind spoke of your misfortune, my queen," he said, ignoring my previous comment. "Something about choosing to sacrifice your own mother for the blood moon. Has it always been an obvious choice?"

The weight of his words pressed on my chest, a painful reminder of what I did. "Oh, but you did save us all. What's one life in the face of a realm? You did the heroic thing," he went on, aware of my tenseness. His words taught me an important lesson: heroes are nothing more than cheered villains. And I was one of them.

Spore whimpered, tugging at my hair strand as Caz and Vironnos stepped closer to me. I noticed the way Lord Damien and Liam stiffened. It was clear that they were looking for a weakness, and I wasn't about to give it to them.

I smiled, stepping closer to Lord Damien. "It wasn't only my misfortune the wind spoke of," I said, and just as I'd hoped, their faces paled. I would never forget their attempt to have me killed in the mortal world. The Spring nobles began to whisper among themselves, and their whispers quickly spread like the plague. They would have to try harder if they wanted to intimidate me.

Liam regarded me with disbelief. I wasn't the same lost girl he'd met before in the forest. Nothing scares me anymore. Lord Damien cleared his throat. "I sure hope my burden of a son was of good use to you," he said, looking at Caz like he's scheming his torture. "He would've spent the rest of his life rotting in the dungeon if anything were to happen to you, my queen."

"He was," I answered. A moment later I regretted giving him the pleasure of answering. I turned back to Caz, but he wasn't in the least worried about his father's threat. "And perhaps your future ruler of a son could teach you and your other son how to bow before your queen. Next time I will not overlook your disrespect, Lord Damien, Liam," I said, passing by them without looking back.

The silence was quickly replaced with laughter among the subjects. I knew right then I'd officially made them my enemy, but that was the least of my concern, I wouldn't have trusted them to be my friends anyway.

I sat still while the satyr sisters braided half my hair and twisted it into a crown. I had completely forgotten how much I admired their work. Beyond the walls of my room, I heard the distant chanting of fairies, singing a rhythm in a foreign language. The same one I'd heard after drinking the pixie brew.

The sisters sang along, and a wave of nostalgia swept over me uninvited. I remembered how strange everything seemed to me in Everlynia, but now, I'm shocked to find how things have changed for me in that regard.

Once the sisters stopped singing, I asked them about it. "It's a song for you, my queen," one of them answered briefly.

"The promise will come to pass, when the daughter returns to last. Her fate will not be the same, for her flames cannot be tamed. She will ride the darkness through the clouds, and in her reign the truth will prevail," the other said, letting a few strands of hair slide off hands and onto my shoulder.

I watched her in the mirror, awestruck that they'd chosen me as their promise from the very beginning.

I stood up, turned around, and met King Alrick at the

door. He let himself, dismissing the sisters, who bolted without another word.

"Father," I muttered, stupidly. My heart sped as he approached me, his eyes carefully studying the gold vines that crept from the bottom of my ivory gown to my waist.

The Solmark King's face was emotionless, and his eyes gave nothing away. I remembered we didn't exactly depart on good terms, not after the way I raged at him in the presence of his nobles. Any man wouldn't like that, *especially* the king.

I opened my mouth to form an apology, but he spoke first. "You disobeyed me, daughter, when you left to find your mother," he said, power rippling with his voice, "yet you returned without her." Beneath the calm mask he wore, I felt his pain, his mourn for my mother.

"I had to," I said, not knowing how much the wind had whispered about my mother's curse or the destruction that would have followed if a ruler hadn't been sacrificed.

"I see," he said, closing his eyes briefly as he knew it must've been done. When he opened them again, they were misted over. "You were right, my daughter, I'm not half the king I thought I was." I lowered my eyes, unable to meet his gaze. "I'm afraid I would've chosen to sacrifice thousands if it meant I would get to keep your mother." Disappointment passed over his face as he confessed to me, but his tone made it clear that he bore me no grudge. I couldn't help observing it was himself that he'd failed, not only his subjects.

The king's hand hovered over the Solmark sun pendant that he wore over his dark cloak. "My time is up," he said calmly, slipping the pendant over my neck. I froze in shock as the Solmark King bowed to me. "Solmark is yours now, my daughter, defend it the same way you've defended the subjects of Everlynia, for you are her true queen."

He straightened, his eyes growing wider as I threw my arms around my father. I looked up at him, and he smiled with relief, as if a boulder had been lifted from his shoulders. "Are you ready, my daughter?" he asked as the chimes sounded, summoning us all to start the ceremony.

I nodded, and he led me away.

In the hall, Queen Rose fixed me with a sharp look, but I didn't give her the satisfaction of reciprocating her distaste for me. She may not like me as King Alrick's daughter, but she will learn to respect me as her queen. Quietly, she joined my father, and together, they walked behind me to the throne room.

The hall was crowded with nobles and high born, standing at either side of the hall. Only for today, the nobles were all clothed in white, resembling not Summer or Spring, but Solmark.

The huge windows were painted with unmatched colors, casting a beautiful pattern over the golden rug that ran from the foot of the Faye Throne and to the opposite wall, splitting the room in half. Pastel banners with artistic needlework and shining tassels draped from the walls, some of which were long enough to brush against the elegant floral arrangements that had replaced the winged dragon sculptures.

My heart leaped with joy as I caught glimpses of Max and Rue swinging from one banner to another, keeping up with me.

Fire erupted at every corner, and the horns blew one by one as I passed by. Many bitter faces followed my every step.

I watched Vironnos whispering to three blushing Summer ladies while winking at me. Beside him, Caz wore a black doublet adorned with silver linings, hiding something behind his back. His eyes sparkled as he clasped a hand to his heart the moment my eyes landed on him. I smiled. It felt good to know what you want, and better to find it waiting for you with a flower in hand.

I stopped at the stairs as King Alrick and Queen Rose took their seats next to a lavish, empty throne in the middle. The wordsmith, dressed in a long, gilded robe, bowed to the rulers before turning to me.

"Today's sun will always shine brighter than yesterday's," the wordsmith said, his voice ringing through the hall. He gestured with his hand as Spore ran up the stairs, holding a crimson pillow in his hands. On it, sat a green laurel wreath. "Kneel, heir of Solmark."

I did. My friend passed the wreath to Queen Rose, who turned it into solid gold, and then to King Alrick, who lit it up in flames.

The wordsmith placed the crown on my head. "To the fairies of Everlynia, I present to you Queen Alexandra of Solmark." He bowed. "Rise, my queen," he said softly to me.

I took my place on the Faye Throne as the crowd bowed their heads to their new queen.

"Long live the queen of Solmark," the wordsmith said.

"Long live Queen Alexandra of Solmark," everyone else repeated.

The music started playing, and colorful feathers showered over our heads like confetti, landing with grace.

My fairytale did not end with a crown on my head, troublesome squirrels climbing my dress, a peculiar raven using my friend as a bait to chase after ladies, causing chaos of his own, or a handsome Summer elf getting down on one knee to lead our first dance.

No, that is how my fairytale began.

THE END

ACKNOWLEDGMENTS

No one told me how much joy I'd feel writing my first acknowledgment. There are many extraordinary individuals who made this feeling possible, and I'm grateful for every single one of them.

First, I want to thank my sister, who read the roughest version of this story and still asked for more. Jessica Rammpersad, my alpha reader—to whom I'm forever indebted—provided invaluable feedback that improved every chapter. Thank you to my beta readers, Elaine Buckner and Ruchi, for your time and support. A special thank you to Brandee Paschall.

To my editor, Ioana Cheldiu, for bringing your magic to every page and every word. You have not only strengthened this story but you have made me a better writer. I am endlessly grateful for your dedication and talent.

To my new family at Azala press, who believed in this story enough to take a chance on it, supported me along the journey, and brought my book to life—thank you. MK Ahearn and Ky Venn, thank you for creating this family and welcoming me into it.

Thank you to my sisters, Whitney Gibbs, Kyla Shinder, Alecia Kirby, Kit Aldridge, Margarita Artista, Rachel Tork, and Sophia Denesi. Had I known this story would lead me to this family, I would have written it long ago. Without these amazing people, my story would have remained nothing more than words in my mind.

Finally, thank you to my readers.

9 781963 836745